CORRUPT
KINGDOM

AVA HARRISON

Corrupt Kingdom
Cover Design: Hang Le
Photographer: Chris Davis
Model: Mike Jukes
Line Edit: Editing4Indies
Proofreader: Marla Selkow Esposito, My Brother's Editor, Gemma Woolley
Formatting: Champagne Book Design

Whoever fights monsters should see to it that in the process he does not become a monster. And if you gaze long enough into an abyss, the abyss will gaze back into you.

—Friedrich Nietzsche

The Devil came out to play, bargaining lives for a price, sending those to Hell who crossed him.

CHAPTER ONE

Cyrus

I'M THE KING. THIS IS MY CASTLE, AND IF I HAD A THRONE, I'D be fucking sitting on it.

I set my cognac glass on the staircase's banister, watching it teetering near the edge. Below me, one of my subjects holds court in my mansion, no shits given, but once I descend the steps, he'll remember his place.

I own him.

I own everyone here.

Officially, my bank is the wealthiest private bank in the world. Unofficially, it is the gateway to the underworld. Every penny earned by criminals passes through me. Unlike most of the banks on Wall Street, I don't pretend to be something I'm not. The money that lies in my vaults is dirty as fuck because I don't cater to a normal clientele.

No.

Mine is of a different breed.

The lowest dregs of life.

They are drug dealers. Gunrunners. They are the cartel and the mafia. At times, they are even the shady politicians who run countries, and the trust fund babies who fuck up.

To them, I'm their savior. No more hiding bags of cash under their beds. Nope. Instead, they all come to me to clean their money and, once it's spotless, grow it.

Even though I'm technically one of them—a criminal—I can't stand them. Although that really means nothing, as I can't stand anyone. But their cash is green. Fuck, theirs might be greener. A new shade stained by the life taken to make it.

Tonight, the money they don't deposit in my bank will be brought here instead. It will arrive dirty, smeared with the sins from which they earned it, but by the time the evening ends, the tainted blood will be gone, and they'll leave with bills as clean as freshly washed laundry.

My house is ready, and the staff is prepared. The game will begin soon, so all I have to do now is wait.

I hate this shit, but it's a necessary evil. Here, I'll learn secrets. Possess fortunes. I will amass an empire.

This is my corrupt kingdom, where I am a god.

Time comes to a halt as I wait at the top of my stairs. My gaze drifts across the foyer as each guest arrives. The crowd assembles in the center of the room, waiting for instructions, but really, they're waiting for the poker game to start.

Sometimes, I only observe. Sometimes, I don't even bother to come down. I'm not always needed. The fact that I host the game is enough to keep the players in line. Today, I'll venture downstairs.

I want to monitor a new guest who will be attending. Someone I have been luring for years. He hasn't arrived yet, but my sources say he has taken the bait. Once I have the opportunity, I'll set the trap.

As I wait, I notice a few unfamiliar faces that I need to vet before they can play. I can tell tonight will be worse than most nights, and that is saying a lot. Some of the seediest men I know are among the crowd.

I see the irony. Judging men who are no different from me. They kill.

I kill.

But there is one difference. I only kill when I need to.

Some of these dipshits kill for sport.

To prove they are men.

None of this shit makes them a man. Since they don't see that, there really is no helping them. So, I just clean their money and bleed them with interest instead.

Yet even knowing this, they stand here in my house, offering me their souls. I have enough leverage to bring them all down. But there's only one I'm looking for.

With a shake of my head, I walk in their direction with slow and deliberate steps. Sizing them up, one by one.

Until I find him, I'll search for the big offenders and then signal Z. He will be my second pair of eyes and ears and watch them.

At first, I notice the usual crowd—rich douchebags who have nothing better to do than spend their daddy's money. I know the type, and I fucking hate the type.

On the other side of the room are the drug dealers, mafia members, and dirtier than fuck politicians.

Each group is important to my operation. One washes the other's hand. Most of the people in this room are on my client lists. My banking does the heavy load of cleaning, but what I can't clean that way, I clean through my poker game. That's why the rich boys are here. They don't know how to play; they know how to lose.

With drinks in hand, the men sit at the tables. The crowd tonight is not as large as usual, so only a few tables are set up, each ranging from eight to ten players. It's a healthy mix of legit versus illegal.

Slowly, but with precision, I make my way over, skating my gaze across the tables.

I take in each guest tonight.

At the far left is Matteo. He runs the East Coast mafia, and I do a lot of business with him. Beside him is his right-hand man, his cousin. I don't care too much for him either, but he's a necessary evil.

Alaric, Tobias, Mathis, and James are also in attendance. Even though they are some of the fiercest men around, they're also the only clients I can tolerate.

To the left of them is just another rich pretty boy. I say this because that's what he is, a trust fund baby who's perfect to clean their money. Also known as Trent Aldridge.

He's been coming for years, even though he sucks at cards. His motives don't differ from my motives for being here. He wants to get more clients. Recently, Z mentioned he works in hedge funds, and apparently, he's been funneling clients out of here.

Regardless of why he's here, he's harmless. I look at who sits next to him. I've never seen him before, and he stands out from the rest of the crowd. He looks older than my norm.

Like he could be my father. Or, better yet, Trent's father. They have the same eyes, same coloring, and same hair. Trent is a younger version of him. Except Trent isn't weathered. Trent does not look haunted. Interesting. Why is this man here? I need to monitor him.

I pull my gaze away, and my eyes land on the man I have been waiting for.

He's here.

Looking at Z, I incline my head, and he nods his understanding. Hook, line, sinker.

"Welcome," I say, all eyes on me. "Boris"—I turn to the man in question—"how good of you to come."

Boris.

AKA: The Butcher.

The man I hope to entrap tonight. He is one sick fuck. He and his friend are not clients. Even I have some limits. I don't clean money for men who traffic women, but he is a means to an end.

Now to figure out a way to get him to tell me what I want.

To tell me about his organization and where his boss is.

That's why he's here. The best way to gather intel is to get him drunk, make him money, and wait for him to get comfortable. He might not disclose exactly what I'm looking for, but men talk, and all words are clues. Like a game of chess, look for the advantage, learn to spot patterns, and then play the board in front of you. He'll give something away and I'll take it. I've waited too long for this chance to let anything fuck it up.

With a drop of my head, I give my approval to the dealer, and the game begins. From the sidelines, I watch, observing and gathering information about each person's character. Especially Boris.

As the pot continues to grow, some players act reckless while others are more confident.

One server comes over and takes the drink orders. Most of the men have stopped playing to look at her. I glance over too. She's pretty, but she's not my type.

As the rest of the men sit out the hand, Trent's father is apparently all in.

He's reckless.

From where I am, I can see a line of sweat drip down his brow, and when I look at who he's playing, I understand why he's nervous. He's playing Boris.

This is more than just fear that The Butcher might chop him up. This is something more.

This is desperation. *Interesting.*

I hope for his sake no one else notices. He needs the win. For the money.

Millions are in the pot.

Things will get interesting now. I step closer so I don't miss a minute. He's really sweating. It pours off him, and no one misses it. Trent especially.

"Father." He tries to intervene, but his father doesn't listen. Instead, he pushes forward on to his elbow, throwing more chips into the fray. The gleam in Boris's eyes is predatory. He has him right where he wants him.

He's all in.

Trent's father looks toward Trent. He has no more chips to throw in. Trent shakes his head.

"Father." Nothing. "Dad." His eyes implore him to stop, to halt the insanity. He can't, though. It's clear as day in the old man's eyes. He came to win. He needs to win.

"I have to," he whispers to his son. "It will be okay."

Father and son are at a standstill. A silent argument. Trent won't win. I know men like his father . . . I had a father like that.

"So what's it going to be?" Boris asks, pulling me from my inner thoughts and back to the present. I watch as Trent's father fumbles around.

"I call." There is no conviction in his voice. Boris leans onto the table, resting his elbows on the surface. Cocking his head, he lifts his eyebrow. "With what money? It looks like you are out of chips."

"I have it . . ." His voice breaks. "Just not on me."

"No good." He shakes his head. "Something else . . ." he leads.

Aldridge Sr. lifts his wrist. Red and flashy. A Richard Mille watch.

"No." Boris shoots him down again, boredom etching away at his face.

"B-But it's worth almost six hundred thousand dollars," he stutters.

If I was a better man, I'd step in and stop this shit. But I'm not, so I nod to Z, allowing it to continue. It's entertaining me, at least. Plus, this could be what I need on Boris. I'll see where it goes.

"What else do you have of value . . . because I have watches."

"My house?"

"I already have a home. I have multiple." A sinister smirk spreads across his face. "Something of real value . . ." He trails off.

"Cars."

"You have nothing I want." The answer is final as he places his hands on the table to pull the pot to him. The game will be over before it's even started.

"My daughter."

Fuck. This is not what I want.

Silence descends on the room, hovering over us like a cloudy smog, clinging to everything in its path. I feel as his words enter through my mouth into my lungs.

He would sell his daughter.

To this man.

The man people call The Butcher.

A man known through the underworld to capture and play with his prey. His favorite pastime is carving flesh. Hence the name.

"You would sell your daughter to me?" He's not surprised. This is what he does. He barters and steals.

"Father . . ." Trent tries desperately to interject.

"Shut up," the old man shouts at his son, who's now ghostly white. If possible, Boris's grin becomes even bigger, spreading farther across his unshaven face. "Yes." He tries to appear strong, but he's bluffing. I know this. Trent knows this. To be fucking serious, everyone in the room knows. Except for him. He's so desperate, he truly believes his lies. I should put my foot down. This is not what I intended when I started this game.

"We don't trade flesh here." I step forward, and from the corner of my eye, I see Z shake his head. He doesn't agree with me intervening. Knowing him, he thinks this is exactly what we need on Boris. But even I have limits, and I won't condone it. My word is law here, and no one would be dumb enough to cross me.

"Is there something else of value you have?" Boris leads. I don't listen to them talk anymore. A new deal happens, and the game continues.

It always does.

It's inevitable. This man will lose, and he will owe the Russian his life.

I raise my hand to Maggie, the woman who owns the company I hire for waitstaff. She knows what I want, so without a word, she scurries off.

The game is back on, and as Maggie rushes up to me, her heels clinking against my marble floor, she hands me my glass of Louis XIII.

I take a swig. It burns as it trails down my throat, scorching old demons that once lay dormant.

They deal.

Words are spoken.
Cards are flipped.
The winner revealed.
I know the victor without looking.
I know the prize too.
A life.
The question is whose?

CHAPTER TWO

Ivy

I T'S AN UNUSUALLY WARM DAY FOR THE END OF WINTER.
Normally, the ground is still frozen and fresh snow covers all the surfaces this time of the year.

But not today.

Today, the sun is out, and I can feel spring in the air.

It invigorates me. Breathes new life into my heart. Something I need right now with everything going on. My mother isn't getting better, and it's silently killing me.

It's a good day, though. She always does better when the outside world is beautiful. It's as if she is a flower, and when the sun is out, she blooms.

I live with my parents in the brownstone they own in the West Village. I'm twenty-two—old enough to move out and old enough to live on my own—but leaving this place would mean I leave a piece of my heart.

My garden.

Her garden.

I'm the only one who takes care of it now. Like everything else in this house, they would leave it to wilt and die if it weren't for me. So, instead, I'm on my knees pulling all the weeds and dead plants from the ground.

It's the reason I stay. My mother lost her will to tend to it years ago, around the same time she lost her will to live. She might still be here with us, but she is a shell of the woman she once was.

So, now I tend to it. Using everything she taught me, I bring it back to life, year after year.

My hands touch the withered stems, then I grab them. The hard ground loosens as I free the dead plants and place them in a garbage bag.

After I finish pulling the weeds, I stand from where I'm kneeling, grab the garbage bag, and then turn toward the back door to the house. Through the large bay window, I can see my mother standing there. She's in the kitchen, and even from where I am outside, I can see the blank look in her eyes.

She's vacant. Hollow.

Some days are worse than others.

From what I can gather, today will be one of those days.

My father never came home last night.

It's not unusual for him, nor is it unusual for my mother to be more despondent the day after.

He's probably having an affair. Whenever I ask him where he's been, he says he had to work late. I know better and, unfortunately, so does she.

"Hi, Mom." I walk up beside her and place a kiss on the top of her cheek. She inhales me, probably smelling the fresh air that clings to my skin, and then she looks up as if it invigorates her.

"Where is your father?"

From where I'm standing, I can see straight into her eyes. They used to be a vibrant blue, much like my own. I've always been told I look like her. Sandy blond hair that falls in loose waves down my back and large blue eyes. Now, we no longer look alike. Her blond hair has gone gray, and her eyes have lost their sparkle.

But at least they're no longer blank. Staring at her, looking into her eyes, I can see recognition. I give her a tight smile, taking a step closer to her, and reach for her hand.

"I don't know, Mom," I answer, my voice low with uncertainty.

She pulls her hand from mine, lifting and running it through her disheveled hair. She pushes the strands around as if trying to tidy up and look presentable for him. If my father wasn't such a prick, I would think it was cute. But unfortunately, he is, and she deserves better.

She deserves to be someone's everything.

"I saw him before. He was here . . . angry." Her voice dips on the last word.

My eyebrow lifts. I didn't see him, but he probably was here. I don't doubt it.

It would make sense; he comes and goes as he pleases without a care in the world. He gives no shits of the havoc he causes Mom. Especially when he is angry. And he has been furious recently.

On edge.

Another reason I stay here. Her being alone here is not an option.

Just in case.

I don't trust my father. It's not that I think he'd hurt her, but something is off with him. I've often wondered if Trent realizes something is up. I'd ask him, but he's too busy running around the city, and we don't catch up that often.

No two siblings could be further apart or more different.

I'm a homebody. I like the simple things in life. I live at home and tend my garden and work part-time as a florist.

He's all about the money and prestige. The nightlife. Living fast and hard. He's so cliché.

The paps love him.

He's their favorite "billionaire trust fund boy." Although by the looks of the house I live in, I'm not sure the title fits anymore.

Listen, I don't judge him. If he wants to party and play the field, that's fine for him. I want none of that, but that doesn't make me miss him less.

"Are the flowers blooming?" My mother's voice pulls me out of my faraway thoughts. It's nice to hear. It sounds so crisp, reminding me of good times. When Dad was here, and the madness hadn't taken root in her mind yet. It reminds me of when the backyard is speckled pink and lush and vibrant.

There is hope in her voice. Reaching my hand out once again, I take her frail one in mine. "Not yet, Mom. But soon."

She nods her head, and then like a channel changing on a TV, she's no longer here with me. She's gone somewhere else. Somewhere far in her mind. A heavy sadness weighs down on me, filling my veins slowly. The sound of her footsteps leaving the room makes me take action, and before I know what I'm doing, I'm back outside.

The first flowers won't bloom in our garden for another few months. But I still welcome the balmy winter day. Because days like today bring her back, even if only for a short time.

With my knees back on the hard, weathered grass, I pull again, lifting the earth with my hands. Loose soil sifts through my fingers like grains of sand passing the time.

A noise coming from in front of where I am, has me looking up to see who's there. "Trent?" I say, lifting my hand up to cover the sunlight. My older brother steps out from the shadows. "What are you doing here?"

"Can't I come to check on my sister?" He tries to say this in a joking manner, but his tone doesn't match his words.

I lift a brow in speculation. "You could, but then you wouldn't be my brother."

"What is that supposed to mean?" He halts his steps and then stares at me.

With the bright light gleaming down on me, I can't see him well. I place my shovel on the ground, and then I stand before making my way to him. When he's directly in front of me, I look at him closely and then shake my head.

He looks like shit.

Normally handsome, he seems rundown and tired. Large dark circles and dull eyes make it appear as though he hasn't slept in days.

"Did you come here straight from the bar?" I incline my head to get a better look before narrowing my eyes. On top of his appearance, Trent is acting strange. He's bouncing from foot to foot, almost as though he's high or in withdrawal from drugs. "Why are you acting like this?"

"Like what?"

"Cagey," I respond. "Are you high?"

"No, Ivy." His voice is stern, not even trying to mask his annoyance at my question. "That's ridiculous."

"Is it, though? You show up out of nowhere, and you look like . . . shit," I deadpan.

He takes a deep breath, then shakes his head. His signature smirk appears on his handsome face, and a glimmer of his normally playful personality pops through. It reminds me of when we were kids, and we used to play in the dirt together. Trent would grab Mom's watering hose and sprinkle us like it was raining. After playing for hours, we would both be drenched, and Mom would watch us as she gardened, laughing. "You're not being very nice, sis."

"And you are being shady as fuck." I place my hands on my hips and purse my lips. "What's going on?"

"Nothing. I told you." He stops talking and starts to pace back and forth on the patio in the backyard. His short-lived good mood fading faster than a mirage in a desert.

What's going on with him?

This is odd behavior, even for Trent. I watch as he walks, his mouth moving as if he's talking to himself, but no words come out, and then he's pulling out his phone from his pocket. His shoulder tense as he reads what I assume is a text message.

"Everything okay?" I ask him.

He looks exhausted and beat as he lifts his free hand and runs it through his light brown hair.

"It will be," he says before letting out a sigh. Whatever the text was about is obviously not good because he looks worse off than when he first got here.

"You're worrying me. Are you sure? If you need help—"

He raises his hand to stop me from talking, and I do. Normally, I would fire back a witty comment about how rude it is to butt in, but something tells me I shouldn't. Maybe it's the circles under his eyes or the way his brow furrows, but I decide to shut my mouth instead and hear what he has to say.

"I'm not using drugs, Ivy, but I appreciate the concern. Can't I just be here to see my baby sister?"

I opt for a joke, trying to cut the tension hovering in the air between us. "Yes. If that brother is anyone but you." He chuckles, and then I begin to laugh too. I love the sound of his laughter. He places his hand against his chest in mock disbelief. "Just keeping it real, bro." I miss this version of my brother.

We both go quiet after our momentary reprieve from the tension. It's once again awkward and uncomfortable, and although I'm not close with my brother anymore, it feels wrong. With his shoulders slumped forward, he kicks the dirt with his shoe before looking up and meeting my stare.

"Is Mom okay?" He finally breaks the silence.

"You can ask her yourself, Trent."

He looks back at his phone before his pale blue eyes meet mine. "On that note, I think I'll be going now."

"Please, Trent, what's going on? Are you okay?"

A shadow of something passes over his features before he rubs his temples as if a headache is forming. "I'm just checking on you. I was here to talk to Dad . . ."

"He's back?" My stomach muscles tighten. I have no desire to see him today.

"No."

I shake my head in confusion. "I don't understand. Mom said he was, but I didn't see him."

"Stay away from him." His tone has my back straightening.

"Why? You're scaring me. Did he do something?"

"Just promise me you'll stay away from him. I'll go find him, but in the meantime, can you go back inside? And if anyone comes here looking for him, don't answer."

"What? No. Look at it outside, it's beautiful."

"Please."

"Listen, Trent. I appreciate you being here. I love to see you, but I think I can handle Dad."

"It's just—"

"No," I cut him off, lifting my hand. "You aren't here. I am. I deal with him. His mood. I have done a good job raising myself, regardless. But as much as I appreciate your concern, I need to take care of Mom, and right now, that means getting her garden ready."

"She's not getting better?"

"Her depression is worse in the winter, but when the sun comes out, she does."

He looks down and then looks off in the direction of the pile of dirt I've made.

"I love you, sis."

"I love you too, big bro. Now let me get back to this. It will be dark soon." With one last nod, he leaves.

I can't help but think something is wrong with him. He said he's not using drugs, but I'm not sure I believe him.

Sometime later, when I'm about to stand and head inside, I hear noises. The sound of a car door. Footsteps. From the corner of my eye, I see a shadow. My body pivots to see who's coming toward me. My mom? My dad?

Maybe it's Trent again.

But when I'm fully turned in the direction of the noise and shadows, no one is there.

I fight off the foreboding feeling that I'm being watched. As my fingers pull at the remnants of last summer, I swear I see movement. As if the world around me feels it too, the sky darkens.

I can smell the rain before it starts. The damp, musty air infiltrates my nostrils.

I should move, but I don't. Instead, I wait.

I wait for the crack in the sky, and then I wait for the first drop. Most people don't enjoy being in the rain, but I love it. It invigorates me. It reminds me of the beginning of spring.

Rebirth.

CHAPTER THREE

Cyrus

L AST NIGHT WAS A SHITSHOW.

It wasn't until early this morning that I finally went to bed. I lost track of how much money traded hands, not that it matters. All I really care about is how much money I made.

Taking a rake will do that.

Sure, it's illegal, but not one motherfucker who comes into my house will open their mouth to complain. Not the patrons, and certainly not the staff.

That move would sign their death certificate.

But no matter how much money I skimmed from the pot, last night was not successful. The objective of the night was never met. We never got any information from Boris that we could use in order to take down the organization he works for. We are no closer to finding *Alexander,* and that thought pisses me the fuck off. All the information my men have collected have ended up as dead ends. No one knows where he is, where he lives, or how to get in touch with him. The only man that can provide that intel is Boris, but he would die before giving up his boss.

My phone vibrating next to my bed has me lifting my arm to grab it. It's an unknown number. The clientele I work with don't have numbers that are trackable.

"Speak," I bark into the line. Everyone who knows me knows not to bother me. Period. Especially in the morning. What time is it, anyway?

With the phone next to my ear, I glance at the clock. The red glow of the numbers reflects off the pitch black of my room.

It's like a tomb in here.

It's like hell.

My own personal hell.

Eleven fucking a.m.

"Cyrus," the familiar voice says. It's Z, my right-hand man.

"What number is this?"

"New one."

He doesn't have to clarify. We go through burners like candy, depending on new clientele and whatnot.

"Why are you calling this early?"

"It's almost noon." He chuckles, but I don't respond to his comment. It doesn't matter what time it is; unless it's an emergency, I don't like to be bothered when I'm sleeping. When he realizes I'm not going to respond, he continues. "It's about Trent Aldridge. From the game last night. You know who I—"

"I know who you're talking about," I cut him off. I know exactly who he is. His father was a degenerate last night. Z has known me for years, has been my most trusted man for most of them, so the fact that Z would bother me over something to do with him makes me move to the edge of the bed, place my feet on the floor, and stand. "What about him?"

"He's demanding you speak to him," Z says, and my head shakes.

Un-fucking-believable.

"No one demands anything of me." My voice is calm, but there's no mistaking the anger in my tone. It's deadly.

The phone line goes quiet.

Very fucking quiet.

The silence stretches between us, and I know the truth is there. I let out a long-drawn-out breath.

When the game ended, Trent's father, Ronald Aldridge, owed Boris a fortune. What happens with the collection of said money isn't my problem. They know the rules, so I'm not sure what he wants.

"You're right, boss, but he wishes to speak with you, and he sounded rather desperate. Maybe this is still our in . . ." He trails off, and that's when the stars align. He may just be right. I've been looking for a way in, the debt that Aldridge owes Boris could be exactly what I need as leverage.

"Very well. Tell him to come here."

Hanging up, I stalk toward the bathroom. I have to get ready for the day. Turning on the shower, I wash the night off.

The phone rings the moment I step out, so I secure a towel around my waist and answer it.

"Speak."

"He's begging for you to come to him."

"The fuck, Z?" I respond. "No."

I don't go to him. That's my one rule. I don't leave my fortress. People come to me, not vice versa. Not to mention the fact this trouble his father got in isn't my problem, it might be my solution, but it's not my fucking place to go to him to solve it.

"Boss. I've never heard him sound like this."

"I said no."

"He said it was life or death."

Interesting. "Go on."

"He was rambling about a sister. I think this could be our ace in the hole." Z's voice rises. The pieces of the puzzle for Trent Aldridge's desperate phone call click into place. This isn't about money. It's about his sister. The fucker didn't listen. I don't condone trafficking. Now there will be consequences.

"Tell him I'll be there."

Today will be an exception. I'll go to him because I allowed this shit to go down, and they'll have to pay the price for going against my ruling.

"Very well, boss. I'll have the chopper readied," Z says. There is nothing more to talk about, so I hang up and head into my closet to get dressed.

Now donning my usual three-piece suit, I head out of the room, down the hall, and then I exit the house. In the distance, I see my heliport. Z is standing beside Maxwell, who will fly it. Once inside, it's fired up, and we head down to the city.

In.

Out.

Soon, we're landing on the roof of a building I own. We hop in my car, and then we are off to the address Trent provided for us.

Fifteen minutes later, we park the car outside a brownstone in the West Village located on a quiet street.

This is good. There will be no witnesses if I have to use violence to drive my message home.

"What do you want to do, boss?" Z asks from where he sits in the front seat beside Maxwell.

"Get him."

A few moments later, I see a very different Trent. Not the same man who comes to play in my Friday game each week. Normally, he looks like the rich playboy next door. Today, he looks like a disheveled mess.

Like he hasn't slept in days.

Even from here, nestled in my car, I can see through the car window how he shakes. Rage? Fear? I'm not sure. But he doesn't look like he'll be able to sit long enough to tell me what the fuck is going on.

I fling the door open to the car and step outside. It's unusually warm today. I walk to where he's pacing.

"What's going on?" I ask.

"I can't stop him," he mutters under his breath as he buries his hands in his hair. "I don't know what to do."

"How is this my problem?"

He takes a deep breath. His chest rising and falling. "My father."

"Again, I don't see how this concerns me." I clench my jaw. I knew that fucker would be an issue. The moment I saw him, and as I watched the game, I knew. Fuck. "I'm not seeing how this is my problem." But it is. And no matter what I say, I know it is.

"Your game—" he starts, but I don't let him finish as I grab his jacket in my hands.

"This has nothing to do with my game," I grit. "Your father shouldn't have been there. This is on you." I'm pissed, and it should scare him. Trent does something I don't expect and pulls away from my hold. He's bolder than I first thought, but even with this new bravado, I can still tell that my words crush him.

"I need your help."

"There is nothing I can do for you." I move to turn and go back to the car. I don't need to stay for this, and I'm pretty fucking pissed that I left my fort for this. Even though I came here in order to figure out a way to spin this in my favor, it's not worth the hassle to deal with this level of stupidity.

"Stop." His voice is strong. "Yes, it is my fault, but I can't let him take her."

I knew this is where it was going, but the words have me halting my movements.

"I said last night . . ."

"Yeah, you did, but it didn't mean shit to my father. He lost everything. He has nothing . . . and last night, apparently he lost what little was left, that and more."

"What else? There's more, or you wouldn't have risked your life to summon me."

Trent looks me straight in the eye and nods. "I heard him. He's selling her. For the debt. And Boris said she would be perfect."

Perfect? For what? Or, better yet, whom?

"And this is my problem how?" I keep my voice steady, never showing emotions, but his words cut me to the bone. No woman should have that fate. I might do a lot of evil things, but a woman on the auction block is not one of them. Especially not a block with Boris calling the shots. In this case, her best chance of survival is him selling her because if Boris keeps her, he's nicknamed The Butcher for a reason. There is also the possibility—

"I thought . . ." Trent's voice cuts through my inner thoughts. "What the fuck did you think?"

He looks down. The arrogant shit looks devastated.

"The bank . . . I know . . ."

Trent starts to pace, and there is a long, brittle silence before he speaks. "You think my bank would bail you out? Listen, pretty boy, there is no collateral you could give me to cover it."

He flinches at my words before righting himself. But even with his newfound composure, there is no denying the unease etched on his face.

"I'm good for the money. I'll pay you back. All you have to

do is give the money to Boris. Help her . . ." He points to the right. I can't see what he's pointing at, so I take a step closer.

My eyes find their intended destination.

There, amongst the bleak earth recently frozen by snow, is the most beautiful woman I have ever seen.

She's young, much younger than a woman I should be looking at, but it doesn't stop me from staring.

"How old is she? Is she even legal?" I grit through clenched teeth.

"Yes. Twenty-two."

Thank fuck.

She looks ethereal, like a goddess of spring come down from the heavens to bring life.

"A means to an end," Z mouths to me, echoing the idea that has also taken root in my head.

I nod to my men. "It's done. I won't be loaning you the money to fix your problem. There is only one solution."

"What? I don't understand?" Trent asks, following my gaze.

"I'm taking the girl."

CHAPTER FOUR

Ivy

MY HEAD THROBS.
Why does it hurt so bad?

It feels like a jackhammer digging into my skull, reminding me of a construction site. My scalp being like the first bit of gravel to break before all the stone crumbles.

I reach my hands up to rub the sleep out of my eyes. The weight of my arm is unfamiliar. It's as if I'm weighted down to my bed and can't get up.

What's wrong with me?

My eyes won't open properly, but even with my temporary blindness, I can tell something else is off.

My limbs. My stomach. Everything aches, but it's my head that scares me. It feels like a thick fog has descended over a mountain, making the visibility limited, but instead of a land-scape, it's happening to me.

When my eyes finally open, I'm met with little light. The windows are covered, making it hard to see. The sparse beams that stream across the room don't do much to illuminate the space. An instant wave of nausea hits me at the same time that reality sinks in.

I'm not in my house.

The room is unfamiliar.

I lift myself to a seated position. My muscles scream as if I had drunk too much booze. But that makes little sense. The room comes into focus. Beautiful and ornate. It looks straight out of a castle. High ceilings, marble floors. Even though it's dim, I swear I see gold leaf on the walls. What is this place, and what has happened to me?

I lift my hand and run my fingers through my hair, trying to remember.

Nothing comes to mind.

The last thing I remember is being in the garden. *Odd.* But that makes no sense. I must have done something else. Otherwise, how could I be here right now?

I'm in a house. In a bed. Alone.

I pull the sheet down, checking to make sure I'm not naked. A long-drawn-out sigh of relief pours from my lungs like the steam from a train.

Fully dressed.

I'm still in the clothes I wore when gardening, which means I didn't get drunk, nor do I remember going out.

What happened then?

Throwing the sheet all the way back, I climb out of the bed. My body shakes uncontrollably. Something is wrong with me. It's almost as if I have taken a sleeping pill.

But that wouldn't explain where I am?

Unless . . .

My limbs begin to quiver as fear twists inside me. Cold as ice, the thought chills me to the bone.

I was drugged. *Taken.*

My head moves back and forth frantically as blinding terror drips into my veins. It pours like a rambling river with no end. The farther I walk into the room, moving toward the door, the faster the current moves inside me.

By the time my hand touches the metal handle, I fear I might pass out from the way my blood pumps.

Swishing.

Pounding.

Begging me to turn back, but go where? The only way out of this unknown room is through that door. The metal is cold to the touch, making me shiver. Slowly, as if to creep out of the room, I turn it, but what I'm met with forces my ears to ring with terror.

I'm locked in. I shake the door handle now, desperate to escape.

When that doesn't work, I kick. I scream.

I pound on the door with my fist. Flailing as pain radiates through my arms. The scene is straight out of a bad Lifetime movie. The harder I try, the more frail I feel. It's as if the door is made of steel. In the movies, it looks so easy. The heroine bangs on the door with all her might, and lo and behold, it cracks, except in my case, there isn't any indication that my efforts are fruitful. The wood looks just as intact as when I first started this endeavor.

All the oxygen in my lungs feels depleted as I try desperately to break through.

Nothing.

There has to be another way out. Peering around the room, I look at the window. There. That. I can climb out.

Maybe.

I have to try.

I run toward it, and then pull back the curtain. There is a metal handle that I grasp to unlock it, and then I swing it toward me.

As soon as it flies open, the cold air hits me in the face.

Could it be this easy?

Could I escape?

The muscles in my stomach tense as I lean up onto my tiptoes to peer out the window.

I look down.

That's when I realize this is worse than I thought. From my window, the ground drops beneath into a bluff. Open water crashes against the beach.

I choke back a sob that threatens to escape. There's no time for tears. Even though my chest feels like it will burst, I need to stay calm and figure out a way out of this room.

I have nowhere to go, but I have to try. I can't just lie in wait for my fate. I can't stay in this bed, waiting for whoever took me to come back and hurt me.

With my hands on the edge of the windowsill, I move to climb out. Maybe once I'm farther outside, I'll notice another way to get away.

My head and chest are almost through the window. There must be a rail somewhere? Maybe a window beneath that I can shimmy down. I push forward until I lock my arms. But I'm still not seeing any easy solution for my salvation. Lifting a leg, I move to crawl out.

"I wouldn't do that if I were you." I hear from behind me and I freeze in fear. *I'm not alone.* I thought I was, and in my rush to leave, he had slipped into the room. How had I not heard him come in?

"Get down from there." The voice is cold, making me shiver as if an arctic blast has blown through.

Slowly, I step down, the drapes moving back into place as I turn to see who is here.

It's almost pitch black again. Hard to see. I squint my eyes, trying to adjust to the darkness that surrounds me.

Only small slivers of light shine in a tiny beam, but it's not enough.

He's in the shadows.

Tall and dominating.

Like the angel of death come forth to pull me to the other side. *To Hell.*

A chill runs up my spine.

I haven't seen his face, and I'm already afraid. His presence alone is enough to have me cower in the corner.

I can't, though.

He is the only thing blocking the door to my escape.

So, I need to be smart about this.

I step forward, resting my hands at my hips. I might be petrified, but I won't show him my fear.

"Who are you?" I ask.

He doesn't speak.

"Why am I here?" My voice is louder this time than before. When he doesn't answer again, I wonder if I had even heard him before. I take another step.

"I said, why am I here?"

This time, he steps out of the shadow, and his face comes into focus.

Handsome. Devastatingly handsome.

A god among mortals.

Sharp lines. Strong and powerful. Dark hair. Pressed suit. Not just any suit, though. This one screams money.

Power.

He screams power with dark eyes that have no soul.

"Why am I here?"

The silence that descends upon the room is deafening.

Talk to me. Answer me. Acknowledge I've spoken.

Anything.

But instead of giving me what I look for, he steps back into the shadows.

Closing the door. Locking it again.

With him now gone, I sit back on the bed and pull my knees into my body. I wrap myself up in a protective cocoon. It's hard to stop the tremors that run through my body at what just happened. Who is this man, and what does he want?

I continue to shake as fear knots inside me.

A gasp escapes as realization hits; there can only be one reason I'm here. I've been kidnapped probably because he wants to rape, and maybe even kill me.

Disturbing thoughts start to play out, building images in my head that I can't stop. A sob escapes as water cascades down my cheeks. No. I shake my head back and forth. I can't cry. I won't cry. Reaching up, I wipe my damp cheeks.

There has to be a way. I look back to the door. The *locked* door.

I'm trapped.

I'm in a cage. A gilded cage, but a cage, nonetheless.

CHAPTER FIVE

Ivy

WHEN I OPEN MY EYES SOMETIME LATER, MY HEAD shakes back and forth in confusion.

The door is now open. I must be seeing things that aren't really there. But as my eyes adjust to waking, there's no mistaking the gleam of light penetrating the crack in the door right now.

It's open, and a light in the hall reflects into my room.

What the hell is going on? Why would he lock me in, only to then leave the door open?

It makes no sense.

Is this the twilight zone? An alternate universe? I'm so confused by this new turn of events that I just sit here, staring like an idiot at the route I can use to potentially escape.

Yet when my limbs don't move, I shake my head. What am I doing? Move. Taking stock of my surroundings, I note that I'm still dressed, still have my sneakers on, and am still wearing a coat. Nothing is stopping me from walking out that door. Except fear.

I need to leave. This is my chance. I will my body to go, and with that, I propel myself as if I'm a runner in the Olympics.

I lift off the bed. My shoes hit the floor, and I'm out the door before I can think better of it. By the time I'm in the hallway, I realize my mistake.

I could find anything out here.

This could be a trap.

I halt my movements, taking slow, meaningful steps. I don't want the sound of my feet to alert anyone to my presence. That's my worst nightmare, to come so close, only to be stopped by stupidity. I need to be careful to make sure there will be no sound as I make my way out.

In the distance, I see the stairwell. It's grand, but no lights are on in that part of the house. Not one.

I have no idea what time it is, but I have to be careful.

I can't risk him seeing me, finding me, hurting me.

My heart thumps in my chest like a stampede of elephants. It ricochets off my breastbone, rattling. If I don't calm down, I'll hyperventilate.

Lifting my shoulders, I take a soft breath and then move toward the stairs that lead to the front foyer.

Before taking them down, I stop, listening for any signs of life.

There's nothing.

The house or, by the look of the hallway and stairs, the mansion is empty. No one is here. But then why would he leave the door open? Was he in a rush? Was it a mistake?

Is this a trick?

Maybe I should head back to my room?

No.

I'm not that girl. I'm not the type to hide in the corner and wait for the villain to arrive. I won't be a victim. I won't be a helpless lamb waiting for the predator to kill her.

I have to see if I can escape. Or at the very least, find someone to help me.

By this point, I'm not even sure how long I've been here. A day?

One thing I'm sure of is, no one is looking for me. My

mom probably doesn't know that I'm gone. Dad wouldn't care, and Trent is too busy.

I'm not scheduled to work until next week, so my boss won't even wonder where I am.

I can't sit around waiting for someone to help me. I have to help myself.

So I do.

I don't allow my fear to stop me.

As I tiptoe down the stairs, each step is more precarious than the last. When I finally hit the bottom, I see the front door. It's grand and dark and ominous. It's the door in a scary movie that led to a house of horrors. I know that if I open it, the sound will be terrible. It will squeak, or worse, it will alert him to my escape. This is the part in the movie where the scared heroine runs for her life. Hopefully, in this story, I get away. I'm not dumb enough to think it won't be hard, but the thing is, I have nothing to lose.

I won't be another statistic.

My hand lifts the knob, and as I suspected, the door makes a horrible sound against the quiet of the night. It's awful.

Like metal and wood scraping together.

I'm not sure if it's as bad as I assume, but it hurts my ears, and it makes my heart jump out of my chest.

I don't stop, though, and instead, I fling it open, emerging into the eerie night.

There are no lights outside, it's nighttime now. Pitch black other than the small stars twinkling from above.

Looking up, I see more here than I have in a long time, showing that I am no longer anywhere near the city.

Where am I?

I walk, using the stars as my only light. I can't walk fast, though; with limited visibility, I don't want to hurt myself.

Time passes in a series of heavy breaths verging on a panic attack.

As far as I go and as many steps as I take, it doesn't matter because there is nothing here. I push through branches, and then I see it.

As the light brightens, I see the stars reflecting off water.

But what scares me more is that it's black all around except in the distance. In the distance, I can finally see light.

But it's not close enough, and there is no way to swim there.

It's too far. Standing on what must be a beach, I walk along the coast, looking up at the stars to use them for direction. At some point the beach stops, and rocks and grass replace the sand. It's harder to walk now, especially with no visibility, so I take small measured steps. The terrain changes, and now I'm surrounded by trees and boulders.

Where the hell am I?

I keep going.

With each new step, the light from the water disappears more and more, cloaking me in darkness. At least I have the stars.

I walk for God knows how long.

But before I know it, I'm once again back on sand, staring out across the water into the vast distance at the lights on the beach.

Is it the same?

Am I just walking around in circles?

I need to mark my spot.

Pulling off my coat, I drop it on the ground, putting some rocks over it to keep it in place.

Now, without my coat, my body shivers from the cold. I start to walk in the same path I had just made. Through the beach, then the rocks, then the trees. I walk for what seems like forever, with my arms wrapped around my body to keep myself warm. In the distance, I see something, my stomach muscles tighten as I make my approach.

This confirms my fears. There is nowhere to go.

The blood in my veins pumps so hard it sounds like drums are playing.

Thud.

Thud.

My jacket.

I look up, staring at a sight that makes me shake all over and not because of the cold this time. But because there it is, yet again.

In the distance are lights, and then realization hits me like a ton of bricks.

I now know him leaving the door open was no accident. There was no reason to lock it because I have nowhere to go.

I'm stuck.

On whatever island it is I'm on.

He doesn't need to lock any doors because it appears that there is no way off.

Maybe in the light, I'll find something.

Or maybe . . .

My head shakes back and forth. I can't dwell on the what-if. I need to calm myself and think.

I sit staring at the beach in front of me. It's dark so I can't see much, but there are enough stars in the sky to make the water visible. Each time the waves crash against the shore, little bursts of light dance in my eye as I catch the reflection of the moon.

I don't move as I try to think of a plan.

But nothing comes to me. Not now. Not at night. And especially not on an island probably surrounded by sharks.

That's just what I need, to escape and then be eaten by bloodthirsty sharks desperate for food. Me being lunch.

That would be just my luck.

I should go back.

Admit my fate.

But I don't want to.

I feel I'm suffocating, but at least here I have air.

I stare off into the night sky, wondering how this happened.

Why am I here, and what does he want?

Fear dances within me. My brain's running a mile a minute. The muscles in my heart beat so fast, I fear I'll pass out. I need to calm down. My brain runs through all the techniques I've learned over the years to help my mom through her depression. This isn't the same, but maybe it will help. The doctor once told me to have her breathe deeply, to focus on an object and forget everything else.

I watch as the waves crash against the shore.

As they break and turn to crystals against the moonlight.

Inhaling slowly, I will myself to calm.

Inhale. Exhale.

Inhale . . .

I'll find a way. I know I will.

I have no other choice.

I'm no one's victim.

Exhale . . .

CHAPTER SIX

Ivy

THROUGH THE HAZE OF MY DREAM, I CAN SEE A BRIGHT light peeking in. My eyes hurt. They blink rapidly as I take stock of where I am. Lifting my hands, I rub at them, but as I do, I notice the chill in the air. My body aches, and as the world appears before me, I know why.

I'm not in my bed, nor am I in a bed at all.

No. Instead, the vision in front of me makes me shake. Now the cold makes sense.

I fell asleep outside.

Sitting up, I look around me.

Still on the grass that sits nestled against the beach. Still on an island in the middle of fuck knows where. Still cold.

I pull my jacket tighter.

Now, in the harsh morning light, I can see the land in the distance. From where I am, a giant estate sits on the property. It's too far to be sure if it's a house or even a hotel—that's how large it is—but clearly, I went around in circles last night on my tour, so it's obvious I'm on an island. But if I'm on an island, there has to be a way off.

A boat?

Yes. There has to be one somewhere.

I just need to search.

I'm about to stand when I hear a sound behind me.

My back goes straight because that is not the sound of a person. It's the sound of an animal.

Then I hear barking.

Vicious, loud, scary barking.

My fight-or-flight kicks in. I need to get out of here.

A dog is coming, and it's coming to attack, so I weigh my options. I don't know where to go. On the one hand, I can jump into the water, and on the other, I can run to the beach.

Or . . .

I shake my head. No. I can't run back to the house, but there really is no option. I'm screwed either way, and the water is probably freezing.

Shit.

What do I do?

In the distance, I can see trees. That's the only safe bet. Before I can second-guess my decision, I'm up and running.

My feet pound the grass beneath as it cracks under the pressure. The ground hard and brittle from the cold winter months.

Wind hits my face, and my lungs expel oxygen.

Thud. Thud. Thud.

I'm running so fast, my vision starts to haze from the exertion, but I hear the sound gaining on me.

And then it's right behind me.

I wasn't fast enough.

I fall.

My knees hit the cold earth; hands next. Loose gravel scratches me, causing a burning feeling to radiate inside me. I need to get up.

The sound intensifies, and I know I need to get up *now.*

I'm just about to push off the ground when I hear the words.

"Stop," he bellows, and I know I have only spoken to him once, but I know the sound. I would know that voice anywhere.

I might not know his name, but I know his voice. Not

heeding his warning, I push off anyway, but the growling stops me.

I turn slowly to find the scariest dog I have ever seen, and he's poised to attack.

Looking down his long nose at me.

Teeth bared. "*Liggen.*"

I have no idea what he's just said to me, but then I realize he's not talking to me. He's talking to the dog.

The snarling dog who is now in a down position staring at me.

"What are you doing out here?" he says, and I look up at him.

At this man I don't know.

Nor do I want to.

In the light of the early morning, he looks even more handsome than he did last night. I know I shouldn't think that, but even if he is a killer, it doesn't change the truth. He might be psychotic, but maybe that's his lure.

I shake my head back and forth; his appearance or mental capacity shouldn't be on my mind. The only thing I should care about is how I'm leaving.

"Did you sleep out here?" He steps closer, and I try to retreat, but that elicits another snarl from his watchdog. "Answer me."

"Yes."

"You tried to escape?" I can hear a hint of dismay as he nods to himself. "Even in the dark."

"Yes," I hiss back. "Even in the dark."

"You're lucky you didn't get hurt."

"Better drowned than . . ." A shudder draws down my spine.

"I will not touch you." His words come out with conviction. Unwavering, with no trace of a lie. It doesn't make me feel any safer, though. He might say he won't rape me, but can I really believe him?

He took me, so how can I trust anything he says?

"Then why am I here?" My eyes narrow suspiciously as he steps closer. His stone-cold features give nothing away. Then he turns on his heels and starts walking back to the house.

"Are you coming?" he says over his shoulder.

"No."

"Not a very smart answer. A storm is coming. If I were you, I would take shelter in the house."

"And you? Will you be taking shelter in the house with me too?"

No way in hell am I getting stuck in closed quarters with him. Who knows what this man will do.

"No."

The breath I didn't know I was even holding releases, but then another thought hits me. If he's leaving . . .

"So, I'm stuck here alone?"

That makes him stop walking and turn to face me.

"Would you rather I stay?" He lifts a seductive brow.

"You said you wouldn't touch me."

"And I won't. Not unless you ask."

"Well, then, don't hold your breath because I'll never ask for that."

"If you say so." And with that, he keeps heading toward the house, his dog beside him. Although, I'm not sure I would call that thing a dog. More like a beast that wants to kill me.

Weighing my options, I can either try to escape again or follow him.

I shouldn't trust him, and I don't. The options are limited, though.

The truth is, I don't know if he will keep his word . . .

Then another thought hits me straight in the stomach. My legs almost give out under the weight of the train of thought driving through my head.

I have seen his face.

Multiple times.

If asked, I could sketch it, describe it. I could tell the police who he is. I'm a liability, a potential loose end to a crime committed.

Kidnappers only show you their face if they're planning to kill you.

My feet stop, no longer able to walk a step.

I pray he doesn't look back, but he does. Staring at me intently, but it's not a normal look though. It's dark and predatory, and if I don't move, he will make me, but my fear has me stuck in quicksand.

"Let's go."

"No."

He arches an eyebrow, and it's almost as if he's smirking at me. The line of his lips is a flat line, but it appears the right side is lifting a little bit higher. Or maybe I'm just reading into things, probably from dehydration and desperation.

"I'm not coming with you."

"Don't make me come get you. You won't like it if I do."

We are at an impasse, but I have no choice but to succeed first.

"Will you kill me?"

"No." I don't know if he's telling the truth, but I guess I have no choice but to believe him.

CHAPTER SEVEN

Cyrus

WHEN I SHOWED UP THIS MORNING AND SHE WASN'T IN her room, I thought she had maybe escaped. That faded fast when I realized there was no way off this island.

No one could come or go without my permission.

The island sits close enough to the land that it isn't in the direct view of passing boats, and my property is large enough that the nearest neighbor is too far to see what happens on the island.

They would have to be close, and anyone who gets that close will be noticed. I have men watching the waters now.

Normally, I don't.

But this isn't a normal occasion.

I've never taken a woman captive before, so the added security is necessary.

It doesn't matter why she's here; her obedience is required, and trying to escape will not be tolerated.

I turn around and watch as she trudges after me. She's disheveled from sleeping outside. The beach was the last place I looked when it should have been the first.

If I was taken—obviously, that would never happen, but if I was—you bet the first thing I would do is try to escape. I just figured she was in the house somewhere.

But after I looked everywhere, and it was obvious she wasn't there, I went to the front door. Nothing was there to indicate she had left.

The door automatically locks from the outside.

A part of me wonders if she ever tried to come back last night. Her quest would have been fruitless.

She wouldn't have been able to get back in, even if she tried, but something tells me this girl didn't even try.

She would rather freeze to death sitting outside than admit it was safer inside.

I stare at her as she makes her approach. Standing by the large front door, I dangle the metal key from my hand.

"After you." I swing it open and step aside for her to enter. When she doesn't move, I lift my hands in surrender. "I will not hurt you."

Meeting my stare boldly, she doesn't flinch, just speaks. "Like you would admit to it."

I could answer her, but I don't. It would be easy to put her mind at ease. I don't do easy, and I don't explain myself. "It's your choice. Stay outside and freeze or take your chances inside with me."

She looks back toward the beach, unsure of what to do. She's weighing her options, but from the way her jaw hardens, I know she's come to the conclusion she doesn't have any other option.

"First, I have a question."

I knew she would. She's too fiery not to. I admire it.

Not that I'll tell her shit.

Instead, she'll stay here locked up in my fortress with no clue why.

"Inside. Now."

She should shake in fear at my tone, but she doesn't.

Nope. Not her.

Instead, she straightens her back, keeps her head held high, and walks through the door.

Her steps halt the moment she's in the foyer, and with the strength reserved for a superhero, she glares at me.

"Now that I came inside, why am I here?" she asks firmly.

"For your protection."

She steps slowly forward as if pondering my words, then glances down at the floor. Halting her movements, she once again lifts her eyes to meet my gaze. Those blue eyes, deep with thought, read me, challenge me. I shouldn't like the way she narrows her eyes and tests me, but I do. More than I should. It's like a losing game of chess. She should cut her losses, minimize the outcome, but yet she presses on.

It's admirable.

"My protection. That's rich. You kidnap me and lock me up, and then you claim it's for my protection." She inclines her head in thought. "Okay, I'll bite. From whom?"

I don't answer her question. Again, that would be too easy. I prefer to watch her get angry. To watch as her skin turns a vibrant red and her cheeks suck in when she bites them. It's probably a reaction to anger that she doesn't even realize she does. It's cute. Watching Ivy get angry might be my new favorite pastime.

"So that's it. You make some ridiculous claim and don't back it up."

"Exactly."

I really could tell her, but I almost like this better. The attitude, her strength. No one challenges me. Regardless that she is my captive, she still has the strength and will to challenge me, and it's invigorating.

Men clamor at me. Women fawn.

But not her.

Yeah. Decision made.

This is the most alive I've felt in years, and I'm not willing to give this feeling up. No. I can't tell her the truth, and I can't let her go. Instead, I let her pass and follow her as she heads to the stairs.

"I'll leave you." I look toward the front door and then back at her. Her eyes widen because she thinks this is her chance. I stifle my laughter because there is no getting away. "I won't lock you in," I confirm. "You have free rein of the house. You'll find nothing here to help you."

"But how will—"

I hold my hand up. "There is food. Water. Everything you need is here. But there is nothing in this house or on this property to help you leave."

"Why are you doing this?"

"Because I can." I walk toward the door. "*Bescherm*," I say, and my dog moves to stand beside Ivy.

"You can't leave me with him. He might kill me."

"He will protect you. Which also means no one but me will come or go from this house."

"What's his name?"

"Cerberus."

She laughs, a full-body laugh, and when she throws her head back, I stare at the curve of her neck.

"How cliché are you? Cerberus? Really. Jeez, you have to be kidding."

I shake my head at her words.

"Who do you think you are, Hades? You are no king."

I advance toward her, stalking over like a lion ready to devour its prey.

"I'm Cyrus Reed, and that is exactly what I am."

And on those parting words, I leave her standing in my foyer with her pale blue eyes still wide with fear.

Good.

She should be afraid.

Back at my estate, I'm sitting in my large chair in my office that faces the ocean. In the distance, I can see the outline of the manor that sits on my secluded island.

No one knows it's there.

No one but me. Well, that and the limited people I trust.

There are only a handful.

I wonder what she is doing now. Is she searching for a way to escape again? Probably. I wouldn't put it past her.

If it was me, I would never give up. I wouldn't cower in fear either. *She never cowered.*

When I first saw her, she left me breathless. Something that rarely happens to me.

Sure, I fuck a lot, but more often than not, I barely care to even look at the woman when I do. I choose instead to take her from behind, a hole for me to sate my own baser needs in.

But Ivy is different.

I won't fuck her.

Not unless she begs for it. Not unless she gives herself to me willingly, but I can't pretend I don't want to. Even with her sun-kissed hair matted with dirt, and her fair skin pale from exhaustion, she is still more beautiful than anyone.

Couple that with her inner strength and she is irresistible to me. Temptation at its finest.

When the phone rings on my desk, I welcome the distraction. It can only be one of a few people.

"Yes," I answer.

"Tobias is on the phone."

Tobias, one of my clients, will give me business to work on. That way I'll no longer be preoccupied with the fiery blonde an ocean away. "Put him through." The phone call connects. "Tobias," I say.

"Cyrus Reed. You are a hard man to get in touch with."

I recline back in my chair and chuckle. "I am. But I'm also the best at what I do."

Tobias laughs in return. "Hence, why I wait. And I don't enjoy waiting."

"And I don't like false pretenses, so tell me why you're calling," I respond.

Tobias might be the leading distributor of cocaine on the eastern seaboard, but I don't fear anyone.

He needs me more than I need him.

"Also, to the point. I like that about you."

"Good to know," I respond as my mouth twitches with amusement.

"I need to make a deposit."

Leaning forward, I type into my computer, pulling up his embedded file. "Figured as much."

"A fairly large one."

"Again, not surprised," I deadpan.

"Ten million."

"That can be arranged. Cash?"

Dumb question, but hey, you never know. Maybe drug dealers deal in credit now. But to be honest, you would be surprised by how often I get diamonds or gold. Fuck, drugs too. I don't deal in humans, though.

Well . . . Ivy is the exception.

This girl is fucking poison.

"Yes. Are you in the office?"

Even dumber question. I'm never in my office.

I never go into the city unless it is necessary, and if he wants to give me a fucking briefcase with ten million dollars, he can fucking come to me.

"Don't ask stupid questions," I respond. "My estate. Tonight."

"Any chance there is a game going on?"

I shake my head. They are all the same, and I'm okay with that. He'll come with ten million but only deposit half.

Works every damn time. The good news is, less to clean. Funneling five million is much easier, and plus, I'll make a better cut if he spends it.

Not that I need money.

I have more money than I can spend in five lifetimes, but what I like is the power.

These men need me, and that is priceless. I rule the underworld.

Ivy was right.

I might not be Hades, but I damn well run the show like I am. I own these men, and they fucking know it.

Before he can say anything else, I hang up. I'm not one for small talk or talking at all. Instead, I prefer to sit back and observe. That's my strength.

I was hoping I could observe her tonight.

But alas, work comes first.

I refresh my computer screen and prepare the proper funnels to hide his money.

It will be a long night.

Hours pass.

My eyes are burning, but once Tobias shows up with his

suitcase, I have all the paperwork in place. By the time I rid him of his satchel, it will look like he struck it rich on the stock market.

See, this is why it pays to have the seediest of clients.

Take Trent, for example . . .

He needed my help.

I gave him said help, and now, in turn, he will invest a percentage of the money Tobias brings as well as some of my other clients, without a blink of an eye. It will appear on the up-and-up, but he'll know it's not.

I pick up my cell and scroll through the contacts.

Hitting him up.

"Is she okay?" he answers.

Regardless of the fact I think he's a self-indulgent douche-bag, I have to admit he loves his sister.

I let out a sigh. "Yes." It's not his fault that his father got him into this mess. That's something I know way too well. My nostrils flare at the memory threatening to surface. The less I think about the man who gave me life, the better.

"Where is she?" There's an edge to his voice, one I hope for his sake isn't aimed at me. He'll learn rather quickly that no one talks to me like that.

"The less you know, the better," I respond matter-of-factly.

"I want to speak to her."

I've got to hand it to him, he does have balls. The more I talk to Trent, the more I can see that stubbornness might, in fact, be a family trait.

"Not going to happen. She doesn't know the full story, and unless you finally came up with something to tell her, the answer is no."

He goes silent for a minute. "Maybe I just should . . ." he

says, resigned to the fact that there is no other way. "Have you made any headway to fix it?"

"No."

"Are you even trying?" He scoffs.

This has gone on long enough. If he was in the room, my gun would be out and aimed at his head right now, but he's not, and there are bigger issues at hand at the moment, which means, I'll rein his attitude in and not kill the son of a bitch.

"Listen, you fuck, do not question me." My tone brooks no argument. Have I tried to fix it? Truth? No, I haven't. Why? Fuck knows why. Maybe I don't want to. Maybe I want to keep her all to myself.

I haven't even tried to come up with a solution. I don't tell him that, though. He's clearly unhinged over his sister, and I don't need the complication.

I wait for a few seconds and then speak. "I'm not calling regarding your sister."

"Then why are you calling?" he replies without inflection, as though he's come to terms with the fact that he has no power here and recognizes all the power is mine.

"Because you owe me. Regardless of anything, I fucking saved your sister's life, and now it's time to pay up."

"What do you need?"

And then I tell him exactly what I need.

I imagine he's wishing he never brought his father to my poker game.

CHAPTER EIGHT

Ivy

I EXPECTED HIM TO STORM THE ROOM—TO SHOW UP AND demand something I'm not willing to give—but he doesn't.

He never appeared.

I should be relieved, but I'm more on edge. It's like I'm waiting for the other shoe to drop. Normally, I'm not one to be scared, but now I'm feeling petrified. The uncertainty is killing me. I would rather know what my fate is. Why I'm here. But seeing as I'm still alone, I know that will not happen.

Yesterday, I sulked for the rest of my night.

Today isn't much better. I'm still sulking. A fact that I hate.

I am not that girl.

But desperate times call for desperate measures, and right now, I'm having a goddamn pathetic pity party for myself.

I miss my mom.

I miss my friends.

I miss my brother.

I don't miss my dad.

But other than that, I want out of this place, stat.

I walk around the large estate. It's odd how it sits here vacant. It's old, older than Cyrus Reed to have built, so he must have bought it, but for what? It reminds me of a smaller version of a medieval castle.

Except this one is located in Hell.

A small but nervous chuckle escapes my mouth as I realize I referred to him as Hades and remember that not only is his dog named Cerberus but also this island can only be accessed by boat.

It seems my host must have an affinity for Greek mythology. Seems fitting as I do too.

No. We are not the same at all. One little detail doesn't make us similar. No, I could never be like him.

He's a monster who probably kills. And I like to give life, helping things grow and flourish. He probably stops the light. Blocks it with his large, powerful frame. Snuffing out life.

I tiptoe around the corner, waiting for his dog to attack. He knows I'm coming because he's there, turning the corner. He must have some good hearing. I expect him to pounce, but he doesn't. Instead, he gives me a large berth to walk.

He shadows me as if I commanded it, which I guess since Cyrus did, he's just following orders.

My eyes roll of their own accord. Even though I have been here for a few days, I haven't checked out the house much. I need to explore.

There must be a boat somewhere. First, though, I need to eat, so I head to the kitchen. Walking into the large pantry, I find slim pickings. Barely enough to survive.

He said I had food and water, but clearly, that's a stretch of the truth. The food here won't last more than a few days.

I grab bread and then open the fridge. If I thought the pantry was empty, this is post-apocalyptic. Not a stitch of food.

Great. I have bread and water. That's not called food. That's a form of torture in some cultures.

With my prison meal in hand, I take a seat. Better make it last since who knows how long it will be before I get more.

I take a small bite of the bread. He didn't even include something to put on it.

What an asshole.

He really is the devil.

Conserving it, I continue to nibble. The slower I eat, the faster I'll grow full. I just need to chug water and force myself to believe I'm not hungry.

As I eat the tiny morsels, I notice that Cerberus stands guard. Hovering by the table.

Against my better judgment, I rip a piece of my bread and hold it out to him in my hand.

He doesn't move. Instead, he snarls. Probably trained not to accept food from strangers.

If only I could stick to my guns too.

"Cerberus," I say to him, but he doesn't look at me. He doesn't even acknowledge that I've spoken. If I didn't know better, I would think he didn't understand. But seeing as with one command, in who knows what language, he's followed me around, watched me, and apparently not eaten my scraps, it's obvious he knows more than the average dog. What else could I expect from the dog that guards Hell?

When I'm done with my bread, I stand and start my mission. I begin with the door right outside the kitchen. Then after that, I walk the main floor. Opening every door and every cupboard, I'm not sure what I'm looking for, maybe a key for a secret door or something. Although that won't help me. Only a boat will, and it's not like he would have a boat in the hallway. But I keep looking. I hit the jackpot when I find toiletries and women's clothes. A part of me doesn't want to use the clothes I find. Who knows who they belong to? For all I know, it's another captive of his. But desperate times call for desperate measures, and I need to shower and change. I'll wash the clothes I have on, but while I wait for them to be clean, I can't be sitting around here naked.

My body trembles at the thought of Cyrus coming back and finding me in that state. Reluctantly, I strip down and get in the shower in the bathroom of my room. I bring my dirty clothes in with me. I'll wash them with soap and water until I can find out if there is a washer in my prison. That will take more exploring, but at least it passes the time.

CHAPTER NINE

Ivy

T HE DAYS MESH TOGETHER, BLENDING LIKE THE STROKES of an impressionist painting. When I'm hungry, I eat. When I'm tired, I sleep. I'm always hungry, though. That's the problem with living on bread and water for days.

The sound of the door opening has me bolting from my bed. I quickly slip on my sweater over my leggings and head down the stairs. What I'm met with once I hit the bottom landing has me halting to a stop. It's not Cyrus.

My brain can't even register what is happening.

Has the moment finally come?

Is this it? The moment I've been waiting for.

All the what-ifs bounce around like a pinball in my brain.

Before I can second-guess myself, I'm running toward her.

She can help me. The sound of my approach must take her by surprise because she holds her hand to her chest.

Yes.

This is exactly what I need.

"Help me," I say as I run to where she is standing. Her eyes go wide as she looks me up and down, and that's when I finally look at her. She appears to be around my age, maybe older by a few years.

I expect her to say something, but when I move to touch her, to beg her, she takes a step back.

Her hand rises to stop me.

"Please," I implore. "Help me. I'm being kept here. I've been kidnapped." My voice cracks as my emotions threaten to overcome me. I'm petrified that this might be my only shot.

She looks at me with wide eyes, and then she does the unthinkable. She shakes her head back and forth.

"*Não falo inglês*," she responds.

The language sounds like Spanish, but it's not. I remember taking Spanish in high school. This is something else, but regardless of the fact that I can't understand her, it's rather clear that I have to assume she is saying she doesn't understand English.

"Please help me," I implore again, but this time, she doesn't answer.

I lift my hand to my ear. "Telephone." I gesture my hand to pretend I'm calling someone.

"*Desculpa*," she whispers.

I continue to stare at her as my heart beats frantically in my chest. I can escape. Even if she doesn't understand me, this woman must have keys to a boat. Could I be that lucky? Maybe? But then my stomach bottoms out as another thought crosses my mind. What good are keys when I have no boat?

She was probably dropped off.

The sinking feeling festers, spreading from my belly to all the other parts of my body, including my heart, that now pounds heavily. My plan won't work. It's hopeless. This woman can't help me.

With my shoulders slumped forward, a sigh escapes me.

She bites her lip at my clear show of defeat, and then she walks through the house, leaving me stunned in the foyer. As she trails off, I force myself to calm down and follow her to the kitchen. There has to be something I can do. Some way she can help me.

Once I'm standing in the doorway, I observe her. That's when I finally notice she has bags in her hand.

Food.

She's here to make sure I'm fed.

Shit.

That means I'll be here for longer than I wanted to believe. If he's feeding me, he has no intention of letting me off the island anytime soon.

This is bad.

Really bad.

There is a pressure building in my head, and my jaw starts to tremble. I'm about to cry in front of this woman if I don't pull myself together.

No.

Pushing all thoughts of my predicament aside, I sit at the kitchen table and watch her. She puts some food away, but the rest she cooks.

It's like I'm a stalker, or at least that is how I feel, as I sit at the table and just observe.

It must be hours that I watch her.

A part of me is hoping if I stay long enough, she will turn around and say "surprise, I'm here to help you."

That won't happen, but a part of me is so desperate to believe that, so I just watch as she cooks and then sections off the food into small plastic containers for me to eat.

One. Two. Three. Four. I lost count after ten because it's too depressing to think about. If she has to cook that much food, then there is no way he's coming back for me today or tomorrow.

There is no way anyone is coming for me for days, at least.

I must have lost track of time because the next thing I know, the woman, who I have to assume works for Cyrus as a cook, is standing beside me. She has a plate in her hand.

She tries to hand it to me.

But I shake my head.

"No." My voice is more forceful than I intend, but I need to get my point across. I am not eating.

She pushes the plate at me again, rambling something in her foreign tongue.

"No."

This time, she places the plate on the table, but I don't touch it. I don't even acknowledge it sitting in front of me; instead, I turn my head blatantly to look away. Then I lift my hand.

The lady stares at me, and then she lifts her hand to me, the one with the fork in it. The movement makes the sleeves of her shirt pull back, and that's when the breath leaves my body.

On her exposed skin are scars.

Deep scars. But also old scars. It looks like someone sliced her forearm open.

It feels like snakes are crawling up my body as the ramifications of what those scars can mean beat down inside my brain.

Is she like me?

Was she kidnapped?

Did the man who took me make those marks on her?

I can feel bile running up my throat and coating my tongue. I need to swallow a few times and will myself to breathe in through my nose to make sure I don't throw up right here on the kitchen table.

My hand lifts to touch her. I expect her to move away like last time, but she doesn't. She just stares at me as I take her hand in mine.

"Help me," I say for what must now be the billionth time.

Again, she talks, but there is no way to get my point across, so I drop her hand. If she won't help me, there is only one person who can, and that person is myself. I just need a plan.

Any plan.

Don't eat.

If I don't eat, he'll have only two choices—come here or let me die. It's a big risk, but it's the only chance I have.

I won't eat, not until I speak to Cyrus.

"No food. Not until phone. Not until he comes," I say as I stand, making my back appear ramrod straight. There must be a way for her to get in touch with him.

I head back to my room, and once inside it doesn't take long for my body to object to my new approach on my kidnapping. My stomach sounds like an earthquake is happening inside it.

Rumbling and shaking.

It takes every bit of resistance to object.

But this is a hunger strike.

I have no choice.

As time passes, the pain doesn't get any better. I was never good at going hungry. As a kid, before my mom faded away, she would joke that when I hadn't eaten in a long time, I would become angry and hostile to everyone around. Seems not much has changed over the years. Now starving, I want to throw something to make the cramps subside. Instead of being destructive, I throw my body on the bed and try to sleep.

It might hurt to lie down, but at least if I'm out cold, I won't feel the pains any longer.

Unfortunately, the plan is bad. Before I can second-guess myself, I'm standing in the kitchen with the fridge open.

Fuck this.

I can eat if I want to, and he'll never know. Or will he?

A thought pops into my head as I stand there with the cold air hitting my face and stomach groaning. *What if there are cameras?*

He will see me eat, and then there is no strike. He won't come.

Making sure I don't move too much, I pop open one lid. My whole torso is inside the fridge. The slight chance that he can see it here is worth taking the smallest bite. Using two fingers, I take a tiny scoop of the chicken salad she made. The food tastes amazing against my tongue, making my mouth salivate.

I have to stop myself from eating more. If I touch or take too much food, he will know, so I don't. Just that one bite and then I grab a bottle of water and head back to my room.

Cyrus will have to show up.

If he appears, I'll have a chance at convincing him to let me go.

Later that night, and after just enough food to let the pain go away, I fall asleep with a smile on my face. This plan will work. It has to.

The next morning comes, and not eating is harder than I thought, especially when I'm sitting there watching the dog eat.

Apparently, he has an automatic feeder. *Must be nice.*

Storming out of the room, I decide to search the estate to see if I'm alone. After going over every square inch again, I can't find the lady from yesterday.

Good thing? Or bad thing?

As much as I hated that she couldn't talk to me, it was nice to have someone else around, even if she didn't exactly come across as friendly. The only thing I can hope at this point is that she goes back to Cyrus and tells him how I'm faring or, better yet, how I'm starving.

A laugh bubbles up at the thought of the arrogant bastard finding out his captive is being defiant.

With no more rooms to search, I head back into the kitchen, take a seat at the table, and then I stare at the fridge.

My stomach growls loudly in protest.

It's loud enough to have the dog stop eating and look up at me. He cocks his head at the second growl that leaves my body.

"I know," I say to him.

This will be torture.

I can't survive on water and the small bites I took last night. Maybe I can take more without showing anyone I'm eating from the containers.

When another loud sound emanates from my stomach, Cerberus stands from where he is eating and drops something at my feet.

Kibble. He's trying to feed me.

"As much as I would love to eat this, I think it will kill me." Standing, I head to the fridge, opening it and popping the lids of the food that is there.

I take a bite from each one, but still a small enough amount that no one would notice it's gone.

It's enough to keep me alive, but my brain is fuzzy, and I feel weak.

———————————•———————————

It's getting harder and harder to pick food out of the containers without it being obvious. But the only hope I have of this plan working is being able to sell my hunger as real.

Today, I hear the door, but I'm too weak to approach her in the foyer. Instead, I wait for her in the kitchen, sitting in the same spot that I sat the last time I saw her.

When she walks in, I notice that once again she has groceries. She sets about with the same routine as last time. Putting a few bags down on the counter that she will eventually unpack in the pantry and then walking to the fridge. When she opens the door, she stops.

The food in the bag in her hand hits the floor.

I don't need to see what she's doing to know. She's opening each one, making sure I'm telling the truth. The evidence is there. All the containers of food she cooked are still full. Or so it would appear.

If I wasn't so weak, I'd smile at my victory. Too bad, I am.

The sound of the fridge slamming has me looking at her. She turns to me and begins to speak in quick succession.

"No. Call him. I will not eat. Not until he comes here." I know she can't understand what I'm saying, but I hope she understands my hand gestures. I lift my hand to my mouth, pretending to eat, then I shake my head and gesture to the phone. Her eyes are wide, and she looks scared.

A part of me feels bad. The scars on her body twist at my heart, but I can't back down now.

I'm a fighter, and I'll fight with whatever I have to.

Once I'm sure she understands the message, I stand and leave her once again. Staring at my back.

Let's hope this works.

CHAPTER TEN

Cyrus

WORK HAS BEEN KEEPING ME BUSY FOR THE PAST FEW days, and I haven't been able to check on my prisoner.

I always knew I was a monster but leaving Ivy alone on the island just confirms it.

You're as bad as him.

No. I'm not the same. I don't take something not clearly offered.

I did what I had to do to protect her. Taking her was the only way to keep her safe.

But why do I even fucking care? The answer screams at me in my head, behind distant and buried memories, but I refuse to let it resurface. I push the thought out of my mind. I can't think about that now. I have other, more pressing matters.

Like what the fuck am I going to do with the girl? I told her brother I won't hurt her, and I meant it.

I'm a man of my word, so I won't touch her.

But what will I do with her?

I shove my hands in my pockets and finally walk to the window, the large window that faces the water. The waves crash against the shore. Each time one hits the rocks, white bubbles to the surface like small crystals. Beside that, the ocean looms in the distance. Dark and menacing. A perfect storm is brewing.

A minute passes as I look out into the dark abyss.

"Boss." I hear Z's voice. "What's the plan?" he asks, and I shrug at his question. "Are you going to bring her here?"

That has me stop and look toward him. "No."

I couldn't. It's not safe here. Not that Boris knows I have her yet, but he will.

He can come here all he wants. No one knows about the island. No one but Z and Maxwell and me. I trust them with my life, so there is nothing to worry about there.

"I know it's not my place . . ." he starts to say, and I lift my hand to silence him.

"No. It's not."

When he doesn't move, I shake my head, but then I let out a breath. The man has been with me since the beginning. His father worked for my father. He lived in my house; he was like a brother to me. He's been with me since before I lost everything and then after I burned myself to the ground. He was still there with me when I rose from the ashes to build all this.

"If you have something to say, then please, by all means, talk."

"What are you doing, boss? We can end this now. Call Boris, broker the trade. Saving her won't—"

I was wrong. I don't want to hear what he says.

"Enough." My voice booms. "I saw her. I wanted her. That's it."

"Keeping her will ruin—"

"Stop," I cut him off again. Z might be the closest person I have to a friend, but it is not his place to question my authority and rule.

A tense silence stretches out between us as he waits for me to say more, but I don't. I don't even know why I did this. Why this girl is stranded on my island.

When I saw her . . . there was so much about her that . . . I shake my head. "I couldn't let her have that fate," I answer because that's the only thing I can say. "No one should have that."

Many things about me are evil, but not that.

An hour later, Z and I are still sitting in my office when the phone rings on my desk. It's one of the landlines from within the house, probably Maxwell.

"Speak," I answer.

"Mariana wishes to speak with you, sir."

"Send her in." I hang up the phone and look up to see Z staring at me. "Mariana."

He nods his head in understanding. Mariana works in my household, but she is also providing my little captive her food.

The sound of the door has both me and Z looking to the left.

Mariana walks in, timid as usual. She's been with me for only a few years, but it doesn't matter how long she's been here, she still acts like a scared mouse when I'm around.

"Mariana."

"Hello, Mr. Reed."

"Cyrus, please," I tell her. I might be a dick, but there is no reason to be one to her. She's been through enough. "What can I do for you?"

She looks down at the floor, but it's when she worries her lip that I know something is wrong.

"What's going on, Mariana?" I speak softly so I don't send her shaking with fear to the corner of the room.

"She won't eat."

My hands ball into fists, but instead of losing my shit, I inhale deeply. "What do you mean she won't eat?"

Fear, stark and vivid, glitters in her eyes. "S-She . . ." She stops, probably petrified of me. Even trying to be calm, I'm still scaring this poor girl. "She said she won't eat until you come."

The room goes quiet. If a pin dropped on the floor, the sound would be as clear as day right now.

I give her a reassuring smile. "Did you speak to her?"

Mariana was given strict instruction not to engage. To pretend she didn't speak English.

"No, sir. I did just as you asked. But even if I didn't understand her, she made it quite clear."

Interesting. A hunger strike. My parted lips spread farther. She is quite the conundrum, constantly refusing to do what the norm would do in her position.

I like it. Fuck that, I love it.

"And she is following through with this?"

"Yes, sir. I came back, and none of the food was touched."

A change of plans is in order.

"Thank you for bringing this to my attention."

Mariana nods her head and then leaves the room, after which I stand from my desk and straighten my jacket.

"Where are you going?" Z asks.

"The island."

"Why? Because she isn't eating. If you go, you are playing into her hand."

"Be that as it may, I'm going."

"It's a bad idea. Why don't you just let me make the phone call? The longer you hold her, the bigger the risk to you. Let's tell Boris we have her . . ."

I halt my steps and turn around. "I'll let you speak out of turn this one time because I know that you think you are looking out for me, but remember your place, Z."

He nods his head, but his words still ring through my mind. I know what he wants me to do.

"This will start a war when it gets out. We can use this to our advantage now," he states, and I consider his words.

"War is already upon us. It has been for years. Ever since . . ." I stop myself, not wanting to feel weak.

"So then let's use her. You could have her by your side at the next poker game, he's sure to come out of hiding if he hears that."

"No."

I know Z feels loyal to me, protective even, and I know he thinks this plan is our best option, but I disagree.

I watch as he opens his mouth and shuts it. "You know, boss, after what you did for me . . ." His words trail off. He is referring to helping him get back on his feet by giving him a job and mission in life after he too lost someone he cared about like I had. It bonded us, the loss. We were both alone in the world with no direction. I gave us both a common goal. Ever since then, Z has been by my side. I know he has my best interests at heart, and normally, I would agree, but not this time.

He's overstepped, and he knows it. Without another word, I head toward the docks. Time to see what my little prisoner is doing.

The small boat is ready to go in no time with Maxwell at the helm. It doesn't take long to get there.

"Do you want me to wait?" Maxwell asks.

No one knows about this island, but I can't take any chances now that Boris wants her.

"Offshore. Not visible."

"Got it, boss."

Stepping on to the dock, I make my way through the path up to the estate. When I open the door, I'm not sure where I'll find her. I'm actually surprised when I hear her padding down the stairs.

Her hair is pulled into a ponytail, and she has a tight-fitting sweater on that she must have found in one of the drawers.

She looks younger today, but when our gazes pass, I know it's all an illusion. She is still the headstrong and brave woman I have come to admire.

I wouldn't tell her that, but in the time she's been here, I have to admit she's not at all like I thought she would be.

"You won't eat."

Her full pink lips part and then spread into a large smile.

"So, she does talk. What language?"

I ignore her question. "Enough of the shit, Sun. You will eat."

She looks at me confused by the nickname, and I expect her to ask, but instead she puffs out her chest, and I can't help but look at their full shape under the tight-fitting gear. Her back is straight, and I can tell she is trying to be tough. Good fight. I like that.

"No," she says.

"Very well, I guess I have no choice but to make you."

Her eyes go wide, bulging from the sockets. In all the times I've seen her, she's never looked as shocked as she does now. Which, seeing as she orchestrated this whole thing, is not expected. However, as much as I want to read into it, she pulls herself together faster than a race car driver on the last lap of a race, schooling her features and placing her hands on her hips.

"Or" —she cocks her head— "you can let me go."

"Any other requests?"

"You dead." She shrugs.

"That would leave you in a predicament. I'd be dead, and then you would die here too."

Like a blazing inferno doused by a fire hydrant, she sizzles. It's true. I die; she dies.

"Come with me."

My demand should squash her remaining defiance, but instead, in typical Ivy fashion, she responds, "No."

I move toward her, towering over her small and lithe frame. "I said move."

Then off I go, prowling to the kitchen, and shockingly, she follows.

"Sit." I point at the table, and once she is sitting, I go to the fridge and grab a container. "Eat."

She doesn't move to follow my orders. She doesn't do much of anything. Staring at me with hatred in her eyes, she commences a silent battle of wills.

There is no hope for her, though. I always win.

I lean forward in my chair. "We can do this one of two ways. I can force you . . ."

"Option two, don't eat," she chimes in.

"No, option two is not that."

"What's option two?"

My lips spread into a large and thoroughly pleased grin.

"I'm happy you ask, Ivy. Option two is I chain you to the table until you do." Her mouth drops open at my words, so I continue. "I have been easy on you."

"Easy? You call this easy? You locked me in your scary home."

"I hardly call living in a mansion, roughing it."

"I'm all alone. The only companion is that dog." She points at Cerberus, who chooses that moment to bark at her, and I can't hold back the chuckle.

"You think that's funny?"

"Yes."

"It's not funny that you have left me alone with a dog that wants to chew my face off."

My lips keep pulling up. Watching her get so angry over the dog is fucking hilarious.

"How about this . . . why don't you tell me why I'm here? Tell me why you took me, and I'll eat."

"Interesting idea." And it is, but Ivy doesn't know me. Everything comes with a price. Leaning forward, I rest my weight on my forearms. "Fine, I have one stipulation. You cannot ask me why I took you."

"But—"

"Option two it is. I'll just tell Cerberus to watch you while I get the chains."

The shiver that runs down her spine is obvious. It's as obvious as the fear that reflects back at me from her large blue eyes. Ivy is scared, and she should be.

"Fine." She lifts her hands in acceptance. "Fine. One bite, one question."

I nod. "I agree to those terms."

She lifts the fork off the table and looks at me and then the food.

"Cyrus Reed, you better not be lying."

"Ivy Aldridge," I counter, "I don't lie."

"How did you take me, and before you say anything, the question is not why? It's *how*."

"Chloroform," I answer truthfully. By now there is no proof, so she can't do anything with this information.

"You have access to chloroform?"

I lift a brow and dart my eyes toward the food. "That's two questions. Now you owe me two bites."

She takes the two bites, and I can tell she wants to say how good it tastes after not eating for so long, but she's too strong to do that. So she stifles the moan threatening to escape and swallows.

"Yes."

She places her fork down and furrows her brow.

"That's not an answer."

"Well then, you should probably ask better questions," I deadpan.

A groan of displeasure pours from her mouth as she shakes her head. She rights herself quickly. I'm not sure if it's because she is hungry and wants to eat more, or if it's because she really wants to know the answer.

"How do you have access to chloroform?"

"A store."

Cue the groan again.

"This isn't fair."

"And you owe me another bite."

She huffs in annoyance but takes the bite.

CHAPTER ELEVEN

Ivy

A FEW DAYS HAVE PASSED SINCE CYRUS CAME HERE AND forced me to eat. I'm no longer starving, but I'm still annoyed. The man is infuriating. Never in my life has someone evaded questions quite like him. The whole thing was a giant waste of time.

Searching the property has also proven fruitless. I still have yet to find anything useful for a potential escape.

The worst part, cabin fever has set in.

I'm bored, have no one to talk to, and my only companion wants to eat me for breakfast.

Things aren't looking good for me these days.

No. Not true. There has been one bright light in all this darkness. During my latest search, I did find one thing. Off the side of the house, I stumbled upon a door. It was jammed, and I almost broke my arm trying to bust in, but it was well worth it.

A greenhouse.

Not a very nice one, but still it has the potential to make my days better. Everything inside is dead and unkempt. But I did find seeds and will plant them in the abandoned pots I found. Maybe I'll even be able to grow flowers.

I'm not sure what plants or flowers the seeds are, but I'll plant and water them, nonetheless. As soon as they sprout, I'll know.

Or maybe I won't.

Hopefully, I won't be here that long. My stomach drops at the thought. Will I?

At first, I would've said no, but seeing as I've come no further in a week, there's a good chance I will be. At this point, I'm so desperate I had full conversations with Cerberus. As if he will answer.

I have made it my lifelong goal to turn him from the dark side to my alliance. At every meal, I try to feed him, and at every meal, he rejects my advances. I will win him over. I'll get him to like me. Today, he guards me once again as I tend to my new flowers. It's hard to plant anything, seeing as there're no shovels. Cyrus was smart; he left nothing that could be construed as a weapon.

When I'm done in the greenhouse, I make my way back into the main part of the house. On the first day, I had noticed stairs, and today, I'm finally prepared to search. There's no light, so I leave the door open and head down. The dog follows me, and when I get down there, you can smell the dank air.

It's an old storage room, maybe for wine. When I look around, I notice old metal chains on the floor. A shiver runs down my spine as I realize this didn't hold wine; it holds prisoners. They're too old for Cyrus to have put them there. My curiosity piques. What was this place, and how did he come to purchase it?

Is this his family's house? Is kidnapping in his blood?

No. I refuse to believe that. If that was the case, why hasn't he come back?

He muttered it was for my protection.

From whom or what, I don't know.

But why is the better question. It's the question that has plagued me for days. I need to find out.

I wake the next day to a sound in the house. The sound of something that sounds a lot like the door opening. This could be my chance to escape . . . I look out the window, but I don't see any boats.

It doesn't matter, though. Even if there is no boat, and I can't escape, I don't care. No, but what it does mean is that maybe someone is here.

Someone who can help me.

Or even just someone to talk to.

Never in my life have I been much of a talker. Often, I have chosen to be alone, but I still miss the companionship. Even before I came here, after my mom had succumbed to her depression and stopped talking to me, I at least had her presence. Here, I have no one. Well, that's not true. Here, I have a dog, but he doesn't answer me. Though that doesn't stop me from talking to him.

The idea of not being alone has me quickly putting on my clothes, and then I find myself running down the stairs.

As soon as I reach the landing, I realize no one has come to save me.

It's Cyrus in the foyer, and Cerberus is beside him.

A strange feeling works its way down my spine as I take him in. It's terrifying because it doesn't feel like fear. It feels like something entirely different.

Excitement.

It feels a lot like excitement as butterflies start to swarm in my belly.

Shit.

I'm actually happy to see him. I hate how *happy* I am.

No. It's not him. This isn't about him, in particular. It could be anyone, and I would be internally jumping for joy. That's what happens when you have no one to talk to for days. Hell, the Grim Reaper could walk in this door right now, and I'd probably ask him to join me for dinner. Or in this case, make it *Hades*. I tone down my thought. No matter how starved for attention I am, I won't let him know.

"You're here."

His expression darkens when our gaze meets. "I am."

"Do you ever speak in full sentences?"

"Didn't I just now? I am. That's a *full* sentence."

"Yes. But not really." The man drives me crazy. I take a deep breath and try again. "*Why* are you here?" It's really a dumb question, but I ask anyway. I know why he's here, to make sure I eat.

"Have you forgotten our deal? I'm here to fulfill my promise, Sun." I'm perplexed by why he keeps calling me that, but by the time I open my mouth to ask, he's already heading toward the kitchen.

Like Hansel and Gretel looking for breadcrumbs, I follow him and then take my seat at the table.

He's already pulling out whatever he brought for me. Bare bones. That's what he does. He gives me just enough to live, and then like the asshole he is, he takes days to return.

I'm not an idiot, but I still play the game. He knows he doesn't have to answer any questions in order for me to eat, but he likes wielding the power.

I grab the fork out of his hand and scoop a bite of the rice in the bowl. He walks over to the fridge and places the rest of the containers to last me until he returns in a few days.

I take a bite, swallow, and then place my fork down. "What is this place?" I ask, gesturing my hands around the space.

He turns from the fridge, directing his attention on me now.

"I thought a girl as smart as you would know what a house is." Deep, smooth, and laced with sarcasm, his voice washes over me, making me clench my fist and try my hardest not to punch him.

I could try, but something tells me it wouldn't end well for me.

"I wouldn't do that if I were you." I follow his gaze and see that he's talking about my right-hand fist that is balled and ready to strike. If it were possible for my eyes to roll out of their sockets, they would.

"I meant why is this 'house'"—I air quote—"on its own island?"

"Two bites."

"I just took one . . ." Still, I place my fork in the food and then take another bite.

"It's the reason I bought my estate."

"I don't get it." This man is about to make me bash my head into the table with his half answers.

He sits back in his seat and cocks his head. The presence of a smirk lines his normally stone-cold face. "Is that your next question?"

Before I can stop it, a long, audible sigh escapes my mouth. "Jeez, fine. Yes."

"The seclusion and proximity to my estate on the mainland is invaluable to me."

I throw my hands up in the air at his once again vague answer. "You know what . . . I'll just eat this. You can leave now."

And with that, he laughs.

Ass.

CHAPTER TWELVE

Ivy

THIS TIME, I KNOW HE'S COMING. HE'S BECOME predictable. Every three days like clockwork. By the time he gets here, all the food he's left from the previous visit are scraps. It's planned to a T.

Today, when he arrives, I greet him in the foyer.

"When are you going to let me go?" I ask. He ignores me, walking into the living room and checking the logs.

"You haven't used the wood."

"It hasn't been that cold."

Lies. It has been, but I refuse to admit that I don't know how to start a fire. I wasn't a Brownie growing up. Wasn't a Girl Scout. I grew up in Manhattan with a trust fund, so the fact I have a green thumb is a modern miracle.

"Take this," he says as he passes me a bag that I didn't even realize he was holding.

"What is it?"

"Just take it. It's more clothes. Although, there are also more supplies you might need in the cabinets."

I don't tell him I've been through everything. Or how I found the basic necessities I need to live. The fact he hasn't brought shampoo and other toiletries until today leads me to believe he already knows this fact.

"Now that I have seen that you're okay . . ." He starts to turn around, and it feels like a red-hot poker is being jabbed in my chest. I'm not ready to be alone again.

"No. You can't leave yet," I plead before catching myself. "I haven't eaten." I hate myself for the desperation.

"You made it clear last time that you didn't want to play my game." He sounds smug as shit as he says this. The worst part is, now, I need to grovel because I don't want to be alone again. I won't tell him that, though.

"I still have questions, and I won't eat this if you don't answer them."

"Do you want me to stay?" he asks, lifting a suggestive brow. Nope. He saw right through me.

My head shakes back and forth. "Not like that."

"Pity, Sun."

That nickname again. "Sun?"

His lip tips up into a dangerous smirk. "Yes. It's fitting."

"For my sunny personality? I find that hard to believe."

Something tells me he's toying with me, messing with me somehow. I don't like it one bit.

"If you knew why I called you Sun, you'd understand."

Does this man ever speak in clear sentences, everything out of his mouth is like a damn riddle.

He starts back toward the front door.

"Please don't . . . I can't take much more time alone."

He turns in my direction, scanning his eyes over me. It's only then that I remember my precarious spot. Although I got dressed, the clothing was slim pickings. All I have are the clothes on my back and some soap I have been using to wash them. I did find the clothes in the bedroom, but I've used them only when I'm desperate. I was about to get dressed, but ran down so quickly, I forgot to throw on the rest of my clothes.

So here I am standing in the cold foyer in nothing but a flimsy camisole and barely there shorts. I was so excited I had forgotten. Shit.

I can feel his eyes dancing across my skin. It's unnerving. And I fear that in my insolence, I have pushed the boundaries. He was going to leave, and now he'll defile me.

I have dangled a piece of steak in front of a lion. If only I had a weapon to fight him off.

"I thought you said you wouldn't touch me without my permission."

"Does it look like I'm touching you, Sun?"

"No. But it looks like you want to."

"Wanting and doing are two very different things. I might be a monster and make no mistake, I am, but I'm not that kind of monster."

"If you say so."

"I do. Now let's go feed you. I don't have all day."

This time when I'm sitting at the table, I use my questions to ask more important things, things that hopefully he will answer. But first I have a demand.

"I won't eat anything unless I can call my mother."

"No." He doesn't even consider granting me this, and it pisses me off.

"Why the hell not?"

"Eat, and I'll tell you." He winks.

His need to drive me crazy is having its desired effect, but I refuse to show it, instead, I place my hands on my legs and squeeze my nails into my thighs to keep me from going off. This is important, and I won't let my anger toward this man ruin my chance of connecting with my mom.

"Please." I hate how desperate I sound. I hate this weak person, sitting at the table, biting her tongue and trying to be a docile little thing.

When he doesn't answer me, I take my fork, stab the steak in front of me, and take a bite.

"Ivy. I'm doing what's best for you. You can't talk to her."

My mouth opens and shuts. I'm not sure what to do, how to get him to tell me more. I'm in a precarious situation, if I push too hard, I'll never find out anything.

"Is she okay?" Despite my best efforts, tears start to form in my eyes, I try hard not to blink, harder for them not to fall.

Cyrus leans in and his finger lifts up. Confusion clouds my brain. It feels like I'm trapped in fog and can't see my way out of this. He's going to touch me, and I don't know what I'll do if he does.

There is a slight hesitation in his eyes, but then I feel it, and I'm too baffled to do anything.

The rough pad of his finger touches my cheek, brushing a lone tear that has fallen. He collects it on his finger. It feels oddly intimate, and I hate it, but at the same time, I welcome the comfort. It feels good and I don't know what that means.

Am I starved for attention? Is that the problem, am I desperate and needy?

Another tear falls. He's the first person to soothe me in a long time and I don't want it to stop, no matter what that means.

I still hate him.

But I welcome the support.

"I might not let you speak to her, but I'll do something for you . . ." His gaze is unwavering, searing me with emotions I can't place. "I'll call your brother. I'll make sure your mom is okay."

CHAPTER THIRTEEN

Cyrus

THE FUCKER IS CALLING ME.

Turns out, I don't actually need to call Trent after all.

I have no intention of telling him I was planning on calling him. The shit needs to be scared of me and seeing as he went against what I said, there will be hell to pay.

"Why are you calling me again?" I grind the words out between my teeth. He should know better. This is the kind of bullshit that will get him, and his sister killed.

"Where is my sister?"

Apparently, he has a death wish after all. Lifting the glass of cognac I just poured myself, I take a drink. As the spicy yet bitter flavor works its way down my throat, my shoulders loosen enough to answer him.

"I thought we covered this, Trent."

"We covered shit." He fires back, the little shit is lucky he's not here right now.

"Careful, Trent. I would hate for your sister to lose her brother."

One thing is certain, hotheadedness apparently must run in the family.

"You threaten, but I see no action," Trent presses.

I slam the glass down. It doesn't break, which is a modern miracle.

"One last warning out of respect for Ivy." My voice is slow, steady, and controlled.

"Don't say her name like you know her."

"I might not know her, but I know that the fucking Butcher wants her. If what you say is true, that she's meant for someone else, it's even worse."

"You—"

"Listen, pretty boy, I know you think you know what horrors are, but you don't know shit about anything. You think over on Park Avenue you know shit?"

"What do you mean?"

"While you're bitching because you want to talk to your sister, I'm protecting her, it's more than just Boris."

"What are we talking about here?"

"Trafficking. Human fucking trafficking. Boris works for one of the largest traffickers in Europe."

"I don't understand."

"He works for one of the largest organizations involved in human trafficking and . . . it sounds like Ivy is already meant for someone. If it's who I think it is, she is better off with me, no matter what you think I am."

That shuts him up, finally. The only sound coming through the phone is the sound of heavy breathing. He finally understands.

Thank fuck.

"You can protect her?"

An odd sense of unease finds me, but I push it down. Normally, I would say fuck yes, but this is different. The leader of the organization has been evading me for years. I don't say that to Trent, though. He's already a loose cannon as is, I need to rein him in, not send him off the deep end.

"Better than you can. But I need you to stop calling me. Stop calling attention to yourself and me. Right now, where does Boris think she is?"

"I told him she was away."

"And how long do you think that will buy you. A week, two? The one saving grace for you, is that they think she's worth not killing you. Not just for the money, but for whoever she's meant for. You need to contact Boris, and tell him you will pay off your debt, tell him you need more time."

"I'm not calling that motherfucker."

"You will. Because if you don't, he will kill you. Tell him you will pay him back with interest. Anything you have to make him not murder you. You understand?"

"Yes."

I'm about to hang up, but then I remember what Ivy asked of me and how broken she was. "Trent." It might make me sound weak to ask this of him, but the look on her face has me asking anyway. "I need you to take care of your mother. Ivy is worried about her."

"I am. She's staying with me."

"Good. Don't call me again." I hang up and pick up my glass and drink the remainder of it.

The door to my office opens and Z comes striding in like he owns the place. I'm too bothered by the reaction I have to Ivy to do something about it. Instead, I grab the bottle of Louis XIII and pour myself some more. Nothing like the earthy taste to bring me back down to the ground.

"What's going on, boss?" Z asks, stepping farther into the room.

"Aldridge again." I motion to the bottle of cognac on the counter. "Want some?"

"Nope. I'm good. What's the problem now?"

Placing my glass down, I lift my hand to scrub at the headache that's starting to form. "He wanted to check on his sister."

"Okay . . ." he leads, wanting for me to go on.

"To make sure she was fine."

"Doesn't he understand what could have happened to her. Fuck. The bastard should be grateful you stepped in. Those bastards would have destroyed her by now."

"I informed him."

Z chuckles, he knows what that means. Typically, it means I threatened his life. Not too far from the truth. "How'd he take it?" he asks.

"Honestly, I probably made him shit himself." It wouldn't surprise me one bit if Trent Aldridge was vomiting right now after our conversation of Boris and his associates.

"Better that than the alternative."

"This is true."

Z's expression hardens, and then he takes a seat across from me.

"Speaking of, boss. I think we should leak to Boris that we have her."

"No." The word falls from my mouth before I can stop it.

"But—"

"Not yet." My voice is firm, but Z now looks confused. His eyebrows have knit together and a large line forms between them.

"That was always the plan. Why not now? Keeping her logistically is a nightmare. Boris will probably kill her family and then we will be stuck with her."

"It's taken care of."

"How?"

"Let me worry about that. You just keep up surveillance on the island when I'm not there. The timing isn't right."

The timing will never be right.

But handing her over as bait to catch a bigger fish, is wrong.

Friday night is here, and the game is on. Tonight, I'm here for no other reason than I need to distance myself from the temptation waiting back on the island for me. Each day that I'm there feeding her, it gets harder and harder not to give in to my primal urge to push her against the kitchen counter and show her just how much she truly wants me.

That's why I'm here tonight, even though I should be bringing her more food.

I've chosen a spot by Matteo Amante tonight.

"Boss." I hear from behind me. "Aldridge is here."

I turn to face Z. Stern as always, he stands behind me with his lips thinned and his arms at his side. Watching. Waiting. Observing. The best man to have covering your back.

"Does he never learn?" I mutter to myself.

One would think after losing his daughter, he would have learned something, but nope, this fucker came back.

"Not senior," he clarifies.

"Trent."

Z gives me a small bob of his head before turning to face where the man must be waiting in my foyer.

"I told him not to come back." I start to walk out of the parlor room of my estate where tonight's game is being played. Trent is in the foyer, pacing back and forth. When he sees me, he halts his steps. "Thought I told you, you were no longer welcome here."

"You did." His nostrils flare, and I take a step up to him. I expect him to step back, to flinch, but I'm actually impressed. It seems Trent has grown a pair of balls.

He doesn't even look like the same Trent I've met in the

past. Instead of being funny like when he used to play poker or disheveled like the last time I saw him at his place before I took Ivy, he stands up straight today, his face determined to say his piece. "I'm here to talk business."

"And this couldn't have waited?"

"Well, it could have, but I know you don't leave your estate, and I wanted to talk to you about the money I invested for you. I figured you wouldn't want to talk over the phone."

"And you would be right." I nod to my men who flank him, and I allow him to pass. Together, we walk back into the parlor, but instead of going to a table, I lead him to the bar.

"What are you drinking?" I ask as I call Maggie over. She knows what I drink. In no time, she will be getting me my signature glass of Louis. When she approaches, I gesture for Trent to order from her.

"Don Julio 1942 extra chilled."

Maggie smiles before heading off to get us drinks.

It doesn't take long, and as Trent lifts his drink to his mouth a few minutes later, we move to stand far enough away from the tables so no one can hear.

"Now that you have my attention, and a drink, tell me why the fuck you came to my house even though I was clear that you and your father were no longer welcome."

"I thought you would be interested to know that the fund is up forty percent. It is now worth one hundred and forty million."

My hand lowers, but that is the only sign I allow to show he's shocked me. When I commanded this job of him, I didn't expect him to be that successful.

"Now, that is good to know." I lift my glass and take another swig.

"Thought so."

As hard as it is for me to admit, this kid might actually know what he's doing.

"Trent, how would you like to do another job for me?"

"I thought this was a one-time deal."

"It doesn't have to be. I know you came to my game to get clients, but how would you like to get the bigger dogs? Take him, for example." I point my finger to the far table. "He could bring another hundred million to the fund if you play your cards right."

"Doesn't he run the Italian mafia? What do you have to do with the mafia?"

"The Italian mafia wouldn't exist without me. I am the mafia. All the money passes through me."

"I'm not sure I want to get into bed with you."

"Interesting. Working together in the future could be mutually beneficial."

"True, but first I want to know when you are going to take care of Boris."

I step into him, tall and powerful. "Don't question me."

"What does that mean?" He doesn't back down. Instead, the muscles in his neck flex.

"Keeping her hidden is the best option right now."

There is no hiding how he clenches his teeth. He hates this. Hell, he should. I hate it too.

"You better not touch her," he grits out.

"What I do with Ivy is none of your business."

"There is no you and Ivy, because if there was, you would be no better than Boris. Maybe you aren't different. But you won't be screwing my sister. Not if I have anything to say about it."

His words hit me in the stomach.

As much as I want her, I can't have her.

Because despite what Trent says, he doesn't know how accurate his words are. If I touch her, I'm no better than Boris.

It's been a few days since I've been to the island. After the morning I've just had, the last thing I want to do is check on my little prisoner.

She is a perfectly wrapped gift box that I'm dying to tear into. Unfortunately for me, she's not mine to open. Since I won't take her, I try to stay away from her.

But she needs food, and I need to make sure she hasn't gotten herself in any sort of trouble. There is a good chance she's locked herself in the room, which is fine by me. The need to reach out and touch her pisses me the fuck off.

Why couldn't she not evoke emotions in me?

No one does.

Why her?

It's bad enough that I'm going on about this, but it would be much easier if I didn't want to sink into her every time I see her.

I shake my head. It's fine. I have control.

Plus, I doubt I'll even bump into her. The past few times I have come by, I haven't seen her.

For all I know, she's dead in her bed.

That would probably make my life easier.

But then I couldn't use her to get what I need from Boris.

The truth is, that's fine by me.

There are other ways.

I'm not sold that the plan to use her as bait is the way to go anyway.

Z keeps saying she's a means to an end, but for some reason, it doesn't sit well with me.

It's because I want to fuck her.

Maybe if I did . . .

Nope.

Not going there.

Trent's words about Boris are still too clear in my head. In order for that to ever happen, she would need to beg for me to take her.

I'm a lot of things, but rapist, is not one of them.

Today will be a fast trip to the island. Maxwell will wait offshore for me to do what I need to do.

Then I'm off to a meeting with my client Alaric; we need to discuss his acquisition of a new territory for the distribution of arms.

First, though, to check on Ivy.

Metal key in hand, plus a bag that Z filled with God knows what, but knowing him, a bomb, I step into the house set on my private island.

To think, this place was once a summer getaway for my family.

Then it housed all kinds of shady deals.

Now, it holds a captive hostage. Life has gone full circle.

Moving farther into the space, I find the house quiet. *She must be in her room.* Then I hear a noise coming from the far side of the house.

Cerberus?

Or is it her?

She wouldn't go in there, would she?

The muscles in my back tighten as I drop the bag and head toward the greenhouse.

A part of my house she shouldn't have access to.

It should have been locked.

Turning the corner, I take slow, measured steps through the kitchen to the door that isn't locked at all. It's wide open, but I don't want to alert her of my presence if it is her.

Standing in the doorframe, I see her kneeling over a pot in the corner. She doesn't notice me as I watch her for a minute. The sun that beams in through the glass ceiling illuminates her blond hair, casting a glow.

Like an angel.

So different from the last one to garden here.

The anger I had tried to tamp down from her being here rises to the surface.

Simmering as I watch her touch something that doesn't belong to her without a care in the world.

She's alone in this house. What else was there for her to do?

Not break into a greenhouse that was clearly locked.

"What are you doing in here?" I scoff, entering. She shouldn't be here. No one should. No one has in a long time.

Years.

By the looks of the space, it's obvious, except . . .

Around where Ivy is are newly planted pots. It looks clean and put together, as if she has worked countless hours to tidy and tend to it.

It makes my blood boil. This isn't her dirt to sow.

Soon, I'm towering over her. I need to rein in my emotions because if I don't pull myself together, I'll be no better than the monster I'm hiding her from.

"Leave this room." My voice comes out harsher than I intend, and from where I'm standing, I can see her body go tense.

"No," she fires back, and I want to applaud her for schooling her features. She's a good actress. I can tell she's frightened of me, but she won't give me the satisfaction of showing it.

I reach for where she is kneeling to grab her by her shoulders, but she sees what I'm doing before I connect and moves back while still kneeling.

"Don't touch me," she hisses as if I'm going to rape her in this place. As if I would tarnish what happy memories I have left with her presence.

"I wouldn't think of it."

"Sure," she mumbles under her breath.

"I don't need to touch you." Our bodies are still close, and once she stands to her full height, she's even closer. I'm close enough to see the ring of her irises, and the bright flecks staring back at me.

"What do you want from me?" she asks.

"All in good time," I divert.

I'm not sure why I don't tell her. Probably because it gets a rise out of her. I like to see her angry, and I like to frustrate her. It's a dance, a fight, a war, and I never lose.

"I want you to stay the fuck out of my greenhouse." I take a step forward, essentially blocking her escape now. She'll have to pass me to get by.

Touch me even.

Because I won't move otherwise.

"Let me pass." Her jaw is tight, and her eyes are narrowed. She's trying to stay strong in front of me with her hand on her hip. I know what she's trying to portray, but it does the opposite. Instead, all her little show of defiance does is make me want her more. It makes me want to have her begging for me on her knees.

The vision of that starts to play out in my mind.

"Stay out of my greenhouse," I grit again through clenched teeth. She has me all worked up, and I hate it.

"Get out of my way."

"Agree."

"And if I don't?"

"You won't like my response." I let my eyes trail over her exposed skin. As cold as it is outside, it's sweltering inside the greenhouse, and Ivy is wearing only a tank top. A light sheen of sweat glistens on her neck.

I want to lick it off. Taste her.

I devour that moisture with my eyes and then lift my gaze. She must read my thoughts because I watch her neck as she swallows and goose bumps break against her hot skin.

Interesting.

She's not immune to me after all.

I file that knowledge away before turning and leaving her in the greenhouse.

"Next time I come back, I don't want to see you in here."

She groans.

Good.

Hate me, *Sun*. It's easier this way.

CHAPTER FOURTEEN

Ivy

I NOW MEASURE MY TIME ON THIS ISLAND BY MY VISITS from Cyrus. However, unlike the last few times he's come, he's spaced this trip longer than normal.

"Time to eat, little Sun."

"Oh, now it's time to eat. Now, after you have starved me for days." I lift my brow up at him from where I'm perched at the kitchen table.

"Days? Hardly." He walks farther into the room. The smell of whatever he's brought wafting through the air and making my stomach growl.

At first, I was picking at my food to get him to come here, but ever since I started getting answers, I've been eating more and more. Apparently, Cyrus didn't want to give answers more than he wanted me to eat because he's been taking longer and longer to come back. He used to have his lady come cook and restock the food every other day. But now I haven't seen her in a long time. I've already gone through most of the food, even though I've been trying to ration.

It's like my damn plan backfired on me. Not only am I starving, but I'm also not getting answers.

And now, I'm also so hungry that I have shown him my hand. He knows he has one on me.

"Just give me the damn food."

"No. I don't think I will." He smirks, and if I wasn't so dizzy right now, I would probably throw something at him. Unfortunately, my strength is not what I'm used to.

"I know you think you're clever. But I know what you're doing."

"And what, pray tell, would that be?"

"You're spacing out my food to be a dick. You don't want to answer my questions."

His eyes darken, and he steps closer to where I am.

"I don't lie. And I don't play games. If I wanted you to die, you'd be dead. Choose your words carefully, Sun."

"You won't kill me," I say with false bravado.

"Is that so?"

I stand from my chair, feigning strength I don't have. "No."

He approaches me. His large frame towering over my frail one. "Do not make me angry, Sun."

"I wouldn't dare," I mock.

"Sit."

"Or?"

"I'll make you. I'll give you this one pass because I know you're hungry."

"Whatever you say."

I sit back down, but he's right. I'm way too weak to stand my ground with him right now, and if I push, he'll see my weakness. That is something I can't have.

Once I'm sitting, he pulls out a container from a bag he brought with him today.

"Where is your slave?"

"My slave?"

"The woman with the scars."

Cyrus's fist hits the table, startling me. "Sun, I will say this one time. I do not take slaves. She is no one's slave."

"I-I . . ."

"The proper sentence is . . . I'm sorry."

"I'm sorry," I say sheepishly.

For the first time since being here, I feel the weight of his anger, and I realize I don't want to be on the receiving end of it.

We both sit silently for a few minutes before I decide to break the ice.

"What did you bring?" I keep my voice neutral, gauging how he'll react.

"Lasagna."

My mouth waters at the idea.

Cyrus brings over a fork and a plate.

"Aren't you going to eat?" I ask before I can think better of it.

"Why, Sun, did you want me to join you?"

I stare at him for a minute. If this were any other time, I would say yes. Who wouldn't want him to? He's gorgeous, sinfully so, but not without answers. Which is why I take a bite.

"First question," I say, mouth full of food.

"Chew before you talk, Sun."

I swallow. "How long will you have me?"

"That depends."

"That's not a real answer."

"It's the only one you'll get."

"Then I'm not eating."

He stands from the chair, and his arm reaches to grab the food.

My arm reaches out, landing on his skin.

"I-I . . ." I stutter as I look down at where my hand is and I freeze. It feels like an electric current of energy courses through me as realization hits that I am still holding on to him.

"Please don't take it," I whisper.

"Sit down," he says through gritted teeth that make no sense to me. I do as he asks and drop his arm.

I scurry to grab my fork again, but he still won't give me access to the plate.

"Change of plans. I'm going to tell you one thing. You can't ask any questions after I say what I have to say, after, you will eat—"

"What? No. That's not fair," I interrupt.

"No one ever said I was fair. But trust me, you want to hear what I have to say."

I let out a huff of oxygen. I don't want to trust him, but I really don't have any other choice. "Fine."

The way he looks at me is unreadable. I don't know if it's good or bad. My stomach knots as I wait. His obsidian orbs smoldering with unspoken words that scare me.

"I spoke to your brother," he starts to say, pausing for a brief second. A second long enough to make my pulse accelerate. "Your mom is fine. She's staying with your brother."

Oxygen expels from my lungs in a heavy relief filled pant. I open my mouth to ask more, but he lifts his hand, silencing me. "Now, tell me something about yourself, and after you do, I'll let you take a bite."

As much as I don't want to do this now, I must. He did what he said, and now I need to honor the agreement. The thing is, that doesn't mean I have to tell him anything important.

I think about what to say. I don't want this man knowing much about me. I don't want him using anything I divulge against me, so I decide to beat him at his own game.

"My favorite color is pink."

He inclines his head, and now it's my turn to smile. "You never said what I had to tell you."

"Touché."

He hands over the plate, and I go at it like a starving child in a candy store whose parents never let them eat sweets.

I don't even come up for air until I'm halfway through.

"Tell me more."

I finish chewing my bite. "I love to read."

"You're really divulging a lot," he deadpans.

"I learned from the best." I shrug.

I look up at him, waiting for him to ask me to tell him more about myself, but he signals down to the plate. "Just eat."

"Thank you," I whisper before taking a bite, and we both know I'm not talking about the food.

CHAPTER FIFTEEN

Ivy

KNOWING MY MOM IS BEING TAKEN CARE OF HELPS TO KEEP me at peace. I think about her often, think about my life back home, I wonder if I was replaced at my job; I wonder what Trent told them? It doesn't matter. Nothing matters from that life right now. As long as my family is okay, I can't let it get to me. I need to stay positive.

It's hard though when I feel like I'm not getting anywhere. Yes. I'm getting bits and pieces of answers, but the one question I want to ask, I can't.

Keeping my spirits up is almost impossible in this house. It's like I'm stuck in a mausoleum.

Preserved and untouched.

Cobwebs and dust from years of neglect litter the rooms, and it's apparent no one has frequented any of them in some time.

I need to get out of here, but there is nowhere to go. I need to talk to someone, but there is no one to talk to. I would even eat a full pie at this point just to hear Cyrus speak. Not that he speaks all that much.

I'm not stupid. He barely answers any of my questions, and he's evasive as fuck.

It's almost like a giant game to him, and it pisses me off. Then there was the moment with the dog.

Cerberus.

For a man who shows very little emotion, he sure did find it entertaining that his dog hates me.

If only I could wipe that grin off his face.

Turn his dog around.

Ideas take root in my brain, and before I know it, I'm in the cupboard of the kitchen. Spoon in hand, I dip it inside the jar of peanut butter.

"Cerberus!" I shout, even though it's not necessary. For a dog that doesn't like me, he never leaves my side. I should change his name to shadow, because that's what he is.

Something tells me the dog that only speaks God knows what language is not going to answer to that name.

I'll need to ask him that next time he is here.

It's been days, and I'm running low on supplies, which means he'll be here soon. I have to work fast.

When the dog cocks his head at me, I kneel on the floor, lifting the spoon up. Growing up, I never had pets, but I've always assumed or at least heard no dog can say no to peanut butter, but apparently, I found the dog.

He looks at me with his dark eyes. Dark eyes that have probably seen worlds of things I have no idea about, and then he turns his head away from me.

Not interested.

There isn't much more to offer him.

"Cerberus," I say again, and this time, I dip my finger in the peanut butter.

Again, he looks at me like I'm batshit crazy. As if he is trained too well to fall for my shit.

When he refuses to eat it, I lick my own finger, tasting the peanut butter. This is hopeless.

The weight of my situation comes crashing down on me. Here I am, so desperate for attention, for someone to talk to, for anything, that I'm trying to win over the dog that is named after the protector of the underworld.

There's no way it will work.

Suddenly, my chest feels like it's tightening. It's like I'm suffocating. Standing from my spot on the floor, I run toward the front door and swing it open.

Air. I need air.

Before long, I'm sitting on the beach facing the ocean.

The chill in the air has me wrapping my arms around my body tightly.

In front of me, the vastness of the dark abyss reminds me how hopeless this is. There's no way to escape. I'm at the mercy of a man, and I don't even know why.

The water starts to blur as my eyes fill with tears.

No. I won't cry.

I can't.

Once I cry, there's no coming back from that. I am stronger than that.

Inhaling, I try to force my walls up. The walls I have learned to erect over the years. When my mother needed me to care for her, I learned how to build these walls, and I refuse to let them go.

My mother.

Despite how hard I try, a tear slips down my cheek at the thought of her.

Does she know I'm gone?

Is she okay?

I'm the only one who can help her through her depression.

With me not around, are there any good days?

Or are they all bad?

Like a busted faucet, water leaks from my eyes until the tears come out strong and fierce. My breathing becomes erratic, hard, and choppy as everything I have been trying to push beneath the surface comes pouring out of me in breathless sobs. Every wall falls down. Crashing against the beach.

I'm not sure how long I sob.

But then I feel it.

Something I never thought I would feel, the gentle nuzzles of something. No, not something, it's Cerberus.

I look up at him through tear-lined eyes.

His brown ones hold my gaze.

"I'm okay, boy," I say, but he only cocks his head in confusion.

I don't know how to speak to him, how to tell him I'm okay.

He continues to stare, and I continue to cry.

Looking away from the dog, I stare back into the horizon. It's too far to that land. I have to wait.

But I am not the girl who likes to wait. I am the type of girl who never waits, who does it herself, which is why this is even harder.

I know I need to pull myself together and stop this bout of hysterics, but I can't seem to get myself to. Each thought pops into my brain, making it harder.

I cry and I cry until I feel Cerberus approach me again.

This time, he stands directly in front of me.

Blocking my view as if he knows this hurts me.

He sits down and then lifts his jaw. That's when I see a twig in his mouth.

Then he nudges it forward. I take the stick in my hand. "What do you want, boy?" I ask. He cocks his head. I really need to figure out what language he speaks. Because this is ridiculous.

He looks at the stick and then looks behind me.

"Do you want me to throw it?" I ask, knowing full well that

he can't answer, and he probably doesn't even know what I'm saying. But I might as well try because when I lift the stick in my hand, I think his tail wags.

I saw it from the corner of my eye, but I think he wants to play fetch.

Without a second thought, I throw the stick back toward the path to the house, and off he goes. A smile breaks across my face.

That's all he wanted.

Someone to play with.

When he runs back to me, stick in mouth, he drops it on the ground in front of where I am sitting. Once again, I pick up the stick and play. This time, my smile widens, and a laugh bubbles up.

Like me, Cerberus is lonely.

We play fetch, and I laugh, and he might not understand what I am saying, but we have passed that because he understands what I need—a friend—and he gives that to me.

Eventually, we move off the beach and back toward the house; I keep throwing, and he keeps fetching.

Flinging it this time toward the trees isn't a good idea because when Cerberus runs back up to me and licks my face, I lose my heart to him. It also very well might have resulted in me losing my sweater because when I look down, I notice that a now muddy Cerberus is licking and jumping on me. "Great. Boy. Time for a bath . . ." This should be fun.

CHAPTER SIXTEEN

Cyrus

I'T'S A FEW DAYS LATER WHEN I DECIDE TO COME BACK TO THE island. I've been busy. Things are going well with both Tobias and Alaric.

Alaric has made a sizeable deposit, which has taken up a large portion of my time. Fifty million will do that. His business is apparently doing good.

Which is fine by me. What the future holds with its competitors is not my problem; eventually, a war will come. My business is strictly holding the money. I have too much other shit to think about, say, for example, my prisoner.

Captive.

Sun.

She thinks I call her that because of the obvious reasons. If she only knew what it meant, she'd probably throw a pot at my head.

Speaking of pots, she better not be in the greenhouse when I arrive.

From where I enter the room, I find her leaning over the bathtub.

But it's who she is washing that has my movement stopping, and my eyes going wide. There, in the tub, is Cerberus.

My dog.

My guard dog.

He's sopping wet, and she is scrubbing behind his ears.

There is no way this is happening. The dog is licking her face now, and her head is thrown back as she laughs.

He's transfixed by her, and I understand why.

Fuck, I'm transfixed by her, and she's not even rubbing me.

She's a goddess come down to Earth, thrust into my hell, and making me feel things I shouldn't.

Staring at her is like looking at the sun. Ironic, really.

As if she can hear my thoughts, she looks up at me.

Her large blue eyes widen in surprise.

She doesn't understand the precarious situation she's in. I'm a monster. She is the prey, and if she knows what's good for her, she will run.

Cerberus wags his tail back and forth when he sees me. Who is this dog? What has she done to him? Only Ivy.

Cerberus chooses that moment to jump out of the bath and shake before Ivy can grab a towel. Water sprays everywhere, and Ivy is drenched.

Her nipples pebble beneath that damn tank she always wears.

"Why don't you ever wear clothes?" I say gruffly.

"Um. Kidnapped."

"I gave you some."

"I'm not wearing your shit."

"Is that so, Sun?" I say, stepping out from the doorway and into the bathroom. She steps back, but she has nowhere to go because behind her is the bathroom counter.

Her hands reach out until they are hovering close to my chest. I step forward, toward her, and her skin collides with my shirt.

"Get out of my way," she says, more like pleads.

I look down at her, and a smirk lines my face.

"Do you really want me to?"

From my vantage point, I can see the way her chest heaves at my words. "I-I." she stutters.

"Yes?"

She shakes her head, righting herself.

"Are you done staring?" She asks.

"No."

"Well, I'm done letting you."

She lowers her body and escapes under the space in my arms where I had bracketed her in.

One thing is clear, though, from this interaction. Ivy isn't immune to me. She feels the pull, and she wants it too. She just won't admit it to herself.

I love a good challenge.

CHAPTER SEVENTEEN

Ivy

I'M PATHETIC. I KNOW I'M PATHETIC. BUT KNOWING THIS doesn't stop me from now being so eager to see this man that I'm sitting outside waiting for him. As soon as I heard the boat approaching, I headed down here, and now, like the idiot I am, I wait.

"You're more trouble than you're worth," a new voice says, and I turn my head in the direction where it's coming from. A man I've never seen is standing there, glaring at me. He looks at me as if he wants to kill me. The way you would look at your worst enemy just before you slashed their neck, but that makes no sense. I don't know him.

My back goes ramrod straight, and my fists ball at my waist. This man might be scary, but I won't back down.

"What did you say?" I ask the stranger, my eyes meeting his, but what I see there makes me shudder despite my false bravado. Dark eyes full of hatred. It really looks like he wants me dead.

"I don't know what you're talking about," he answers, and my anger rises to his blatant lie.

"If you're going to talk smack, you should own it." Snarky is probably not my best course of action with this man, but snarky is my best form of defense at the moment. My only defense, if I'm honest.

"You don't think I own my shit, little girl?" He steps closer, looking down his sharp but crooked nose at me. I can't imagine how many fights he's been in for it to look like that. I don't want to, especially since I'm throwing attitude at him. I square my shoulders, refusing to back down to fear.

"Well, apparently not." I let my lip tip up, calling him out on the lie.

"I know what you want me to do. You want me to tell you something. Anger me enough, right? But let me tell you this. You are a distraction, and I don't like you. If it was up to me, I'd get rid of you. Because, believe it or not, I don't give a shit what happens to you. Only him. And I will take you out if need be."

His words drip with so much malice I know I need to believe him, and while I want to be scared, I refuse to. Instead, I stand taller and smirk. "Do your worst."

He looks me up and down, and I know without a measure of doubt this man would squash me like a bug if given the opportunity.

Luckily, the moment ends as footsteps can clearly be heard approaching. It must be Cyrus, finally.

I look toward the beach, but still I don't see the boat. Is that what this goon is doing? Running interference?

Interesting. The boat must be my best bet for survival. If I can swim to it, I have a chance of escaping.

"What is going on here?" I hear, and we both turn in the direction of Cyrus. "Z?" When he doesn't answer, Cyrus's jaw tightens.

"Go to your room, Ivy."

"I'm not a little girl."

"I said leave." His deep voice bellows, leaving no room for protest. Whatever words that are about to transpire, I want no part of. I normally wouldn't turn tail, but even as stubborn and bullheaded as I am, I know when to pick and choose my battles.

CHAPTER EIGHTEEN

Cyrus

"WHAT WAS THAT ABOUT?" I STORM UP TO Z, AND HE has the audacity to look confused. I don't like the fact that he's here, nor do I like the fact that he spoke to Ivy.

"Nothing." He shrugs.

Once I'm standing directly in front of him, I stare down at him with my eyes narrowed, and his widen in return. "I know you don't agree with what I'm doing here, but it is not your place to question me," I snarl.

He looks toward the house, and something passes over his features. It's too fast to gauge what it is, but eventually, he nods his head in submission. Good. He should know his place. This is my business, my operation, he needs to know where he stands.

"Z, you are one of my most trusted men. Is this going to be a problem?"

"No." His mouth opens and then closes. He has more to say. Probably something that will get him killed if he's not careful one day.

"Speak," I order.

"It's just . . ." He pauses, thinking, and then he must decide it's worth the risk to his life to continue because he opens his mouth, and says, "We are so close. I don't want this to be fucked up over a girl."

He's not wrong. Fuck. I agree. But I'm not going to let him know that.

"We'll do things my way. Do you understand me?"

His head bounces up and down again in agreement.

"Good." I look toward where Ivy went and back at Z. "Now leave. I'll call you when I need you to come back."

The air around us is tense, and I can tell he wants to say more. Instead, he doesn't speak. His shoulders rise and fall, and then he sighs. I watch as he walks away, back down the path toward the docks where Maxwell will pick him up.

I, on the other hand, head back to the house.

Once inside, I head up the stairs toward where her room is. I had ordered her to her room like a petulant child in a time-out. I wonder if she followed that order or if, once again, she will be a problem.

Ivy is a distraction, but there is something about her that makes me want to keep her locked up here, even if it's not in my best interest.

You like her fire.

She's like the sun.

Both definitions of it.

When I finally get to her room, I lift my hand to knock and then pull my hand back. This is my house, and she's my prisoner, so I don't have to alert her of my presence. Throwing the door open, I notice that all the lights are off. It's pitch black in here. Other than the small streams of light coming in through the curtains, it's hard to see.

"Why are you in the dark?" I move into the room, standing by the foot of her bed. "Sulking?" I ask with a smile she can't see on my face.

"Hardly. I wouldn't sulk over you."

"Then why are you in here?" I start to walk over to the light switch. When I flick it up, I realize the problem. "They're dead."

"Bingo. Ten points for Hades."

"Keep up that mouth, and I'll punish you."

"Promises, promises. Do your worst. You stole me from my life, what more are you going to do with me?"

"There are a lot worse things than being my captive."

"Punish me then and get out." I step away from the bed and head out the room but not before I hear her say, "Thought so."

Truth. I would punish her. I'll starve her if need be, and if she proved to be an enemy, I would do a lot worse. But the reason I leave the room is because I need to take a deep fucking breath.

Her fire, attitude, and refusal to cooperate does something to me.

I ball my hands and head down the hall. Once I make it to the closet, I grab a light bulb. In the dark of the closet, I allow myself to breathe. It wouldn't be smart to go in there and show her the true force of my strength; however, making her fear me a little could prove beneficial to tame her.

Even though I'm calm now, I still go through with my plan and storm back into her room. The door slams shut as I pass through, and the walls shake from the force. Regardless of how dark it is, I can see the shadow of her body jump.

Good.

Mission accomplished. I scared her.

I prefer her be scared than tempt me with the flames.

Once I'm standing right by where she's lying in the bed, I notice something else.

Fuck.

She is wearing next to nothing. It's dark, but not dark enough to cover up the fact that she is practically naked. All she has on is that damn fucking camisole. I trail my eyes lower, noting an outline of material covering her, maybe boy shorts too.

How am I supposed to do anything with her looking like this? Here's the thing about Ivy—she's not even trying to be sexy, and she's sexier than any other woman I have met. She's certainly not trying to drive me crazy and entice me, but she does anyway. The feeling she evokes in me makes me feel equal measures of anger and desire. I want to strangle her for confusing me. She's too much temptation.

I give myself a shake and pull all thoughts away from the naked girl on the bed, so I stand on the mattress. The bed shifts with my weight.

Ivy groans, "Seriously, couldn't you grab a chair?"

"No."

"Come on, please." The way she asks has me hopping back off. Hearing a woman beg will make even the toughest men weak.

I grab the chair, the one I purposely forego in order to piss her off and then make quick work to change the light bulb. Once it turns on, I look down at Ivy who is reclined in the bed beside where I am. Her eyes are wide, and I follow her line of vision.

When I was changing the light bulb, my shirt rose, and Ivy now has a perfect view of my torso, and apparently, she's eating it up.

I can't help the shit-eating grin that spreads across my face.

"Like what you see?" I'm back to being a dick because it's easier this way. She shakes her head, but now bathed in light, I don't miss the blush crawling up her skin. I also don't miss that I was right about her attire. She is wearing that fucking damn camisole and small barely-there boy shorts.

I'm about to jump off the chair and stop looking at her when Cerberus runs up and bumps me where I'm standing.

"Fuck," I snarl, but it's too late. The chair is tipping.

I catch myself, though, and being the dick I am, I opt for where she is, directly on top of her, all my weight balancing on her bed, slightly hovered above her.

We're close enough that I can feel the rise and fall of her chest.

"What are you doing?" she breathes out, and her words tickle my chin. Her body stiffens, and I push back a little to stare into her eyes. Silently, she begs me to move, but instead, I continue to hold my weight on my hands and watch as she breathes in my air.

We're both locked in a trance. Her breathing. My breathing. Her exhale. My exhale.

It's a wicked dance, but neither of us pulls away.

We're two flames, burning brightly to merge and become one. The type of fire that scorches everything in its path and causes mass destruction. That's what we'll be if I cross the imaginary divide between us.

Logic dictates the need to pull away, but instead, I lean toward her. We are now close enough that if I move a fraction of an inch, our mouths will touch in a kiss. Her eyes are large, the blue almost completely gone, hidden behind wide eyes, filled with desire. Lowering my gaze, I notice how she trembles beneath me and I ache to close the distance, to put us both out of our misery already.

"You can go now. The light bulb is changed."

I know I should get up, but I hold myself there for another second, watching as she swallows, watching her mouth. Memorizing the look in her eyes, and then, when she licks her lips, I get up.

Z might be right after all. She might be too big of a distraction.

Now to figure out what to do with this distraction.

CHAPTER NINETEEN

Ivy

O NLY ONE DAY PASSES WHEN I HEAR THE FRONT DOOR opening. I head out of my bedroom and down the stairs. He's here. Why? Usually, he makes me wait days. When I approach the foyer, I stop, cock my hip, and raise a brow at Cyrus. "For someone who was trying to starve me into submission, you're doing a horrible job."

"And why is that?" A ghost of a smirk appears on his handsome face.

My hands rest on my hips before I answer. "Because you are here yet again to feed me." Then I smile at him, an overly fake one, and his once upturning lip pulls down into a straight line.

"The first thing you have to know about me is if I wanted you submissive, you would be submissive." The way he says the word submissive should be illegal.

Get a grip, Ivy. Head in the game.

"And the second?"

Then he smiles.

Shit. It's not a smirk or a grin, but a full smile that makes my heart flutter in my chest. Damn. Why does he have to be so good-looking? No, I chastise myself. He's not good-looking; he's evil. The devil. The devil can't be handsome. Who am I trying to kid? He's delicious when he looks at me like this. There is an unfamiliar glint to his dark eyes.

"What?" I ask.

"Your smart mouth will get you in trouble." He starts to walk to the kitchen, and I follow behind like a lost little puppy.

"Yet you're here, feeding me," I chide, trying my best to feign indifference to the butterflies now flying in my belly.

He lets out a small chuckle. "Do you have your list of questions handy?" His voice sounds different than normal, and that's when I realize he's playing with me. Poking fun at me.

"Was that a joke?" I ask as I take a seat at the table.

He shrugs, moving toward the fridge.

"Wow. I didn't know you had it in you."

And I'm going to need you to stop acting like this.

I can handle gruff. I can handle asshole. What I'm not sure I can handle is playful Cyrus Reed.

He's deadlier than the rest.

"Well, apparently, you bring out all different sides of me." His tone changes and his eyes darken. I'm not exactly sure what he means.

Not wanting to read more into it, I lean forward, placing my weight on my forearms.

"What language does Cerberus understand?" I ask, changing the topic.

"Is that your question? Because that will cost you a bite."

It's probably pretty obvious at this point that he doesn't need to answer questions for me to eat, but we keep up the pretense anyway.

Not sure why.

Maybe it's easier for me to talk to him under the guise that it's for food.

"Done."

He opens the container he has set on the table and then brings me a fork.

My eyes narrow at the food in front of me. It looks like rice and veggies, but there is a sauce on it.

"What is it?"

"That's two bites."

I roll my eyes. Why would I think he would answer? That would be too easy for Cyrus Reed. "Fine."

"It's Biryani. A popular Indian dish."

I take a bite and swallow. It's delicious, but I won't tell him that, though.

"Dutch," he says as I take my second bite.

I quirk my brow at him. No wonder the dog thinks I'm crazy every time I speak. "Dutch?"

"Cerberus is a Dutch Shepard. He's trained to understand Dutch commands."

"You speak Dutch?" I ask.

"You don't?"

"How many languages do you speak?"

He skims his eyes down my body. "All of them."

"Why?"

"Because of my clients."

"Well. Um. That's not helpful at all. I was hoping you would say Spanish." I take another two small bites. Technically I owe him three, but apparently, he's not counting. After I swallow, I place my fork down. "Teach me commands for him."

"That will cost you."

"Okay . . ." I trail off, afraid of what I'll have to do.

"You eat the rest of the meal. No more questions. I'll teach you Dutch, but that's all I'm answering."

"Well, that's not really fair."

"Life's not fair."

I bite my lip, trying to think of a witty response, but when I come up short, he leans forward. "Do we have a deal?"

"No."

"I'm a fair man. If you want to learn how to command my dog, that is all you will get from me tonight."

He's right. He doesn't answer any important questions anyway. It's not like I'll be getting anything else from him.

"Deal."

Cyrus turns to the center of the kitchen, then sweeps his hand in a half-circle motion in front of his body while saying, "*Kom*."

Cerberus comes pounding over. "*Zit*," he says next, and I notice his pointer finger is pointing up.

It's pretty obvious what he means with these, but I still turn to Cyrus for clarification on the hand gestures.

"*Kom* means come. When I give the verbal cue, I also use hand gestures."

That makes me lean forward. "Really? Why?"

Cyrus looks at Cerberus and then with his right pointer finger traces a command in the shape of an *L*. Cerberus lies down on the floor by his feet. "If it's loud, and he can't hear my words, he will still come. He will sit, and he will lie *down*."

That's what he was just commanding him without words, down. The shape of an L, the lower part of the letter, tracing the floor.

Interesting.

I nod because this all makes sense to me. "And *zit*? I must assume that means sit."

"Yes. Correct."

"Those were easy. I could have figured that out eventually. What else can you tell me?"

"I won't teach you all my tricks, Sun." The corner of his lip tips up into a smirk. A very sexy smirk that I shouldn't think is, but it doesn't stop it from being true. Cyrus Reed should smirk more. Rewind. No. No, he shouldn't. He's way too sinful for him to be making me think that.

"Fine. What about what you told him the first day?"

"*Bescherm*?"

"Yeah. That one. You told it to him before you left me."

Cyrus looks over at the dog and then back at me. His features seem to soften. "Protect. I was telling him to protect you."

The words make me feel light-headed. I'm on the top of a roller coaster, about to spin out of control. I should be scared, but instead, I'm excited.

Standing from my chair, I try to get distance, but the room feels too small for all the emotions propelling around inside me.

"Why are you pacing, Sun?" His question has my movements stopping. I hadn't realized I was.

Cyrus is now standing right in front of me.

His large and masculine frame, pulling in all the oxygen from the room. He's too close, and I need air.

"Was it something I said?"

I look up at him. What I see is unnerving, he's watching me, but it's the look in his eyes that has my pulse pounding in my ears. He's stares into my soul as if he can crack it open. What he'll find is unknown. I'm treading in deep and dangerous waters and I'm sure I'll drown.

I know I need to pull my gaze, but as we look into each other's eyes, there is an electric pulse between us.

Silence stretches with a million unspoken words. I have so many questions, but the only one I can ask is...

"Why?"

"Why what?" He steps closer, and our bodies are practically touching now.

"Why did you tell him to protect me?" I whisper, tilting my head down to the ground to not look into his eyes, but he's not having it. His hand reaches out, his fingers brushing against my jaw, then my chin.

He draws my gaze back up. "Because you're mine to protect."

"I'm not yours to protect."

"That's where you're wrong."

My pulse skitters alarmingly fast, and I lick my lips. I don't mean to, but Cyrus doesn't miss it. His blazing stare now lingering on my parted mouth, I try to ignore how my heart flutters as he looks at me, how it ping-pongs in my chest.

But it's impossible.

There's no way.

He's larger than life.

He's too much.

He's everything I shouldn't want, and yet the way he stares at me makes me feel alive. It scares me. It scares me so much; that before I can think better of it, I run.

I don't get far.

I don't even bother to leave the house. Instead, I open the door to the library and slip inside. He needs to leave the island. Once he's gone, I can rein in these emotions that have taken on a life of their own. I shouldn't want him, I shouldn't crave him, but I do, so he needs to get back on that boat of his before I do something, I know that I shouldn't. I can't have him on this island, not in this house, and definitely not near me.

He does strange things to my body whenever he is around. I feel warm and tingly. I hate it.

I'm like a bad romance novel.

He's my captor, and I refuse to have Stockholm syndrome. The problem is, he hasn't gotten the memo that he needs to stay the hell away from me.

I swear he's everywhere I am.

When I'm in the kitchen, he's there. When I'm taking a walk . . . there.

What does he want from me?

And after all this time, he still refuses to talk. To tell me about his cryptic words.

Protecting me? From who?

It makes no sense, and I refuse to find him and ask. Because even though I am so starved for attention at this point, I don't trust myself with him near me. As if summoned by my thoughts, he steps into the library. The room I was hiding in.

"Don't run from me, Sun."

"I can't be here." My voice is fragile and shaky. I need space, but he doesn't give me that, instead he steps closer. I raise my hands in the air as I take a step back. "You can let me go," I whisper. "I won't tell anyone. But you have to let me go." *I can't control the way you make me feel.*

"I can't let you go."

"Why?"

I take another step back, and my butt hits the desk in the corner of the library.

"Because you're mine now, and I won't let anyone have you."

His words shock me, making my muscles freeze. I've felt the heat of every stare, but this is more, and the look in his eyes scares me.

"You don't even like me. You hate me." I shake my head, not wanting to let my brain go there. Denying the truth that is right in front of me. He moves closer, his body touching mine.

"Does this feel like I hate you?"

"You kidnapped me . . ."

"I did what I had to do." His answer is cryptic, as usual. I want to bash his head against a wall for not telling me what he means, but my brain and arms aren't working properly due to the proximity of our bodies. I know I should push him off, but I can't think of anything but the feel of him.

I hate him, but most of all, I hate myself for feeling this way.

"I'll tell you the truth," he says, "but it will cost you more than food."

"What?"

"You have to earn it . . ." His words hang in the air, mischievous, sinful, and full of dirty promises.

"What do you want?"

"You."

"I thought you wouldn't take something not given?"

He lifts his hands, touching my jaw.

"Who says anything about taking?" He smirks.

"But you just said . . ."

"I said I wanted you, Ivy. And I do. I want to taste you. Feel you. I want to know what it feels like when you come apart under my tongue."

"I hate you."

"You don't hate me. Let me show you just how much you don't hate me. Your body will show you."

He lifts his hands to cup my jaw. His fingers trail against my skin. "Does this feel like you hate me?" He continues his path down the hollow of my neck. "How about this?"

"Why then?"

"I have my reasons."

My breath comes out in shallow pulls, and my body shakes under his ministrations. "I won't hurt you, Sun."

"Why do you call me that?"

He doesn't answer my question, though; he just keeps up the path of his fingers. I stare at him. Shocked by what I see.

The passion in his eyes screams that he's telling the truth. Screams for me to allow this. But what does that make me if I do?

You want him. I shake my head, and as if he can read my mind, he speaks the words.

"You want me."

I shake my head again.

"I don't." My voice cracks pathetically, even I can't pretend.

"You do, and you want to hate me for it."

"I do . . ." Not even I can believe myself.

"You don't. Because deep inside you, you know the truth."

"And what truth is that?"

"That you are here because you need to be here."

His words are still cryptic and still make no sense. But when I look into his eyes, I know he's speaking the truth, or at least a truth he believes.

His hands continue their path to the center of my chest.

I think he will stop touching me. Lean forward and kiss me. He doesn't move forward, though; instead, his hands cup me.

"I can feel how wet you are . . ."

My chest rises and falls.

He's right; I am. I'm so desperate for him to touch me that I hate myself. What does it mean that I want my kidnapper?

"I don't want you. You kidnapped me."

"I saved you."

"You have delusions of grandeur."

His hands are still on me, warming my body and making me feel alive under his touch, blossoming. Blooming.

I need to push it down and stop it.

He's lying.

He's crazy.

Then why does he look at me like this?

Like I'm his salvation.

And he'll do anything to protect me.

It doesn't make any sense.

He leans forward, his lips hovering close to my mouth. His fingers touching me between my thighs. One swipe against the inseam of my pants has my breath hitching.

I shiver. A soft moan escapes my mouth.

My brain is rapid-firing why this can't happen. Why I need to push him away and say no, but as his breath tickles my lips, I can't find any words.

I do want him to touch me.

Desperately.

I want in a way I've never wanted anyone before, and I don't know what that says about me.

It must be Stockholm syndrome, or maybe his words are true. Maybe I recognize them for what they are, for the conviction in them.

He hasn't hurt me.

Lust.

It's just lust talking.

He kidnapped . . .

His finger touches me again, and this time, my head lolls

back. I shouldn't want this. I shouldn't want him. But I bask in his touch, regardless.

Because with a touch of his hand, I forget why I'm supposed to hate him. I forget why I'm fighting this.

I forget everything but the here and now and the feeling inside me.

He's like the storm that batters the island outside. Like a hurricane, growing, gathering strength until it strikes. I'm the eye, and he is the storm.

His lip tips up.

I wait for him to kiss me, to do something. Anything.

I want to beg him to finish what he's started. To soothe the burn that has been building inside me. But I don't say anything and neither does he.

He just stands in front of me.

Not speaking. Just staring. A look passes through his gaze. I can't put my finger on it, but if it was anyone else, I'd say it was regret.

Silence looms between us like a heavy mist as I wait for something to happen. Finally, it does as he inclines his head down and shakes it. "Nope." He looks back at me. "You don't hate me . . ." He trails off before he turns and walks away. "Not at all."

I need to get out of here. My desperation is getting to me. My need for attention making me feel things I shouldn't.

The next time he comes back, I'll leave. I *will* escape. No matter what.

CHAPTER TWENTY

Ivy

HE HAS TO LEAVE THIS DAMN ISLAND. AFTER OUR LITTLE run-in earlier in the library, I need to be alone. I'm a mess. Not only am I confused, but I'm so turned on, I'm afraid at any moment I might hump his leg. Which I can't do for obvious reasons.

My options are limited in places to go. I'm afraid I'll see him, and I can't be held responsible for my actions if I do.

Truth is, it feels like I'm suffocating with him here. I know what he's doing; he's trying to torture me. Well, it's worked.

He is.

A million conflicting thoughts are spiraling in my brain, and that doesn't even touch upon my body. My treacherous body that refuses to take the memo: *You are not allowed to be turned on by your kidnapper.*

I can pretend that I'm not, but then I would be lying.

No point. I know the truth. Hell, he felt the truth.

My cheeks become warm as I think over the things that he said to me.

The bastard.

He ate that shit up. Probably still is.

I wonder if I can hide from him.

Well, I'm already doing that. I'm hiding in my bedroom, but eventually, I'll have to go downstairs, and with my luck, he will speak to me.

Little damn butterflies start to fly in my stomach. Great. Even my stomach knows I'm lying. I want to speak to him.

I hate myself for it, but it doesn't make it any less true. My stomach hasn't gotten the memo that we are avoiding Cyrus and his meals because it starts to growl in protest.

There's no fighting this. I have to go down and eat.

Without a second thought, I head straight for the kitchen. What I'm met with has my breath hitching.

What is going on?

I look around the room, but no one is there. It's the table that has me blinking. The room in general that unnerves me.

The lights are dimmed, and there are candles set in the center of the table. A table that has food placement for two.

"What is this?" Cyrus says as he steps up from behind.

I turn over my shoulder. "If you didn't do this . . ."

"Mariana."

I shake my head, not knowing who that is.

"She brings the food. Cooks it."

Aww. It all makes sense. "She was here today?" he nods. I wonder why I didn't see her. *Probably because you were too busy panting after Cyrus.* "But why would she set it for two?"

"That was my doing. I told her I would be eating dinner. The rest"—he gestures to the table—"that's all her."

The room is the perfect romantic date, if we were going on a romantic date. We aren't, so instead of setting the mood, a heavy tension hovers in the air.

"Sit. Stop thinking. Just sit and eat."

"Always a gentleman," I say under my breath.

"Sun . . ." he warns, and I shut my mouth and sit.

Now that we are both at the table, we both reach for our silverware to eat.

The food, as always, is delicious, but the silence is

deafening. I look down to the floor and notice that Cerberus is curled up against my leg.

Cyrus follows my line of sight. "You really have him wrapped around your little finger."

That makes me smile.

"What did you do to win him over?"

"As if I would tell you." I smirk. Intense pleasure over that fact that he was wrong about his own dog has a laugh bubbling up inside me. I bask in knowing that I have bested him. Take that. A taste of his own medicine.

"You think you have the upper hand? It's cute."

"I do."

"I let you believe that, but you don't."

"Tonight, I do."

He leans forward, placing his elbows on the table. "And how do you figure this?"

"Well. Normally, you make me eat, but today, you're eating. Which means the ball isn't in your court anymore. Actually, I think it's in mine, and you owe me."

Beautiful dark eyes smolder at me, reminding me of silky-smooth satin. The type of satin Cyrus would probably use to tie me up with.

The memory of earlier becomes vivid and clear in my head. The feel of his fingers haunts me. The way they teased and tortured. There is no denying how my body reacted.

My cheeks burn from the images playing in my mind. I try to push the thoughts out, but instead they bury themselves in deeper, making my blood soar through my veins, and the unquenched hunger that I thought I had under control now rekindles in my core.

"What are you thinking?" His voice dips low and only serves to make me feel warm all over.

I shake my head and try to think of something to say. "Um. How about you owe me answers? How about for every bite you take, you answer?"

"Or . . ." he drawls out. "We each answer questions."

"Can I ask—"

"No."

"Why not?" I find myself pouting, and I want to slap myself.

"It's better this way right now. You have to trust me."

That word again. There is no way that is happening. Hell, when he's around I can't even trust myself. "I can't do that."

"Try."

My head drops down and then lifts up. "Fine." At least this way I might be able to find out something about my host and stop staring at him. Maybe I'll find out something that will make me stop fantasizing about the way he touched me. As if he can hear my mind, he starts to drum his *fingers* on the table. A choke escapes my mouth, and I know that all these lusty thoughts have turned my cheeks red from how hot I feel as I stare at his masculine hands.

"You okay, over there?" he asks, sexy grin large and very happy with himself and the feelings he so obviously brings out in me.

There's a part of me, that wants to stand from the table and put an end to this game of cat and mouse, but instead, I school my features, extinguish my desires and pretend I'm talking to a stranger, and not a stranger I want to kiss.

Shit.

Not doing a good job of pretending.

With a deep inhale, I try again. "I'll start the questions. What exactly do you do?"

"I run a bank. Next question." His answer is short, and I file it away as something I want to find out about.

"What is it you do, Sun?"

I narrow my eyes. "I thought you knew this?"

"Nope." His answer doesn't meet his eyes, but maybe I'm reading into things too much.

"I work at a flower shop. Or I did." I can't help but feel the loss as the words pass through my lips. I shake away the thoughts and smirk. "Are you as evil as I think you are?"

"More so," he responds, not missing a beat.

"For some reason, that I believe."

His lips tip up into a heart-stopping grin. "I'm more wicked than you could ever imagine."

"I don't doubt that for a minute."

"And you, Ivy." His dark eyes sparkle with mischief, "Have you ever done anything wicked?"

Don't fall into the trick.

My cheeks turn hot at the inquisition, my body obviously a traitor. "Maybe. But I'm not telling you."

"Live a little. No one's here. It's just you and me . . ." The husky tone in his voice makes me think of decadent chocolate, sinful and delicious and probably not the best thing for you. "I won't tell."

Jeez, this man. The way he speaks, silky smooth with innuendo should come with a warning label.

Careful when engaging, highly combustible.

I need to steer this conversation into safer waters.

"Do you have a girl—" I stop myself before I finish my ridiculous and totally not safe question. Hopefully, before he notices, but unfortunately from the way he grins, it's obvious he heard me.

Someone save me.

Cyrus Reed will never let this go.

"Girlfriend? Ivy. Were you asking me on a date?"

"What. No. That's not what I meant."

He leans in, elbows on the table, head cocked as he stares at me, or better yet undresses me at the table. "No. I don't."

Sinful.

He is sinfully delicious.

I need a life preserver to sit at this table with him. Especially with the ambiance set. At this point, all that's missing is sexy music.

That would be bad.

The longer he stares at me, the hotter my cheeks get, I swear they are going to catch on fire, because he just won't stop.

I can't think of anything else to ask. I need something. Anything.

"Do you have any hobbies?" I blurt.

"Chess."

Of course, that's his hobby. Doesn't surprise me at all. Our whole relationship is one big chessboard, and I'm the pawn.

"And you?" he asks.

"Gardening," I answer, and he shakes his head.

"I was referring to the boyfriend."

My mouth drops open. If we were outside, I'd have a mouthful of flies in it.

"I-I. That's none of your business," I respond, trying to save the last of my dignity I have left.

"Good."

That shuts me up, and the room goes quiet once again. I wonder what his next move will be. Will he steer us back to dangerous waters or throw me a life raft.

His face is impassive as I wait for my fate.

Then it opens. "Why flowers?" he asks, breaking the silence and I wonder why after all we talked about; he goes back to this of all questions. Seems strange, but one thing I've learnt about Cyrus Reed is never to think you can anticipate his next move.

"My mother. She loved to garden. She taught me everything." I close my eyes, and I can almost imagine I'm in a garden. I remember the smell; I remember the feeling of the dirt in my hands. I remember everything.

"What are you thinking about?"

I open my eyes; Cyrus is staring at me. "How much I love to garden. I feel lost without it."

"You can use my greenhouse," he says before standing from the table and severing the moment.

But the feelings I feel from his words have already buried themselves in my soul.

Warmth.

Happiness.

Hope.

There might be more to Cyrus Reed than he lets on.

He might be a good man.

Fuck.

I cannot think these thoughts. This is too much. These feelings are too much.

My resolve is set.

I need to get out of here.

Now.

CHAPTER TWENTY-ONE

Cyrus

"Who's my meeting with today?" I ask Z as I walk down the stairs into the kitchen to grab a cup of coffee.

"Alaric."

Mariana is in the kitchen cooking breakfast, and as soon as she sees me, she sets off to prepare my cup.

The stunt she pulled yesterday wasn't missed. Candles. No, that was pretty fucking obvious what she was doing.

It wasn't enough not to fuck Ivy on my desk as is. Couple that with how fucking beautiful she looked last night, and the ambiance, and I'm lucky I didn't do something I would have regretted in the morning.

Catching up with Alaric will be just what I need to sort myself.

"What time?" I ask as Mariana hands me my mug, and I take a swig.

"Noon."

Taking a seat at the table, I motion for Z to join me. "Let's go over numbers before he gets here. He's probably expanding and needs to deposit more money, but in case it's something else, I need to know everything about his account."

"No problem."

By the time Alaric is set to arrive, I'm standing outside on the dock of my estate. The beauty of my property is most of my clients can come in undetected by boat. Alaric's yacht, for example, can come in from the Atlantic, and no one will be none the wiser.

Which is what he's doing right now.

We hold many of our meetings out here on the dock. Far enough in all directions that no one can listen in.

When Alaric's small yacht docks, he hops off and heads over to me.

"Pleasure to see you," I greet, extending my hand.

He meets mine and shakes it. "Thank you for taking this meeting. I had some business I wanted to discuss with you."

"Don't you always?" I laugh.

"I have guns I need to move, and I need your help."

My brow lifts. "Arms dealing is your business, Alaric. I'm not sure how I can help?"

"I need you to store some," he says.

"Why would I do that?"

"Because we're friends."

"Is that what we are, Alaric?"

"I'd like to think so, and friends help friends . . ." he leads, and I know what he's saying. If I help him with this, he has my back in the future.

"Tell me about the guns."

"They're hot right now. Too hot for me to sell."

"I won't agree until you tell me why."

"We lifted them off the competition, Cyrus."

I nod. "And why are they flagged?"

"They are the same lot and caliber as the guns used in the attack in Italy."

I look back at the house where Z is standing. If we do this, it could come back to bite us in the ass, but the risk is worth it to have Alaric in my pocket.

"Very well. Where are the guns?"

He turns to the yacht. I lift my hand and signal Z, who's standing in front of me not a minute later.

"We need to rid Alaric of a load."

"On it." Z walks toward the dock and boards the yacht. His cell phone is lifted to his ear as he calls my men to help him.

A few minutes later, Alaric and my men start to bring the crates inside, and once they are all out of sight, I turn to Alaric.

"Since Maxwell is helping your men, care to give me a lift?"

"Of course." He smiles broadly. "Where to?"

"The island over there." I point at the island.

"What's there?"

"Nothing for you to worry about. All you have to worry about is dropping me off and grabbing your men once they place your guns in my possession."

CHAPTER TWENTY-TWO

Ivy

I HAVE BEEN A MESS EVER SINCE OUR LAST DINNER.

From the window in my bedroom, I have a perfect view of the ocean. I think I see a boat approach the island. It might not be coming here, but it's been a few days, so it is undoubtedly bringing him back. The thought makes me feel like a million tiny little spiders are crawling all over me.

What will he do this time?

Will he tease me again?

Will he make my body betray me once more?

The last time I almost didn't escape his clutches. My mind screams that I hate him, but my body says otherwise.

I wanted him then.

I want him still now.

A part of me needs him to do everything he promised.

He's a savage. A beast.

He's the devil.

Playing me like a fiddle, he lured me in. The way he pressed himself against me, unabashed. The dirty things he promised. The tiny moments of warmth I saw in his gaze, followed by the utter coldness in his soulless eyes.

He is Hades.

Holding me prisoner on an island and refusing to tell me why.

He says he has his reasons, but not a damn thing could justify what he's done. I don't care if the place is a mansion, and it doesn't matter that my every need could be found here. I'm a prisoner, and he's my captor. That makes him the worst kind of evil.

Surely, I'll never get out of here alive.

He said he couldn't let me go. He claimed I was his. He can't set me free, and because of that, I know I'll die here. Unless I take matters into my own hands.

My best shot of survival is getting on that boat.

Right now, it's still off the coast.

I need to hurry. It will be here soon, and then they will be on their way.

"I'll have to swim," I say to myself, preparing for the task ahead.

Easier said than done.

I take several deep breaths, trying to calm my nerves.

The swim isn't going to be easy, and I need to have my head about me. Another thought pops into my head, making me feel dizzy with nerves. When I get onto the boat . . .

Who will be driving the it?

Will they be willing to help me?

Probably not.

A scarier thought hits me next, stealing all the oxygen from my lungs . . . will they hurt me?

Knowing how powerful and frightening Cyrus is, I doubt anyone will betray him and live to tell about it. But it's not worth the risk. No, I'll have to sneak on board and hope like hell I can find a small compartment to hide in.

The good news is that the boat isn't a small speed boat like usual. No, today it's a full-blown yacht. It's different from the usual boat that drops him off.

This must mean something. It has to be easier to escape on that, right?

My feet pace in front of the window. Waiting. Watching. The boat is fast approaching, so I need to move.

The humming of the craft is my signal that it's now or never.

If I want to get off this island, I need to take my chances and move quickly. But how will I escape him? I might get off this island, but staying hidden from him will be a whole other issue.

One that I can't worry about now.

My goal has to be getting out of here first.

Hide second.

At that moment, Cerberus nudges my leg.

I look down into his big brown eyes and feel a moment's hesitation at leaving him here. "You're the only thing I'll miss, boy," I say to him. It's almost as if he's begging me to take him.

It breaks my heart, but that isn't possible. "I can't take you with me. I would if I could. You believe me, don't you?" His whimpers threaten to break me, but as fond of him as I have grown, I have to go.

I can't swim to the boat if I'm worrying about him, and there is no way he'll make it all the way out there.

With my head held high, I make my way out of my bedroom and down the stairs.

My plan depends on evading Cyrus. If he catches me, I'll lose my one shot at escape from this hellish island.

He's too big. Too powerful.

Shut up, Ivy. You got this. This is your chance to escape.

When the sound of the boat stops for a moment, I know that Cyrus is on the island.

He'll be inside within moments.

I try to think of where I can go to hide as the front door creeps open.

Shit.

"Ivy?" he calls out, and I know I have a matter of minutes to get to the boat before it takes off.

I look down at Cerberus, who is following closely behind me.

"*Gaan*," I prompt him in Dutch. "Go. Get him." I hope he'll take the bait and stall Cyrus. I need the dog not to follow me anymore.

It will give away my position. When Cerberus does what I tell him, I breathe a sigh of relief, and then when Cyrus is distracted, I make my dash for the open door. I run as fast as my feet can go.

Fuck.

All hope is dashed away as Cyrus steps into my path; his eyes wild with rage. He still looks at me with a heated stare. The type of stare that in another time in another life would light me on fire. My skin sizzles, but I tamp it down.

He might be good-looking. But I am not that girl.

I am no foregone conclusion.

What I am is a fighter, and I will not let him leave me again.

A new plan takes root. A good one. Stepping up to him, I lift my hand and then I trail my hands down my chest, all while seductively stepping toward him.

Even I can admit this probably won't work, but I have to try.

I reach my hand out and touch his chest.

His eyes widen. I've taken him off guard.

"What in the hell do you think you're doing?" His deep timbre manages to frighten me even more than his deadly stare. He's angry, and that is more dangerous than any come-ons from the other day.

If the malice he portrays is any indication, I have to change the game. I don't have time to waste quaking in fear.

I squash it down and act quickly. Stepping into him, I throw him off and bring my knee firmly into his groin as hard as I can manage.

It does the trick. He bends over, groaning in pain, and I don't stop to think about it. I pump my arms as fast as I can and don't look back.

When I reach the end of the beach, I dive headfirst into the cold water.

I welcome the icy chill.

It's my savior.

My escape.

I channel all the years of swimming I have under my belt and swim as though my life depended on it—which it does.

It's all going well . . . until it isn't.

A strong current pulls me under, dragging me across the jagged rocks below.

Years at the beach in the summer have taught me how to handle such a situation.

I kick my arms and legs to swim directly into the current and let it take me. I try not to panic as I'm quickly running out of air. My hand skims past something hard, and without another thought, I reach out and grab ahold. I yank hard and am able to pull myself up.

When my head crests the water, I gulp in a lungful of air greedily as I cling to the large branch for dear life.

Every ounce of energy I have is depleted along with any hope of escaping. There is no way I'll make it to that boat now.

I'm going to die.

No. I can't go this way. I have to fight. I need to swim. My legs are cut up, and if I let go of this branch, I'll drown.

"Help me," I cry out to whoever is on the boat, but it's in vain. I'm too far away, and my voice is too weak to be heard.

Tears well in my eyes as I realize that the only option I have is to try to make it back to shore.

But I can't.

For one, I don't have the strength to fight that current again, and for another, Cyrus will be there waiting for me on the shore.

What if he makes me pay for my attempt to escape, and for what I've done to him?

The dread becomes even worse when I see Cyrus race for the shore.

He's coming for me, and I can't escape his wrath. My fear turns to shock as minutes later I realize he isn't coming for me. He's carrying Cerberus in his arms toward the shore.

"Oh, no. Cerberus, you didn't," I say, guilt-ridden. The dog had followed me into the water, and I can't tell if he's been hurt or not.

Based on the way Cyrus cradles him into his chest, it doesn't look good. I have to get back to the shore and help.

It's all my fault.

Now that getting off this island isn't an option, I need to make sure Cerberus is going to be okay.

When he lowers the dog to the ground, he does stand on his feet, but his poor tail sags limply before he collapses to the beach. I cry out at the sight.

I'm an idiot.

Why did I ever think I could escape?

A part of me withers and dies as the realization hits me.

What's happening to Cerberus is my fault, and I'll pay the consequences. I continue to lie atop the piece of wood, unmoving. The goal is to get my energy back enough to attempt to swim back. The sky is getting darker. Large clouds rolling in. If my situation couldn't get any worse, it does, as the winds begin to pick up. A storm is coming, and it's coming fast. The current won't last forever. Soon the waves will pull me out. I'm just not sure for how long until it will pose a threat.

My question is answered as rain starts to pound down from the sky. The waves crashing along the rocks where I've drifted. There's no way to go back, I try to kick to push off from the rocks, but I can't move. I'm barely holding on, my hands slipping. I can't let go. I know if I'm pulled under again, this time I'll die.

CHAPTER TWENTY-THREE

Cyrus

RAGE CONSUMES ME AT HER DISOBEDIENCE. DOES SHE NOT know who I am?

Does she not understand that she belongs to me? Her body had reacted exactly as I had hoped.

She wants me to taste her. To take her. Why is she trying to escape? Doesn't she realize she'll never be able to outrun me?

I clench and unclench my fists, trying to calm down. She'll pay for her blatant disregard of the rules laid forth. Nobody crosses me and lives.

But for her, I'll make this exception.

She'll live, but she'll pay in other ways.

Cerberus whines at my feet. He's laid limply on the shore, not bothering to lift his head to look at me. He's had a hell of a scare, but he's all right. He's strong.

What the hell was Ivy thinking? These waters are dangerous.

I have to figure out how to get her ass back to shore. The boat she's trying to reach is already on its way out to sea.

They can't see her.

They can't help her.

No one can help her but me.

I'm her only savior. If she would just believe me, trust me, things would be different.

She's still trying to make it to the boat, but even if they did see her, they wouldn't come back unless I called them back, and I won't.

Today, I took a different boat. Today, I hitched a ride with men I don't necessarily trust. But they know the consequences of talking. I would not make exceptions for them. They'd die.

Regardless, it would be reckless of me to introduce them to my captive. Getting Ivy back to shore is all on me.

I'll drag her back by her hair if I have to.

My eyes roam the water, landing on the location she had last been, but she's gone. It doesn't help that it's raining over the ocean. The clouds are moving fast, it will be over the house in no time. I have to find her now. My head whips back and forth, trying to find her, but with each second that passes without her in my sight, unease grows heavily within me.

This is an emotion I rarely feel.

I'm usually in control.

I rule my world. Nothing makes me uneasy.

So why does my stomach turn and sweat pool at my temples?

This is beyond unease.

This is fucking panic.

And for the first time in a very long time, it's for someone else's life and not my own.

Her head pops up out of the water, and I watch as her hands flail. She's in trouble.

"Fuck," I yell out as my heart pounds in my chest. When her head goes back under and doesn't come back up, my breathing stops.

Before I realize what I'm doing, I'm running toward the water and diving in.

She's about twenty yards off the shore, and if I'm going to save her, I have to swim faster than ever. My arms burn with each stroke, but I push harder.

When I feel like I'm getting close to where she was, I pop my head up to see if I can locate her. After catching a glimpse of flailing arms, I know where I need to be. She's dangerously close to the cliff. If I don't get there soon, she could crash into it. I dive back under and swim to my right. When I'm almost to her, a large wave smacks against us, pushing closer to the rocks, I brace for impact, trying to protect my body from the sharp shards of rocks that strikes me in the side of my thigh, shooting pain through my entire body. As awful as the pain is, I've suffered worse, and I have to find Ivy.

That part of the water isn't too deep, which is my only saving grace.

I skim the bottom of the water, and finally, my hands brush against skin, and I grab and yank upward until we both reach the surface.

She gasps for air, clawing at my neck.

"Ivy. I've got you. Breathe," I order, trying to calm her down. She obeys, sucking in deep lungsful of air as sobs escape her lips. Her entire body starts to shake, and all I can do is crush her into my chest, willing her to relax.

She'll be okay. As my fear for her safety starts to abate, my anger creeps back to the surface.

"Stop fucking crying," I demand. "You got yourself into this."

"Just fucking kill me," she screams. "You can't keep me here. I'll do it again."

If we weren't treading water and my leg wasn't throbbing, I would throttle her.

She put her life in danger. On top of that, Boris is looking for her. I trust my men, but if the men on Alaric's boat today saw her . . .

I don't know what would have happened.

I start swimming back toward the shallow water where I'll be able to drag her the rest of the way in. With every kick of my leg, the searing pain intensifies.

The throbbing is at an all-time high, and I am at serious risk of passing out.

When we finally get to the shallow shore, I yank Ivy's arm, pulling her to my side and practically dragging her behind me.

She gasps. "The water . . . it's red. Why is it red?" she asks in a panic.

"Nothing to concern yourself with," I say through gritted teeth. I don't need to give her any indication that I'm compromised. She won't get far, but I don't put it past her to try running off again.

"Cyrus, wait, you're bleeding." She grimaces. Her face turns sickly pale as she looks at me. When I finally look down, I see scratches, scrapes, and a big fucking piece of wood sticking out of a gaping hole in my leg. "You hurt yourself"—her voice is low—"trying to save me."

Fuck.

I'll need stitches.

"Stop dragging me," she barks. "Let me look at it."

I let go of her arm, unable to carry her weight any longer. With every step I take, the dizziness becomes more intense.

"Sit," Ivy commands. "I need to get something to stop the bleeding." She removes her sweater. "This will work," she says. "First, we need to get that branch out of your leg. Is it deep?" she asks, looking into my eyes. Her blue irises are as clear as the water, and her blond hair is wet and clinging to her skin. She reminds me of a mermaid, a mythical creature that came up from the ocean to save a drowning sailor. There's never been a doubt that Ivy is beautiful, but at this moment, she looks ethereal. Like the first time I saw her in the garden. The moment took her.

"Why did you do it?" she mutters. "Why did you save me?"

"Because I couldn't let anything happen to you. I said I would protect you."

Her eyes go wide, her lip trembling. "Thank you," she whispers with more sincerity than I deserve.

Light to my darkness. Good to my evil.

"Cyrus?" she repeats. "Is it too deep?"

"It's deep," I reply gruffly. "I have a sewing kit back in the house. I'll need you to stitch me up."

What little color that was left on her face completely vanishes, and she looks like a ghost.

"I'm not a nurse. You need a doctor."

"You'll have to do." I grit my teeth through the pain ricocheting inside me.

"I can't," she screeches. "I'm not trained to do that."

"You got us into this mess, so you're going to get us out of it."

Thunder rolls in the distance, signaling a nasty storm to go along with the rain.

"Let me help you into the house," Ivy suggests, but I shake my head.

"You get Cerberus," I say, nodding my head in the direction of the dog.

"Oh God," she gasps, seeing the beast still lying limp on the shore. He hasn't moved since I had brought him back to land.

"Is he . . . is he d-dead?" she whimpers.

"No. He's alive. Get him back to the house."

"How the hell am I supposed to do that?" she cries. "I can't carry him."

"Not my problem. Figure it out." I stand and limp toward the house.

"Cyrus, wait," she calls out toward my back, but I don't turn to her.

She needs to learn her place here. I've saved her. I'll provide everything she needs, but if she betrays me, she'll suffer the consequences. This would be one of those times. The sky is about to open up and soak the earth. She can't escape that. Not that it matters.

She's already wet. But the wind is picking up, and it promises to be quite the storm.

If she stops bitching, she might get the dog back in time to miss the worst part of it.

Right now, my concern is getting to the house and finding the emergency medical kit and some painkillers. If not, it will be a long night ahead of me because based on this storm, I'm not going anywhere tonight.

When I finally make it to the door, I turn to watch as Ivy crouches down to Cerberus.

After a few moments, she attempts to pick the dog up to no avail—not surprising. What is, however, is Ivy's tenacity.

When the rain hammers down, she doesn't run away and leave the dog to fend for himself like other women I've known would've. She stays until somehow, she manages to get the dog up.

Ivy is a rare woman.

A prize meant for some stuffy man in a cheap suit who could never give her the things she deserves.

The things I can give to her.

I could shower her in the most expensive gowns and jewelry. I could whisk her away on my private jet to places she could only dream of. She'd want for nothing.

But that's not how our relationship would ever be.

Not now.

Ivy is too proud to forget all that I have done to her. All that I have stolen. This thing between us will never be more than me taking everything from her, and her fighting to hold on to what makes Ivy, Ivy.

The strong woman making her way to me would never truly be mine. And for the first time in my life, I don't want to take something not meant for me.

CHAPTER TWENTY-FOUR

Ivy

"OH, BOY. I'M SO SORRY," I SAY, MY HEART BREAKING AT the broken Cerberus at my feet.

It's my fault he's in this shape. "I had to try. You understand, right?" His eyes look up at me, and that's all the movement I get. This is gonna be harder than I thought, and at any moment, the sky is going to pour down on us. "I know you're hurt, but I really need you to get up." I nudge at him a bit.

He whines and shifts, but he doesn't stand. "Come on, Cerberus. Help me out here." I put my hands underneath him and lift. Finally, he stands to his feet. I'm on my knees, nose to nose with the dog, wanting to cry.

For him.

For me.

For whatever is to come once I get us back into that prison. My eyes flicker toward the house, and I know he is watching. I can't see him, but I can feel his eyes on me.

All over me.

I can almost feel his anger pulsing through the air.

Something tells me that Cyrus is rarely on the receiving end of pain. No, he's definitely a giver in that department.

There was so much blood, and that gaping wound will need to be stitched up. There is no way this is going to go unpunished, but what would he do to me?

I don't think he'd hurt me, but I don't know him. I don't understand his motives, and because of that, I'm uneasy.

"Come on, buddy. Let's go see what awaits us," I say, allowing Cerberus to go ahead of me. I watch him hobble as his tail droops, and I want to cry.

Not just for Cerberus, but for me too. At least he's up and walking. Surely, that means he's all right, or he will be at least.

Following the trail of blood from Cyrus, I push down the bile caught in my throat.

When I find him, he's sitting at the kitchen island going through a box of supplies. He has rubbing alcohol and a suture set already laid out. The towel he has pressed against his leg is already soaking through, and I know he needs a doctor.

"Cyrus, call the boat back. We need to get you to the hospital."

"No." He huffs. "They're not coming back. Do you not see the storm outside?" he says, gesturing toward the window. "We're stuck here."

All the air whooshes out of my body as I realize that we're alone in this. He needs to get sewed up, and it's on me. I don't have time to stand around.

"All right. Let's get this cleaned and sewed up. You're getting blood everywhere," I say with a smile, trying to lighten the moment. I have to get out of my head if I'm going to do this.

He nods his head, then sitting back against the chair, he puts his hands out to the side in a "come get me" gesture that sends heat through my body.

"You're um—" My cheeks warm. "You're going to need to take your clothes off. I—" Why is this so hard. "I need to check to make sure . . ."

With a smirk on his face, he lifts his wet shirt over his head.

The man is magnificent. He looks like a Greek god, all tanned and toned.

Despite every instinct, my eyes rake down his pecs and

over his chiseled stomach until they land on the light dusting of hair trailing out of sight.

My mouth feels like there are marbles in it, but somehow, I say, "Your pants too."

I try not to look as he lowers them, but I can't help myself.

Cyrus Reed is in boxer briefs.

Magnificent.

That's the only word to describe the view in front me.

I shake off the thoughts, sidling up to the table and looking for the gauze so I can clean the wound.

Within five minutes, I have his leg cleaned and have begun stitching him up.

Periodically, I look up to gauge how he is doing. His face is blank, as though this isn't affecting him in the slightest. The pure control the man has is unnerving.

"Um . . . so you'll be staying here tonight?" I squeak out the words, sounding like a frightened virgin being eyed up by her prom date.

"Yes," he replies, and that does nothing to calm my nerves.

"Is . . . is this okay?" I ask, nodding my head at my trembling hand. I need to pull myself together or else I'm going to butcher this sew job.

He raises his brows. "It'll have to do, considering you're the only one here to do it."

Does he have to be such an asshole? He could thank me. Would that be too much to ask for?

For crying out loud, he should be happy I'm even willing to help him. After all, he's holding me prisoner. He's lucky I don't stab him with the needle.

"I didn't ask you to come after me."

"You shouldn't have tried to run in the first place."

I stop stitching and look up at him. "You're a fool if you think I wouldn't."

"You're a fool if you think you could ever succeed."

I blow out a harsh breath. "Do you want me to finish this? Or would you prefer to bleed out all over the floor?"

He smirks. "I won't bleed out."

"Pity."

He chuckles. "You're beautiful when you're angry."

I look up at him, searching his face, but for what, I don't know. "Don't say things like that."

"Why?" he questions with a frown. "You are beautiful."

"Just stop. I'm under no delusion that you care for me. And I don't need you trying to confuse me."

"I'm not the bad guy here, Ivy."

"That's not how I see it."

He places his hand on top of mine and looks me in the eye. "You have it all wrong."

"Tell me why I'm here."

He looks away. "Some things are better left a mystery. Trust me on that."

"I don't know your motives, and because of that, I don't trust you. I can't."

We don't say anything after that. I go about sewing up his leg, paying special care not to look up at him. After a solid fifteen minutes, I'm done and cleaning up when Cerberus whines from the corner.

"He'll be okay," Cyrus says. "He's just got a limp tail. He'll be better in a few days with some rest."

"How do you know?"

"I've seen it before. He overexerted himself, and the water was too cold. Trust me. He just needs rest."

There's that word again . . . trust. I look away, not needing to have the same conversation we've already had.

In this particular case, I was just going to have to be patient. If Cerberus doesn't show any signs of improvement within a few days, I'll insist that Cyrus take him off the island to be checked out. Even if I'll be completely alone out here.

"You're all done," I say, turning my back on him to finish cleaning up.

"Thank you, Sun."

I still, his words catching me off guard. Looking over my shoulder, I smile tightly.

"You're welcome. Why don't you go rest somewhere while I clean up the bloody trail you left in the foyer."

"You don't have to do that," he says. "You're not a slave."

"Whatever I am, the blood still needs to be cleaned, and you're in no condition to do it. Go get yourself cleaned up. There's dried blood all over your leg."

He goes to stand but quickly falls back into his chair. "Whoa. What's wrong?"

He inhales deeply. "I'm fine," he barks. "I just got a little light-headed."

"Of course, you are. You lost a lot of blood, Cyrus. Just stay put. I'll clean up the blood, and then I'll help you upstairs."

He considers me for several seconds. "Why?" he finally asks.

"Why?" I parrot, knowing full well what he is asking.

"Why are you helping me?"

I laugh, but there is no humor in it. "The way I see it, my only way off this island is you. If you die, God only knows what shady people will come here looking for you." I shrug. "The devil you know is better than the devil you don't."

He chuckles. "Touché."

"Now, let me get this cleaned up." I turn toward the foyer to mop up the trail of blood. But just before leaving the room, I glance over my shoulder to look at my patient one more time. Every corded muscle is on display, and despite myself, I grow warm, thinking of all the salacious things he said last time we were alone. God, I am an idiot.

CHAPTER TWENTY-FIVE

Ivy

IT TAKES OVER AN HOUR TO CLEAN UP ALL THE BLOOD AND dispose of the ruined towels. By the time I'm done, I'm hot and gross, and in desperate need of a shower, but first, I need to check on my patient.

I walk into the kitchen to help Cyrus move somewhere more comfortable, but the kitchen is empty.

"Where the hell did you go?" I mumble to nobody. I search the lower half of the place, and when I come up short, I decide to check upstairs.

The master bedroom door is open, so I walk in. "You shouldn't have climbed those steps," I lecture, but he isn't in there either. I hear a commotion through the half-opened door to my right and proceed toward it.

"Dammit, Cyrus, you should be in bed, not walking around. You'll split open your stitches," I bark before halting in my tracks.

The door is open just enough to showcase Cyrus lowering his briefs to the ground, as steam from the shower rolls into the room. He doesn't see me, and I take full advantage. He stands bare with his back to me.

My breath hitches at the sight. I know I should turn away. I should not be looking, but I can't force my eyes from him. He's single handedly the most beautiful man I have ever seen, and my body reacts in ways it never has before. Want and need beg me to press forward while my head screams for me to look away.

"Like the view, Ivy?" His cocky remark does the trick. Cold seeps into my once hot flesh.

"I-I just came to help you get settled. I must now bleach my eyes," I say lamely, and he roars with laughter. "It's not funny, Cyrus. I'm scarred for life."

"Liar," he accuses, and I don't say another word.

"Just call when you're done, and I'll help you. You shouldn't be pushing things. If that breaks open, I don't have the proper supplies to help you. You've lost a lot of blood."

"I just need to get this blood off me. I'll be five minutes, Ivy."

I swear under my breath, making my way back into what must be the room he's claiming. I go through drawers and find that it is stocked. I pull out a pair of athletic shorts and a T-shirt, but it's when I stumble across briefs that I once again go down the rabbit hole of want. God, will my body and brain ever be on the same damn page? It's pissing me off.

Sure, he's beautiful, but he's evil. I try to drill that truth into my head, but with every negative thought, two sexual ones take root.

What the hell is wrong with me?

Has it been that long that I'd find just about anyone worth sleeping with?

That has to be it.

My celibacy is the root problem. Well, there are other ways to handle that problem that doesn't include giving my body to my kidnapper.

I need space to clear my head. Being close to him is not a good idea right now.

Once I get him situated, I have to get the hell out of this room.

I'll take care of him for the injury I caused, but I won't spend a moment more with him.

It isn't good for me. I'm beginning to be one of those idiot girls who fall for their captors.

Yep. Stockholm syndrome, it is.

I'm ninety percent sure that's what I'm coming down with. It's a real thing, and I can't be blamed for my lapse in judgment.

He's doing this. It's his fault.

I straighten things on the dresser, dust the windowsill, and turn down the bed. Anything to keep my hands and mind occupied. I'm so engrossed in what I am doing that I don't hear him approach.

I don't know he's there until I feel his touch.

One finger grazes down my spine, leaving goose bumps in its wake. I shiver all over and hate that my body reacts to his touch. There is no denying it. He has to feel my body shake.

"What are you doing, Sun?"

There it is again, that stupid freaking nickname.

I have yet to figure out what it even means. I look at him over my shoulder warily. Droplets of water trickle down his carved chest, and I follow them as they make their way down his toned abs.

A towel hangs loosely on his hips. I swallow, turning my head, but his fingers grab my chin, easing me to look at him. His eyes burn with something I don't want to think too much about.

Not while I'm this close to him.

Not when my senses want to leave completely and just give in to this insane chemistry floating between us.

We are two strangers on a deserted island, completely and

utterly alone. He is beyond attractive. Can't I just pretend he is someone else for just a few moments. Just long enough to get lost in his touch.

"Ivy," he whispers my name like a prayer. "Can you hand me the clothes?" And just like that, the spell is broken.

"U-Um . . . obviously. Please put them on." I sound out of breath and like a total moron. He chuckles again. This gruff man has obviously lost way too much blood if he is laughing so much all of a sudden, and even though I'm sure he's delirious with pain, I still want to slap his face.

Asshole.

"Here." I throw the pile of clothes I have laid out at his head.

He ducks, laughing all the while.

Okay, strike my earlier remark. He's so damn sexy when he's like this that I can't help but smile. Even though I hate myself for admitting it. But he's so carefree at this moment. It's easy to forget he's a bad man.

I'm only human, after all.

"Put your clothes on and then get in bed. You need to rest. I'm going to go shower."

"I'm fine," he counters, sounding annoyed. "This is my place. I'll do what I want." He sounds like a petulant child. It's a bit comical, considering the man is lord of the underworld, but I don't say anything else.

I leave the room, giving him privacy and me the space I need to get myself in check. Hurt Cyrus is almost endearing, and that is not good. I need to hold on to my hatred. That will get me out of here unscathed.

My room is not as nice as the one I've just come from, but it has everything that I need. When I step into the large shower,

I bask in the warmth that cascades over me. I want to wipe off the memories of my near escape just as much as I want to rid myself of the blood and grime.

I moan as I lather my hair with the coconut shampoo.

It feels so good. With my eyes closed tightly, images of a naked Cyrus assault me, and I groan. Whether in frustration or annoyance, I'm not entirely sure. I'm trying to escape him, not pine for the man. But I can't really be blamed. He is perfection personified.

My hands make their way from my scalp down my neck, and I relish in the feeling as

I imagine they're his hands running all over my body. I inhale deeply and sigh on an exhale. Maybe if I give myself release, my brain will start functioning again. Maybe I can beat the building Stockholm I fear I've developed.

"Stop it, Ivy," I chastise myself aloud. I finish quickly, needing to find something for dinner.

My stomach is rumbling, so it's time to eat. Added bonus, eating means I can keep myself occupied for a while. I run a brush through my hair, throw on a white slip dress that I had found in the armoire, and head out the door and down to the kitchen.

Rummaging through the refrigerator, I make a mental note to find out when the boat is coming back.

After the day we had, we're sure to be hungry, so I browse through the freezer and pull out some frozen food that he left the last time he came.

Needing something to make the process less drab, I turn on the meager radio that I had found in the greenhouse and tune it to the first station I find.

It's some upbeat station with dance music that has my hips moving as I heat the food and set the table.

Wine would complement this meal well.

What am I saying?

Alcohol with a criminal is not a good idea. In fact, it's the worst I've had yet. No. I'll be keeping my wits about me tonight.

I'm quickly learning that Cyrus is dangerous in more ways than one.

CHAPTER TWENTY-SIX

Cyrus

I WATCH AS HER HIPS SWAY AND HEAD BOBS TO THE MUSIC. She's captivating, and I can't get enough. Something inside me starts to thaw when this woman is around, and it is hazardous.

My life isn't conducive to such feelings. The more I care about her, the more I have to lose. But here I am, allowing it to happen with every swish of her body.

My mind reels at how her father could've been so careless with something so damn valuable. He deserves to die at Boris's hand, and that I won't stop. She's worth all the fucking shit that would come down on me once Boris realizes that I have taken her.

Fuck him.

They can all come.

All the men he works with.

I'll burn down the fucking world before I allow that man to touch something that belongs to me. And she does.

With every minute we've spent together, I can see her walls breaking down. I'll bend her to my will, and have her, but on her terms. I won't take what isn't offered, but I have no doubt I won't have to. Her body begs for me, and it won't be long before she utters the words herself.

After watching her for several minutes, I pull myself away, not wanting to torture myself any longer. She's coming around, but she isn't there yet. I'll give her time. I will not force myself on her no matter how much I want to. I'll never hurt her.

Instead, I go to my hidden room that is stocked with vintage wines. It was the first thing I had built upon finishing the updates on the place.

I keep my private collection here, as this place isn't frequently used. This is my escape. I come here to get away and to hide out when necessary. . . on the rare occasion, my men will bring in an adversary, but often, we don't have to go that route.

Only a few people know about this island, and they know their life, and that of their families, are dependent on their secrecy. I pay them handsomely for the inconvenience. I sift through my collection and come upon a 1949 Chateau Lafite Rothschild.

It isn't my most expensive bottle, but it's a good one, and I want to share it with her.

If there's one thing I know about Ivy, it's that she was deprived of the finer things in life, all so that her father could indulge in his vices.

I saw the state of the exterior of the brownstone she lived in. Any man who wears a watch like he did but couldn't keep up his shit privately wouldn't treat his family right, and then don't get me started on gambling her virtue away.

The thought of the man turns my stomach and makes me rage.

I return to the kitchen just in time to see her putting the silverware in place. She looks up, smiling when she sees me until her eyes land on my hands. One is holding the bottle of wine and the other, two goblets.

"What's that for?" she says, furrowing her brows.

"To drink," I pronounce, earning a scowl from her.

"I know what you do with it. I asked why you're bringing it

in here." Her hands rest on her hips, and her eyes are in two thin slits as she glowers my way.

Frustration is rolling off her in waves, and I can't help but chuckle. She is adorable when she is flustered and gorgeous as fuck when she is pissed.

"It's a peace offering. For you saving my life," I explain with nonchalance.

She rolls her eyes at me, and a part of me wants to throw her across my lap and punish her. I won't, though.

Damn fucking morals.

"I hardly saved your life. I merely stitched you up."

"You're right." I shrug. "This is for me since you nearly got me killed, along with yourself, and poor Cerberus. Look what you did to him. He looks worse than both of us," I say, nodding my head toward the limp tail.

"Cerberus," she says, looking close to tears. "Is he going to be all right?" she asks for the umpteenth time.

"Ivy, he'll be fine. I was only messing with you."

"Don't joke about stuff like that. I feel terrible about what I did to him."

Now it's my turn to feel like a shit. "I'm sorry. I won't joke about that anymore," I promise. "Cerberus will be fine. I assure you."

She nods her head but doesn't say another word. So, I forge forward, hoping to lighten the mood with my offering. I've never met a woman who didn't like wine, and a vintage bottle at that.

"Now that I'm stranded here, I sure as hell am not going to be denied appropriate drink," I tease, looking down at the glass of water she has sitting out for me.

She rolls her eyes. "Ever the opportunist."

I act affronted. "There are no motivations here, Ivy. I simply want to share a near priceless bottle of wine. With you." I grin. "Is that so bad?"

She mumbles something under her breath but acquiesces and then points at the chair for me to sit. I oblige, not wanting to further her irritation. I want to have a decent meal with good conversation.

"Do you always give your prisoners expensive wine?" she asks, raising a brow.

I groan. "So, we're going to go there, are we?"

"Why not discuss the elephant in the room? Surely, we'll enjoy our food more once this topic is out in the open. Heaven knows I'll feel more comfortable tasting your near priceless bottle with some answers." She mocks my very words, and I have to count to three so I don't lose my temper.

"Must you ruin every moment with your smart mouth?"

Her back straightens. "Have you ever been stolen from your life and held captive? No? Then don't talk to me about my smart mouth."

I can't help the smile that forms on my lips. Her argumentative attitude should make me livid. Bigger men have fallen for talking to me like that, but something about her feisty side makes me crave her even more. I relish in her boldness.

I lean forward, placing my elbows on the table, to give her the platform to voice her obvious disapproval with my actions. It's not like I haven't heard them before, but apparently, she's determined to beat a dead horse.

"Ask whatever you'd like. But just be prepared for non-answers."

She huffs. "Then what's the damn point?"

I shrug. "You'll never know unless you ask, right?"

Her face falls, and her eyes drop to the table. "I'm not even sure what more I can ask? Every time I do, you are evasive," she says, sounding defeated. "I should continue to fight. If I stop, I'm complacent about this whole thing. And I'm not," she basically shouts. "I should beg for my release. If I don't, again . . . complacent. Can't you understand that? Or are you so evil that you have no compassion for the fact that I have been stolen away from my friends and family . . . my life, and without any explanation aside from *you have your reasons*," she imitates my voice, her face growing red under my watchful eye.

I want to tell her.

I might be a monster in her eyes, but this time, there are scarier things at play than me. It was all to save her. Then again, if it wasn't for the poker tournament I had organized, she wouldn't be in this mess to begin with. I'm damned if I do, damned if I don't where she's concerned.

"I know that you want to tell me. It's written all over your face," she says, voice softening. "It's clear to me that you're not a bad guy, Cyrus. So just tell me."

She's lying. I know she is by the way she fidgets when she says the words. She doesn't truly believe them. She is just saying what she thinks I want to hear. She's smart not to believe it. I am the bad guy.

I may not have been the villain in her particular situation, but I am in everyone else's. I am the man you fear. The one you lower your head to when you walk past me on the streets. The one you would never speak out against for fear you'll lose your life. She isn't wrong to doubt me. But fuck if it isn't making me want to strangle her.

I stand from the chair, scraping my knee as I go.

"Fuck," I yell out as the stitches rip open, and blood begins to seep through my pants.

"Oh, God, Cyrus." She jumps up, rushing to my side.

"Stay away," I warn, needing to get my anger under control. This is not her fault.

She only pointed out the truth, but for whatever reason, I don't want to be that guy to her. I want her to trust me. And that is the dumbest thing of all.

The truth is, I don't have the capacity to love her the way she deserves to be loved. I don't even have the capacity to truly like her. So why does it matter how she feels about me? All of these thoughts going through my head are doing nothing to calm my anger.

"Cyrus," she says, softly. Her hand comes up to my arm. "Let me take care of you." Her eyes bore into mine, and all the anger quickly melts away. She helps set me back into the chair, then grabs a napkin and presses it to my bleeding thigh. "I'm going to need to stitch that again. Can you take your pants off for me?"

I raise a brow. I can't help it. I am a man, after all.

She shakes her head. "Just take off your pants, Casanova," she instructs.

As she walks away, I watch as the white dress swishes back and forth. She looks like an angel. My angel.

If only I had a soul worth saving.

CHAPTER TWENTY-SEVEN

Ivy

I CAN'T BELIEVE I HAVE TO DO THIS AGAIN.

If he had just been less of a pain in the ass, he wouldn't be back in this position right now, and I wouldn't be forced to do something I'm not qualified to do. Concentrating, I work to re-stitch his leg, shaking my head the entire time at how careless he is.

The utter bullheadedness of this man makes me want to strangle him.

"Should I be concerned?" he asks, pulling my eyes upward to look at him. I don't answer him. Instead, I narrow my eyes. "You've got such a death grip on that needle, and you're not exactly being gentle."

My fingers tighten. "I told you to be careful. You acted like an animal, and now here we are," I snap. "You really need to see a doctor." I lift my hand in the air. "When will that boat be coming back?"

"When I tell them too," he answers.

"How do you know that? Do you have a phone with you?" Without realizing, I have leaned into him. His eyes widen, and I instantly hate that I've given that thought away.

"Even if I did, you'd never get access to it. Face it, Ivy, you're mine."

If I had to put a definition on the way I'm looking at him, it would go in the dictionary as *a death glare*.

"Do you want me to patch this up? Or should I leave you to bleed out?"

He shrugs. "Whatever you want, Sun."

I huff under my breath but manage to finish the task. When I stand, he goes to stand too, but I shake my head. "Sit down. I'm just getting some water."

He doesn't say anything, just nods. When I get back, he's still in the same position, slouched back without a care in the world. Or so he appears. When I begin to clean off his leg, he stiffens. "What are you doing?"

"I'm cleaning up the blood," I deadpan. "What does it look like?"

He remains silent for several seconds as he considers me. "Why are you helping me?"

I sigh. "Because I'm not like you, Cyrus. I help people. I don't harm them. And besides, if I'm stuck here, I'd prefer not to have to see blood everywhere."

He chuckles at that. "Not a fan?"

"I could live without it," I admit. "I'm not one for violence." I watch him while I say this, looking for any indication of remorse or that he feels the same way, but his blank stare gives nothing away. "I take it violence doesn't bother you?" I press my luck in asking that question.

He shrugs. "Violence is necessary sometimes. It's all I've ever known."

My stomach roils at his admission. What the hell has happened to this man to make him so callous about such things?

"That's . . . sad, Cyrus. Violence should never be necessary," I say. "What happened to make you like this?"

He jerks back. "Like what?"

"Like . . . like this." I gesture at him with my hand. "Gruff, callous, dangerous."

His eyes narrow, and he leans toward me. "You have no idea how dangerous I am, Ivy."

His words, the proximity of his body . . . they do something to me that I can't quite explain. I should be repulsed or, at the very least, angry, but all I feel is need.

I'm on fire.

My stomach flutters, and my core pulses with need.

The way I feel for him is amplified at this moment, and a part of me is disgusted with myself. Am I getting off on the fact that he's a violent man? Do I like that he's dangerous?

Am I sick?

Am I a bad person?

"Let's play a game," he says, pulling me out of my own thoughts. "A game for the *answer*."

The way he says that word has me perking up. "Are you serious? You'll finally answer *the* question?"

Neither of us has to clarify what the question is. It's been hovering above us since the first day I met Cyrus.

"Only if you win." He smirks, looking entirely too smug for my liking.

"What game?"

"You name it," he says.

I tap my finger to my chin, trying to think of the best game. What could I suggest that would give me an edge with this man? "Let's play spades," I finally suggest.

He cocks an eyebrow. "You sure about that?"

I think about his question. No, I'm not sure about anything. I have no idea what this guy is involved in.

For all I know, gambling is his thing. He does run a poker game, but that doesn't mean he plays.

I have to hope that after all those times I played with Trent, I have enough practice under my belt to at the very least hang. Besides, I have nothing to hide. So even if I do lose, the joke is on him. He won't get much from me.

"I'm sure," I say, sounding more confident than I feel.

"Spades it is," he says.

He tells me where to find the deck of cards. I shuffle and set the pile in the middle.

"You first." I offer him the cards to draw from the top. He draws the top card and decides to keep it. We continue to take turns picking cards until we each have thirteen in our hands, deciding whether or not to keep them.

"I'll bid three," he says, looking far too confident.

"I'll bid four," I respond, hoping like hell I can get to five hundred first.

I start the game by laying a four of diamonds. He follows up with a queen of diamonds, winning the hand. As we continue to play over the next twenty minutes, it's clear he is a master at cards. I should have known; you don't host a game unless you can play. I just have to have faith that my luck will turn around soon.

As I look at the cards, a nostalgic feeling rolls over me of a time when I was young, and things were different. "I used to play this with my dad all the time." I close my eyes as I speak, replaying the good times before everything changed. "I remember the first time he sat me next to him and Trent, and they made me play for hours." I chuckle, my eyes opening again. How things have changed since then. I wish my dad was still that man. "That was so long ago. I miss those times," I whisper more to myself than to him.

"Your father is worthless."

My eyes snap to him. "What did you say?" There is no way he said that. He doesn't know my father. Sure, my father was no prize these days, but still . . .

He looks directly in my eyes and repeats the offensive words, shocking me to the core. Malice drips from his tone, but the malice is misplaced. My dad is bad, but he's not a monster like Cyrus is making him out to be.

"Why would you say that? You don't know my father."

"I know his kind," Cyrus answers sternly.

"And what kind is that?" I shoot back, growing more pissed by the second.

"The kind who treats his daughter like a meaningless possession to be handed off whenever it suits him. The kind who wouldn't know something valuable if it were looking him square in the eye. A worthless fuck." He emphasizes the last word so crisply, I flinch.

My lower lip starts to quiver. It feels like the walls are closing in on me. It's the first time I have thought of my childhood in some time. It's one of the fond memories I possess, and Cyrus practically spat on it.

I've felt alone for so long. Even before the island, I have missed the happy times, and finally, when I remember something good, he has to go and remind me of what a pitiful asshole he is.

I stand abruptly. "I'm done."

"Ivy, wait. Please. I-I'm sorry. I shouldn't have said those things."

My chin tips down to meet his dark eyes. They drill into me, and there is an endless depth to them. So many unspoken words and sorrow swim in them, but I don't want to hear them now, so I shake my head.

"Well, you did, Cyrus. Attacking my family won't get you far with me. They're all I have."

"Just sit, will you? Let me explain."

I want to walk out of the room and get as far away from him as possible, but the offer of any type of explanation is too great a promise.

Curiosity killed the cat.

"I . . ." He starts and then stops. Whether he is choosing his words carefully or deciding whether to go back on his word, I'm not sure, but he finally continues. "I didn't have the best home life, Ivy. Things were . . . difficult. I've had to do some bad things to change my circumstances. I didn't have a choice. But others . . . they do, yet they still choose their vices. Their families suffer at their hands and don't even realize it."

My eyebrows knit together. "I'm sorry for that, Cyrus. But I don't understand why your past would make you so hostile toward someone you don't even know," I say. "I won't lie and say my dad has been the best recently. My father might not be the best man right now, but deep down, he's a good man."

He inhales deeply, several emotions playing out on his face, which is a contradiction to the Cyrus I've grown to know.

A man who is anything but readable. Someone who can school his features so well that you can't tell what he is thinking. Or if he's thinking at all. At this moment, he looks almost . . . vulnerable.

"If I were a father, I'd protect my child with my own life. Nothing would ever happen to her. He had you, Ivy, and he let you be taken. That's unforgivable in my book."

I smile at his backward thinking. "I'm an adult, Cyrus. He couldn't have prevented this.

At some point in time, we become responsible for ourselves. I was in the wrong place at the wrong time. Nothing more."

His eyes harden. "It's so much more than that, Ivy," he says through gritted teeth.

"Tell me then," I counter. "If you have something more to say, open your mouth and tell me. Enough secrets." My hand reaches up in the air, angrily. "I'm sick of it."

He shakes his head. "That's all I'm willing to share for tonight."

And with those words, the conversation is cut off, and I'm left in the dark yet again.

CHAPTER TWENTY-EIGHT

Cyrus

MY BLOOD FUCKING BOILS AT THE FACT THAT PRICK YET again is the cause of turmoil for Ivy. I have asked myself a dozen fucking times over the past twenty-four hours why I don't just tell her. I can't quite figure out who I am protecting by keeping this secret. But I know now. I'm protecting her.

I didn't want to break her any more than she is already broken.

In her eyes, her family is everything. She might not like her father these days, but her memories live inside her still. Can I tarnish that?

I know it would kill her to know that the reason she is a captive on a private island is because her own father sold her during a game of cards.

The very thought of it makes me want to kill someone.

She's too good to see the evil that lives in her father. That or too naïve, but I'd like to think it's the former.

I'm not just pissed off about that. I am disgusted with myself. What am I even thinking by suggesting a card game, knowing that this is the reason she's here in the first place? It had just been an idea to pass the time and hopefully get to know her a little better.

There isn't a game out there I don't feel confident I would win against her.

But I wanted to use that to my advantage to get her to

open up to me. I wanted the mood to be lightened. I wanted to see her let loose and have fun.

But like everything I touch, it quickly turned to shit.

I do want to tell her why she's here. I want her to understand that I don't want to hurt her. But for the first time in my life, I care that my truth will hurt her even worse.

It's better for her to think I'm the bad guy. Someone she doesn't know, yet already hates. Knowing that a man she's loved her entire life threw her to the sharks will destroy her.

I'm under no false illusions that I'm a good guy, but I can't do that to her.

I care.

I fucking care, and that's a fucking travesty.

It makes me weak. It compromises my entire empire.

The more I know about this girl, the more reckless my decisions get. I've already lost an entire fucking day to save her. When have I ever cared enough about another human life to risk my own?

Years.

It's been years.

I grab my hair at the roots and pull, wanting to scream, but not wanting to alarm her.

Fuck! I am completely fucked as long as I'm around her.

I need to get off this island and back to work. Back to my sanity. Then I'll be able to think clearly. Focus. Get her out of my system. Or maybe I need to just take her and make her mine. Maybe that's what it would take.

Where the fuck is she?

I haven't seen or heard from her since she stormed out.

Not wanting to upset her more, I remain sitting in the room, contemplating all the things I have to do when the boat eventually comes to get me, when Ivy re-enters the room, pillow and blankets in hand.

"What's that?" I ask, raking my eyes down her body.

She's wearing that tight camisole again, the one that manages to push up her breasts.

Why in the fuck does she have to keep torturing me with it?

My mouth waters at the sight of her round breasts and ample cleavage. She's a sight to behold in simple fucking nightclothes. Her linen pants hug her curves and ass in just the right way to have me hardening. At least she's wearing the pants I brought her. I don't think I could handle it if she was only wearing her boy shorts again.

As it is, it's torture to witness her like this. Her hair is thrown into a messy bun, and I can hardly contain myself. No man can exert this much restraint and not be in serious pain.

"I'm sleeping down here," she says, tersely.

"Why?"

"Do you always have to question me? Can't you just take my answer and keep your mouth shut?"

Her smart mouth has me somehow harder. I lick my lips, running my eyes over her body without an ounce of care. She blushes under my stare.

Good. I hope she's good and wet. I hope she dreams about my hands running over every one of her curves.

Feeling her.

Tasting her.

Fucking her.

"I-I want . . . want to be close to Cerberus," she stutters, clearly unnerved. "I need to make sure he's okay."

I stand, stalking toward her with purpose. Her eyes widen at my approach.

"Ivy," I whisper into her ear.

"Y-Yes," she stammers.

"What are you wearing? I brought you a whole bag of clothes," I rasp, drawing a sharp inhale from her. She doesn't answer me, but her breathing becomes shallow and her chest heaves. I trail my hand up her arm, leaving goose bumps in my wake.

"What are you doing, Cyrus?" She's breathless, and I fucking love it.

"Showing you how good I can make you feel. All you have to do is ask for it."

She shudders and then takes a deep breath while stepping back out of my grasp.

"I don't know what you're up to, but I won't let you do this. Until I have the answer I'm looking for, this will never happen."

"You admit you want it?" I respond arrogantly, wanting to make it clear that she isn't in control despite my raging hard-on. "You admit you want me to fuck you, Ivy?"

Her eyes harden. "Not on your life."

"You can lie to yourself, Sun, but I felt the way your body ached for me. Every shudder, every goose bump told me how bad you want me to fuck you. You want to play puritan? Fine. But you'll have to beg me to fuck you."

She huffs. "You fucking pig. I wouldn't touch you if you were the last person on this godforsaken island," she spits.

"Have it your way." I sit back on the couch and get settled in for the night.

"You can't be serious. You aren't sleeping down here," she screeches. "I need some distance from you."

I smirk at her haughty attitude. She's so damn hot when she's angry, and at that moment, she looks like she could spit fire.

"If you're sleeping down here, then so am I."

She stiffens, looking at me with just barely contained rage. "Why, you . . . you . . ."

With every word she says, my smile grows bigger.

"You asshat!" she finally bellows. I throw my head back and laugh. The whole scene is comical. I haven't laughed this much in years. It feels good.

"Don't laugh at me," she barks. "You are a complete dick."

When I finally get myself under control, I shake my head. "All true. I'll give you that." She crosses her arms across her chest, which only manages to show more of her cleavage. "If there's one thing I've learned over the past day, it's that you do what you want, and there's no use in fighting you." She takes a deep breath and looks at me tensely. "But can I trust you to be a gentleman?"

I frown. "I've told you I will not touch you unless you want me to, Ivy, and I mean it."

She nods, taking deep breaths and seemingly calming down. "Here, you can have this pillow." She throws it at me.

"I don't need it," I respond.

"Please take it. You're hurt, and I'll feel better knowing you're comfortable." This woman is a conundrum. One minute, she looks as though she'll kill me, and the next, she is kind and thoughtful. I've never met a woman like her in my life.

She gets to making up a bed on the couch adjacent to where I'll be sleeping. When she is all settled, I shut off the lights. For several minutes, we just lie in the dark, neither one of us saying anything until Ivy breaks the silence.

"I love the smell of this fabric softener. It reminds me of my mother."

The mention of her mother has me paying attention. I know little about her family, and I always wondered how her mother factored in.

"Smells like lilacs," she continues. "Flowers always remind me of her. She loved to garden. She'd spend all summer planting new flowers, pruning . . . anything to be outside," she says wistfully. "She taught me everything I know."

The reverence in her voice mixed with the tinge of sadness tells me that her mother isn't around. "What happened to her?" I ask. I know Ivy was concerned about her well-being, but I never thought to find out why.

"She's basically dead." She buries her head in her hands and then looks back over at me. Unshed tears linger in her eyes. "Not truly, but she might as well be."

That's all Ivy offers, and I don't press. I don't deserve any more.

"Someday, I want to open my own floral shop. It's always been my dream."

"I think you'll do great," I offer, not understanding why I'd say such a thing.

I know nothing about flowers or what experience Ivy has with them. But now I feel like a dick for screaming at her when I found her in my greenhouse. Thankfully, I already gave her free rein to use it again, or I would feel like a bigger dick. I want to make her happy. It's a strange feeling, but not unwelcome.

"If you want it, you should do it."

"Kind of hard to open a business on a deserted island."

I think about her words for a while. I don't have any intentions of keeping her here forever, but I'm sure as hell not going to let her leave until I know the danger has passed. The reality is, I have no idea how long that will take. What possesses me to say the next words to her, I don't know, but I do anyway. "You won't be here forever, Ivy. I can't tell you how long, but one day you'll be able to leave, and I promise you'll start your business."

She inhales sharply. "Do you promise? I'll be able to leave here?"

"Yes."

"Thank you," she whispers into the dark.

I only hope that I'll be able to keep that promise.

———————•———————

My leg hurts more today than yesterday. I despise that Ivy has to see me like this. Weak and hurt, and not able to stitch my own leg.

Ivy isn't someone I would want to have leverage on me. She might be my prisoner, but I've gotten to know her, if her escape attempt proves anything it's that she is resourceful.

I wouldn't put it past me, that she'll figure out a way to spin this in her favor.

Not that I think she'll try to escape, but she'll probably try to milk a phone call to her mother from me.

That's something I can't do.

From the research I have done on her, and the fact that I know her father, her mother can't be called. Her father is a liability, and there is no way I would trust Ivy's location with anyone in that family. Even Trent doesn't know she's on my island. I can't have anyone breach my trust and tell Boris I have her.

It's been two days since the accident, and I'm still not sleeping in my bed. Ivy doesn't think I can handle the steps yet without tearing my stitches. She's being ridiculous. I've been hurt plenty to know what I can handle.

Taking a bullet to the chest, being stabbed in the back, literally, has me knowing my limits.

A small gash in my leg isn't one of them. However, it's not

awful having someone as fucking gorgeous as Ivy, waiting on me hand and foot.

As if she can hear my thoughts, she stirs beside me. The close proximity has me hyper-aware of what she sleeps in. Basically nothing.

This girl will be the death of me.

"You okay," she mumbles, her voice still drowsy with sleep.

"Yep," I mutter back, distracted with the sight in front of me, and she must notice because she follows my gaze, and then her cheeks go bright red.

She pulls her tank up before she speaks again. "Um, how's your leg?"

"Better."

"Pain."

"Nope." Fuck yeah, but I'm not admitting that. "How's the weather?" Yeah, I just became that guy, the one who asks about the weather.

"Still storming, I think." She stands and heads over to the window to get a better view. "It's awful out. I guess you're stuck here another day. Let me get you some breakfast."

"I can walk, Sun."

"It's probably better that you don't."

"Now who's being ridiculous." I stand from my makeshift bed. Hurts like a bitch, but I bite back the pain.

"You sure, you look a little green."

"I'm fucking sure," I grit out.

She lifts her shoulders. "Fine, have it your way."

Once I'm standing, Ivy takes it upon herself to wrap her arm around me, as if she could hold my weight. I'm about to tell her I don't need help, but something stops me.

When we're in the kitchen, I take a seat, and she stares at me.

"I feel like all we do is eat." She laughs.

"We have spent most of our time in here. I would say we can eat somewhere else, or do something else, but—"

"You think I'm too hurt. Trust me when I say this, Sun. This is nothing. I have been hurt far worse."

Her eyes go wide like saucers, but then she rights herself. "Well, if you don't want to eat yet, why are we here?"

"'Cause you led me here," I joke, and her own lips tip up when I do.

"What do you want to do then?"

"No food and no spades." Now she laughs.

"Yeah, neither of those works, how about I make us some coffee and you think of something else."

My eyebrow raises and she rolls her eyes. "Not that either."

"Our options are rather limited then . . ." I trail off with a grin.

"There has to be something else you do. Come on, what do you do for fun?" When I don't answer her question, she proceeds. "Seriously? Is there anything you do besides being"—she points at me—"you?"

"I play chess."

"Now that makes complete sense."

"How so?"

"Cold and calculated. Perfect chess player." She beams.

"Do you play?" My eyebrow lifts. This could prove interesting.

"No. I don't know how to."

"Then I'll teach you. Meet me in my office, bring the coffee." I stand, the movement still hurts, but I'm becoming used to the pulling pain.

When I'm in my office, I walk over to my chessboard.

Ivy is following closely behind, because apparently, I walk slow enough that she was able to use the Keurig for two cups in the time it took me to walk.

Fuck. I hate being weak.

"This is beautiful," she exclaims, walking into the room, two mugs in hand and Cerberus in tow.

I look at the board where we'll be playing. It should be, seeing as each piece is cast from gold.

"Where did you get this?" Her finger reaches out and touches the top of the queen.

"It was made for me."

I motion for her to sit at the table. She does, and my dog lays down by her feet.

"Seeing as you don't play, today is your lucky day, because you have a very good teacher."

I lean closer to the table and then arrange the pieces. "Do you know anything about chess?" She shakes her head. "Each chess piece can move only a certain way. For example"—I lift the pawn in my hand—"a pawn can only move straight ahead and can only attack on an angle, one square at a time. Make sense?"

"No. But I'm a fast learner." She winks, and so I continue my tutorial. I teach her about every piece. Every rule and I'm sure I've lost her, but she's a good sport. Lifting her coffee up, drinking but never letting her gaze leave mine.

"How did you learn so much?"

My throat closes up, but I push back the emotion threatening to expel. I don't do emotions. "My father taught me."

"Oh—"

"No, *oh*. He was a bastard. He taught me nothing. This is the only thing positive I took from his whole existence." My jaw clenches. Thinking about the bastard always makes me angry. "Now, if you think you understand, let's play."

I'm surprised when she doesn't press, but thankful. "Okay."

She nibbles on her lip as she moves her pawn to f4, opening up her king without realizing it. She's created a weakness; I'll take advantage of.

"In chess, every move has a purpose." I move my pawn, opening up a space for my queen and bishop. "Think of it like life. Every move you make can either bring you an advantage or a disadvantage."

She watches me with narrowed eyes, trying to learn as she goes, but it's too late as she moves her pawn yet again. She's put herself in more danger. Her move allows me to bring the queen diagonal.

"Check." My lip tips up into a grin.

Her king has no safe space. There are no pieces that she has that can capture me.

I've captured her piece in two moves.

CHAPTER TWENTY-NINE

Ivy

A DAY HAS PASSED SINCE CYRUS TRIED TO TEACH ME CHESS. Something I should never do again, being with him, and seeing him like that is dangerous. Thoughts grew in my mind like English Ivy, covering the walls, grasping on tight, and block the view and smothering other plants.

He's not that bad . . .

Smart. Witty, and most of all insightful.

As he spoke, it reminded me of the many layers of an onion. There are too many layers of this man to count, but for some reason, I want to.

Shaking my head, I make my way to the kitchen. The place where I know I'll probably find him. As I step inside the room, my hands and arms stretch up into a long-drawn-out yawn.

"Morning," Cyrus's husky voice calls from a seat at the table. His eyes trail down my chest to my bared abdomen. I relish at the idea that I'm able to affect the hard man in front of me. Licking my lips, I then pull the bottom one into my mouth because I'm thinking about such inappropriate things way too early in the morning. I have several hours to get through day, and if I want to keep my dignity, I need to avoid him.

Jeez. I'm so pathetic. Does it really come down to avoiding him and hiding in order to calm down these ridiculous thoughts going through my brain?

Yes.

Apparently.

"I was thinking we could spend the day together, again," he suggests, and I cringe at the implications of spending the day with him when I'm already keyed up. Okay, who am I kidding? Butterflies are flying in my stomach, and my heart is beating so fast I swear I might pass out.

What has gotten into me? I'm acting like a hormonal preteen. Also, a very confused one, apparently, with multiple personalities. One minute, I hate him, and the next, I want to hump his leg.

Maybe it's his promises mixed with the fact he hasn't hurt me.

The truth is, despite the whole kidnapping thing, he hasn't done anything to give me a reason to hate him or not to trust him. He's said on multiple occasions that he had to take me. I can't claim to understand why, but for some reason, I believe him. Right or wrong, I believe he acted out of a sense of need. The reason? I still need to know that. Perhaps spending the day with him can get me the answer to that question.

"What were you thinking today?" I ask, grabbing a cup of coffee and sitting in my spot.

"Up for another game?"

I want to say no, strictly because watching him play chess was an aphrodisiac, but I don't.

Instead, I smile wide, hopefully hiding the inner turmoil inside me.

"Sure, why not."

A week has passed, and Cyrus seems to be walking normally again. I'm surprised he hasn't left, supplies and food were dropped off, but he stayed with me.

We have spent the last seven days in his office, with him teaching me every possible thing I will ever need to know about chess, but I have also learned so much more.

Without even realizing it, I have grown to care for this man. There's much he tries to hide, but like the Wizard of Oz, once you pull back that curtain, it's all there to see. That's what I think I've been doing this week, yanking back the curtain, and what I've seen, I've liked.

More than I should.

"Let's do something different today. I need to get out of this house."

"What do you have in mind?" I ask, happy to do something *different,* I could use the fresh air too.

"I thought you could choose," he says, taking a sip from his coffee mug.

Us sitting here, drinking coffee and planning our day, feels domestic. My skin warms with the implication.

"It's nice out. Maybe we can sit by the water."

He cringes. "The last time we were near the water, you almost drowned, and I was injured."

"First off, I'm a capable swimmer when I'm not trying to escape," I challenge. "When I was younger, we used to do a polar bear challenge. We would jump into the water when it was still cold out. We should totally do it. It really makes you feel alive." I close my eyes and smile at the memory of my mom and I running into the frigid ocean waters. "Maybe we'll be able to see fish."

When I open them again, Cyrus has put his hands up in surrender. "I have equipment and life vests," he offers as an olive branch. "There might not be great visibility from the storms, but we can try."

I hadn't thought about that. From my time at the beach, I know that storms kick up the sand and typically make the water murky for a day or two following. It'd be unlikely that we'd see anything.

"We could take a walk around the island and see what the water situation is. That is if you feel up to it?"

He nods.

"How's your leg? Do I need to rebandage it?"

"I'm fine, Ivy. I'm not a child you have to take care of."

I roll my eyes. "I was just checking." Quietly I think of what else we can do, when an idea hits me. "I could pack a picnic," I continue, suddenly excited to have a journey. Now that I know he plans to let me go, I don't feel like a prisoner so much. I'm actually looking forward to enjoying the beauty of this place.

"We can do whatever you want," he says, smiling. I cock my head at him, looking at the way his lips pull up. He's a devastatingly handsome man to begin with—even when his appearance is dark and ominous—but when he smiles . . .

It makes me feel alive. Something tells me he doesn't show this side to anyone, and I cherish it. I'm not sure how long it will last, but I want to bask in its glow while I can.

"I have to get dressed. We're wasting the day away." As I rush from the room, I can hear him laughing, and his carefree attitude has me smiling from ear to ear. As I get dressed, I mentally make a list of what I should pack for our picnic. I think another bottle of wine might be good to get him to open up and spill his secrets.

Yes . . . definitely wine.

I take a quick glance in the mirror and smile at my reflection. Despite everything I've been through, I look . . . happy. My cheeks are rosy, and these clothes fit me like a glove. I marvel at how the random attire he brought me plus the clothes I found in the armoire fit me. They are a little tighter than I'm accustomed to wearing, but they make me look good.

I wonder who they belong to.

What girl has Cyrus brought here before? Why would her clothes still be here? Has he kidnapped someone before? I shake off the thoughts running amok through my head. I really don't want to know because it won't change my current situation. In fact, it will just ruin my day. A day I intend to enjoy.

I run down the stairs and package our lunch, eager to get out into the beautiful sun and finally explore the island . . . with Cyrus. I can't help the excitement that flows through me at the thought of spending the day with him in paradise.

Dumb girl.

I internally chastised myself for being so flimsy with my heart. It isn't anything serious. I'm simply attracted to him, but that is still way too much, considering.

"Cyrus," I call out, trying to figure out where he is.

When he walks around the corner, I swear I stopped breathing. He's wearing a pair of jeans and a thermal. The man might look great in a three-piece suit, but lord. My eyes rake over him, and I can't help the way my mouth drops open. He clearly sees my reaction if his answering smirk is any indication. I really need to be more careful about being so blatant with my staring.

"I-Is that what you're wearing?" I ask, looking anywhere but at him.

"What? You don't approve?" he teases, grinning ear to ear.

"It's not that. I just thought—" I blow out too harsh of a breath. He looks too normal, and this feels too intimate. I shake my head. "I just expected . . . a suit," I say lamely.

"Island is the keyword here, Ivy. We're on an island. Would

you expect me in a suit and tie? Maybe a *bathing* suit?" His lip tips into a smirk. "Actually, come to think of it, it's not that cold out. Maybe I should take this off." His hand goes to lift the thermal. "I'll grab a bathing suit for that . . . What did you call it? Polar dip?"

"Um. No. It's fine. I'm fine. You don't have to change."

I can barely handle him in jeans. How would I ever handle Cyrus Reed in less clothes?

"I hope you have a swimsuit under that outfit of yours." His right eyebrow lifts. "Because there's absolutely no way you're not ending up in the water."

"But I . . ." I stuttered lamely. "You can't get wet. You have a bandage on your leg."

"It'll be fine," he assured. "The bandage is secure, the wound is almost healed, and as long as you're not trying to escape, there won't be any issues. We're not going to go far enough out anyway. It's a warm spring day, and I guarantee after walking, you're going to want to take a 'polar dip.'"

Images of water droplets rolling down his firm chest have my hands clenching and wetness pooling in my panties. How in the hell am I going to pull myself together long enough to spend the day with him?

The way my body is reacting to him is absurd. Embarrassing even. "Doesn't matter what I'm wearing under here. Let's go," I say, needing to get some fresh air, but before walking out I hear Cyrus say to Cerberus. *"Blijf"* which I remember as meaning stay. He probably doesn't want him going swimming after the last incident.

For the next hour, we stroll around the island. It's much larger than I had originally believed it to be, and one whole part is dense trees. It's almost spooky.

"What's in there?" I ask, looking toward the dark wooded area.

"I don't know. I've never really roamed that part," he says, kicking at the sand. "I imagine it's just trees and overgrowth."

I remember this spot. It's where I tried to run the day Cerberus stopped me.

"When I come here, it's to relax. I use it to get away from the real world."

"So it's your hideout?" I say, raising my eyes. "Who are you hiding from, Cyrus?" I meant the question to be funny, but by the way Cyrus tenses, I can tell I hit a sore spot. I want to press him on his reaction, but I also don't want to force anything from him.

I know from experience that would only back him into a corner and ruin the entire day. And for the first time since I have been there, I feel good. I want that to continue.

Something flies overhead, swooping down toward me. I yelp, guarding my head, but

Cyrus is already looming over me, shielding me from whatever it had been.

I'm still crouched in a defensive position when Cyrus's laughter burst through my spike of fear. After I untangle myself, I look up into his smiling eyes.

"Are you laughing at me?"

He nods his head, continuing to chuckle. I flick his nose, standing on my tippy toes so that we are almost at eye level. "It's not funny."

"It was hysterical," he counters.

I want to keep the banter going, but when I look into his deep brown eyes, I freeze. We are but an inch apart. If either one of us leans in slightly, our lips will touch. My eyes catch the way his tongue darts out, running across his bottom lip, and I shudder.

His arms come around me, pulling me against his chest, and I want to let go. I want to give in and feel his mouth on mine.

I'm just closing the distance when my stomach rumbles loudly, breaking the spell and darkening my cheeks.

"Hungry?" he asks, and that one word is full of so much meaning. He knows it. I know it. We both want it.

CHAPTER THIRTY

Cyrus

WHAT IS WRONG WITH ME?

Like a fucking idiot, I let her pull away. She wanted me to kiss her. She was practically begging me to, yet I let the moment slip through my fingers.

I've never been such a fucking pussy in all my life.

Normally, if I want something, I take it, but with her, everything is proving to be different.

If this were a different time and a different place, I would have, but as much as I want it, I can't reconcile the difference between me and *him*, if I do.

She needs to come to me.

It has to be her choice.

And most of all, I have to get off this island.

Being here with her is like a kid in a toy store who's been told he can't buy anything.

Case in point, right now.

We are sitting on a blanket in the middle of paradise, and I'm torturing myself by watching as she takes a bite of a ripe strawberry and the juice trickles down her chin. She swipes the juice, smiling at me while she does it.

Temptress.

It's like she is doing it on purpose to torture me.

This is what I get for being an asshole.

Karma is a bitch.

I have to shield my dick from view now.

It's hard . . . so fucking hard. I need to do something, anything to get my mind off her lips.

"Do you like the island so far?" I ask, feeling like an asshole for asking. It's a dumb-ass question, considering how she got here. It isn't a goddamn vacation. She's forced to be here, and I really want to avoid anything that will bring us back to that topic.

But I'm apparently a raging idiot around her.

Everything I say makes me feel like a blundering high school boy who has his first crush, it's an unnatural feeling for me. In the real world, I'm confident to the point of arrogance. I am cold and ruthless. But that's what I have to be.

Considering someone else's feelings and trying to hold regular conversations are not expected of me, and it shows in every normal conversation I attempt to have with her.

I'm becoming frustrated at how hard this is, and I'm not just talking about my dick.

I haven't felt this way since junior high. It's pathetic. Getting off the island and getting back is necessary. Killing someone could help too.

"Are you okay?" Her angelic voice brings my eyes back to hers. Her brow is furrowed, and her eyes are full of concern.

"I'm fine," I lie. "I was just thinking about everything I have to do when I get back." Not a lie. "The boat will be here in a bit, and I need to get some work done."

Her shoulders deflate. "I forgot you were leaving today," she says, sounding disappointed. "Will you be back soon?" Her voice pitches, rises with what I have to assume is hope, and it makes me happy. Another unfamiliar emotion that only she has been able to bring out in me.

"I'm hoping to come back the following day. You're running

out of supplies, so I need to bring back groceries," I say, wondering if there is anything else she might need. "Is there anything else that I can get for you back in town?"

She bites her lip. "Anything?"

"Whatever will make your time here better?"

She thinks on that for a moment before offering some ideas. "I don't suppose I could have my phone?"

"Next idea," I respond, quirking my lip.

She nods her head. "It's fine," she draws out. "Maybe a puzzle?"

"A puzzle?" I ask, confused.

"Yeah. You know. Those things with different pieces that you fit together, and it makes an image." She smirks.

"I know what a puzzle is, Ivy, but you want one?"

She shrugs. "Well, yeah. What else is there to do here?"

I wave my hand around. "You have an ocean and the beach in your front yard. It's an island with more places to explore."

"Yes. But when it rains, it would be nice to have some things to do indoors, and since you'll be gone, I won't have anyone to play chess with."

"All right. A puzzle it is. Anything else?"

"And a couple of books. Your library is kind of dated," she adds. "Something with mystery and romance."

"Mystery and romance," I repeat, chuckling.

"A girl's got her vices." She flashes her beautiful smile at me.

I'm fucked. I'd buy her all the damn puzzles and books she wanted, if only she'd never stop smiling.

"Let's swim," Ivy suggests. "Let's see how cold it is."

Watching her strip down to her bra and panties is a brand of torture I'm not accustomed to. I've been with many women—beautiful, exotic, sexually skilled women who I have enjoyed several nights with—but they never lasted long. I lost interest fast. They were either too eager, too clingy, or just too caught up in my lifestyle. Regardless of all their attributes, not one of them holds me as fascinated as Ivy does.

The black piece of lace hugs every one of her curves, and she looks magnificent. Her golden blond hair shines under the sun's bright rays, and my mouth is dry.

I want her.

I need her.

God, the things I'd do to her.

"Swim with me." She gestures me toward her with one dainty finger.

I oblige. After pulling off my thermal, I remove my jeans, then stalk into the water after her. She squeals, running farther in.

Fuck, it's cold.

Really fucking cold.

But I have to agree with her; it feels amazing.

Invigorating.

"Don't get my hair wet, you Neanderthal," she calls over her shoulder.

"No chance. Going out that way won't save you, Ivy. You're going under whether your pretty ass wants to or not."

"I don't want," she quips. "You stay on your side, and we'll be just fine."

"What's the fun in that?" I call as I charge toward her. "I thought you wanted to swim together."

She stops moving away from me and makes the mistake of walking back toward me. "I can trust you, right?"

The one thing she shouldn't do is trust me because I'll disappoint her. It's guaranteed where this conversation is concerned.

I wait like a shark as she draws in closer. I stalk my prey, and she doesn't even realize I'm doing it. When she's in swimming distance from me, I dive right toward her, hearing her playful screech before I'm fully submerged.

I swim around her in circles until I'm at her backside. I reach out, grab her around the waist, and pull her under with me. When we surface, I turn her so our bodies are flush, and her breasts press against my chest. I inhale, holding in the groan that threatens to break through my chest. It's a perfect moment until I hear the approaching boat.

It's my ride coming to get me and take me back to my life of mayhem.

"Fuck," I say. "That's my ride. I have to get my stuff and go."

Her face falls, but she nods. "Oh, okay."

I want to comfort her, but I know it won't do either one of us any good. So, I release her from my grip and stride out of the water, heading to grab my stuff. The more time I spend with her, the more I want to know about her, and the less I want to leave.

I've watched men fall at the feet of women and thought them the biggest idiots. How could a woman wrap a man so thoroughly around her finger? So much so that he'd give up everything just for her. I've never understood it, and I've always thought them weak, but Ivy has me questioning that notion. Perhaps a better man can admit his weakness and change for love.

No matter how much I may want that, it will never be my life. I'm in too deep in another world. A dark world. One I'll never bring Ivy into. Even if her father has already thrown her into it, I'll do everything I have to, to protect her. To shield her from it. Including keeping my distance. The best thing I can do for her is to leave.

"Boss, I'm in the surveillance room. You need to get in here right away."

I hang the phone up, push away from my desk and stand. Z isn't one to bother me with nonsense, so if he wants me, it has to be something important.

Moving fast, I head toward the back elevator of my house. Not something I use frequently, but something tells me it's important, and time is of the essence.

When I push the door open, I find Z and Maxwell looking at multiple images of the island.

Instantly, my back goes rigid.

"What the fuck is going on?" Now, I'm standing directly behind them. There are different vantage points.

Some are of the house. We also have cameras in the trees and others angled toward the ocean.

We set the computer up with six squares, and carefully I look over each one.

"It looks like a boat is close," Maxwell says, lifting his hand to point to the square on the bottom right.

I see nothing at first, but then Maxwell zooms in. Far enough away to not send out any red flags, but close enough to be worrisome.

"Fuck."

"What do you want me to do?"

"Is there a way to get closer?"

I don't know shit about surveillance.

But I need to know right the fuck now why there is someone sailing too close to my private island that shouldn't show up on anyone's fucking radar.

Best case, it's off track and randomly passing by the island. Worse case, I don't want to think about the worst case.

"Yeah. I think I can. Hold."

Maxwell fiddles around, pulling the image, zooming in. The larger it gets, the more it pixelates.

But it doesn't matter how distorted it gets, I can see the shape of the boat, the style too. If we zoom in closer, I'll see the name.

"The fuck?"

"What?" Z asks, his forehead furrowing with confusion.

"That's Alaric's boat."

Both my men continue to look, and then I hear Maxwell mutter his agreement.

"What are you going to do about it, boss?"

"I'll find out why he's there."

Z pivots in his chair to look at me.

He's still sitting, so his neck cranes up. "How do you want to handle this?" he asks me.

"I'll take care of Alaric," I respond.

Z moves to come with me, but I lift my hand, stopping him.

"I need you to run point on Ivy's safety. She is your number one priority."

He might not speak, but his expression on his face is thunderous. Eyes black, darkened with fury.

"My place is by your side, boss," Z replies with a low voice taut with frustration and anger. His contempt for me placing Ivy in his care clear.

"This is not up for discussion. Ivy is the priority. Monitor. If the boat gets any closer, I expect you on the helicopter protecting her." His lips thin, and his nostrils flare. The silent air around us crackles. "You need to protect Ivy at all costs."

That's the last thing I say as I storm out of the room, and onto the deck. Once I have the island in sight, I pick up my phone.

I don't wait for Alaric to address me. As soon as the ringing sound stops and I hear the familiar click that he answered, I fire away.

"Why is your boat by my island?"

"Hello to you too, Cyrus."

"Fuck hello. Answer me."

"Nothing to fear. With you storing my guns, my men are making sure everything is running smoothly."

"Your goddamn guns are at my estate."

"And the island left me curious. I always do recon when I'm working with someone. Your island is part of that."

"You know what they said about curiosity and the cat."

"Is that a threat, Cyrus?"

"No. It's a promise. Stay off my island. I have your money and your guns. Back the fuck off."

"Duly noted. I wouldn't have been doing my due diligence if I hadn't tried to see what was so special."

"It's nothing. It's an abandoned family home."

"Then why the secrecy?"

"Again, none of your business. But because I value our working relationship, I'll let this go. The home is sentimental, stay the fuck away from it."

"Very well. I'll call my men back."

"Goodbye, Alaric."

I press the end button and as the line goes quiet; I wonder if I have an enemy of one of my best clients. Mentally, I calculate the repercussions if I have to kill him.

I stalk back into the house where I find Maxwell and Z still in the surveillance room.

"I want the island always monitored."

"Boss. The manpower it would take. I think it would be easier—"

"Always," I bellow. My word final.

"Very well."

CHAPTER THIRTY-ONE

Ivy

H E LEFT WITHOUT BARELY A WORD YESTERDAY. IT'S SO strange how quickly his moods shift. One minute, we are having a great time, splashing, playing, and yes, freezing our asses off, and the next, he's back to cold. I'm getting whiplash where his moods are concerned.

Despite all of that, I sit in the empty estate, bored and somehow missing Cyrus. It's an odd feeling to miss someone who I only recently despised, but it is my truth. I miss our banter and the way he looks at me.

As though I'm some valuable item.

Some mystic creature he wants to understand. Someone . . . special to him. It might be absurd, but he makes me think that at times.

I need to find something to preoccupy me until he returns. He had said it could possibly be today, but he hasn't come. I decide to go through the house. Specifically, the room he chose to stay in. I open drawers to find nothing but clothes. Ties, socks, briefs . . . nothing interesting.

I even move things around, but there isn't so much as a hidden item underneath. Looking under the bed proves to be even more of a bust.

There is literally nothing there.

He said this is his escape. Wouldn't you have sentimental personal items in the one place you can get away that nobody knows about?

I open the closet door to find a large walk-in space filled to the brim with clothes.

Why he needs suits and dress clothes in his escape is beyond me, but who am I to judge? If you have the kind of money Cyrus does, I guess you can have anything you want, wherever you want.

Including a stolen girl stowed away on a deserted island.

I sigh, growing bored with my lack of findings until my hand lands on a knob hidden behind a row of suits. Pushing the clothes out of the way, I stumble across a small door hidden in the back of the closet.

What are you hiding in there, Cyrus?

I have a devil on one shoulder and an angel on the other, and each suggests something different. One part of me thinks better of opening that door. The contents behind it could be so many things, and if I've learned anything in my short life, it's that some things are better left unknown.

If I find something terrible behind that door, I'll never be able to unsee it.

The other part of me is eager to rip it open and have some adventure. The problem is, both sides make valid points, and I am stuck in limbo trying to decide which is best.

So, I do what any self-respecting girl would do. I find a coin and flip it.

I call tails is open, heads is walk away.

Tails wins. *Of course, it does.*

Placing my hand on the knob, I draw it down, and the door creaks open.

That seems like a good sign to me, as nobody I know leaves questionable doors unlocked. If this is hiding something big, then surely Cyrus would have it locked.

When it opens all the way, it's hard to see anything.

A little of the overhead closet light filters in, but as far as I can see, there isn't another switch to illuminate the small room.

I run downstairs to the kitchen where I know I'll find a flashlight and hurry back up to the closet. Shining the small stream of light into the room, I'm surprised to find it empty save a small shoe-sized box in the middle of the floor.

Curious.

Popping the lid off, I find a few trinkets inside. Nothing of monetary value, though, as far as I can tell. There are a few pictures of a young Cyrus and a pretty girl, also one of another girl who looks vaguely familiar to me, but that makes no sense. With a shake of the head, I continue to look, and I find a few letters.

I open the first and realize it isn't actually a letter, but a note or maybe a poem.

The handwriting is masculine and hard to read. The letters each appear to have been read hundreds of times. The paper worn, and the ink fading.

The next one I open has me furrowing my brow in confusion. It's a list of names. Some are scratched out, others untouched. Attached to another letter are news clippings talking about area homicides and missing persons.

Oh, God. Was this a hit list?

I continue to sift through the paper-clipped obituaries—most of which belong to well-known mobsters. Their deaths are not tragic in my opinion. The world is better off with them dead. They are horrible men who did horrible things to others.

I sort through the contents and find myself confused as to what the notes and clips have to do with the girl in the photos.

Had one of these men done something to her? Why else would these things be put together in this empty, hidden room?

Behind the newspaper clippings is one more list. This one is different, though. This one doesn't have any scratched-out names. No, this one is worse because it only has names of females. All my prior suspicions are thrown out the window after looking at this list. Maybe the last one was a hit list, but this one might be a list of conquests. My stomach tightens at the thought. A wave of irrational jealousy working its way through me. This is obviously where he keeps things he doesn't want me to find.

"Ivy?" Cyrus's voice calls, and I nearly jump out of my skin. He's back, and I'm snooping through his personal things.

I quickly shove the items back into the box, shut the door, and try desperately to replace everything back to where it was. My hands are shaking as I walk out of the closet. And I don't have enough time to get out of the room before Cyrus finds me.

His brows knit in confusion when he finds me in his room.

"What are you doing in here?" he asks.

He doesn't seem angry, just confused.

"I was bored," I admit. It isn't a lie.

"Are you snooping through my stuff?" He guesses accurately, standing in front of me. I have to crane my head to look at him.

I shrug at his question. I'm not sure what to say. There's no sense in lying because I'm basically caught. What did he expect me to do in this house all alone? Plus, I'm also not sure how I feel about this list. Who are these women?

"You missed me." His statement takes me off guard, and I realize I did.

The fear I had moments ago about being caught is replaced by something else. A warmth travels through my body at seeing him. My pulse picks up, and a smile spreads across my face. He winks at me, and I swear, it makes my knees weak and my brain mush.

"I did," I confess.

His smile turns to something closer to a smolder, and he moves toward me. It's like we're magnets being drawn to each other. He moves toward me as I move toward him. There's no control over it. My body demands I get closer.

When we are a foot apart, Cyrus reaches out and pulls me to him. I sigh as I breathe him in. Spice and mint mixed with sandalwood. All male and so damn intoxicating.

"Ivy, I—"

I cut off his words when I lean up on my toes and run my hand down the side of his face. That's all it takes for him to close the distance between us. Our lips crash together, and we both groan in response.

My mouth opens to him, allowing his tongue to dominate me.

He can take what he wants. I'm his at this moment. His hands grip my hips, crushing me even farther against him. The hard length of his erection presses against my stomach, telling me what I already know. He wants this as badly as I do. His hands find the bottom of my shirt and are beginning to lift it when I finally snap to my senses.

I jump back, gasping for breath and red-faced as I try desperately to control my panting. I've allowed things to go too far.

I want it, but that doesn't mean it is the right thing to do. There are still so many unknowns where Cyrus is concerned. Including the list, I just found. What does it all mean?

What if I give myself to him, and he tires of me? What if he decides I can't go home?

Self-loathing seeps into me, making me question my every move. Have I lost my fucking mind? Despite how gorgeous Cyrus is, he is a kidnapper and God only knows what else.

"Ivy, look at me," he demands, and I shake my head. "Get out of your head. You wanted that just as much as I did."

"That's the thing, Cyrus. This isn't on you. I did this!" I yell. "I kissed you back because I wanted to." Pulling on my hair, I groan in frustration. "What kind of an idiot am I?"

"Stop, Sun. Look at me," Cyrus commands, and this time, I listen. "This isn't wrong. We're two adults capable of making decisions for ourselves. Get out of your head and let go. Just feel," he says, pulling me to him again. His grip tight, face unyielding. "I'm going to kiss you again, and you're going to let me."

But instead, I allow my fears to win, and I push back. I run out of his room, down the stairs, and into the library.

My breath comes out in heavy pants as I fling myself in the chair to calm down.

I expect him to follow me, but he doesn't.

He let me go.

CHAPTER THIRTY-TWO

Ivy

I T'S BEEN HOURS SINCE I EVADED HIM, AND HE STILL HASN'T FOUND me. Or maybe he isn't even looking. A dizzy feeling hits me at that thought.

My hand reaches up to the shelf to grab a book to read. With him being here on the island with me, my time in the greenhouse hasn't been as much as I'd like, but thankfully, there is a fully stocked library to pass the time. Especially now that Cyrus brought new books.

It gives me something to do.

From behind me, I hear him first. The sound of his shoes hitting the marble beneath us. I don't want to look at him. I have tried my best to keep my distance. It's as if he's been summoned by my constant thoughts of him.

"Why are you avoiding me?" he says from behind me, and my back goes straight. "Why are you denying this?"

"Denying what?" I ask as I turn around to face him. He moves in closer, caging me in yet again.

"The last time we were here in this room, I left you unscathed. But this time . . ."

"This time?"

"I won't because there is no denying us."

Words escape me. Like the Sahara Desert, my mouth is dry, parched, and I can't speak. Instead, I try to lull the rapid beat of my heart.

"The need we have for each other. I know you feel it. You felt it then, and you feel it now."

He steps forward again, and I step back again. It's like déjà vu, but a lifetime has passed.

I want to say I hate him, but that would be a lie.

Last time I was here, I said it, but even then, there was no conviction to my words, and now . . .

He's not the man I thought he was.

I still don't know why.

But after he ran into the water and almost died for me, I can't deny that he believes he is protecting me. And there is no limit to what he will do.

I don't know what I'm being protected from or why, but I believe him.

He takes a step forward again, and this time, my butt touches the desk.

We've been here before, but last time, I tried to deny that he was right. My need for him is palpable and all-consuming, but as he's said before, he won.

"How can you pretend you don't feel it?" He steps forward just one step, but it's the last step before our bodies touch and his legs press against mine. "I can't pretend any longer." He reaches his hands out and touches my jaw. "I can't pretend that I don't want you. Because I do."

"I just—"

He lifts his hand to my mouth, silencing me. "Why do you need to talk constantly?" He smirks. "This is what you need to know. You need to know what my lips feel like as I kiss you." He leans forward, placing his mouth on mine.

His hands move to rest on my shoulders, and then he pushes me back until I'm leaning back on my elbows.

My breathing comes out in short bursts of air.

"Since the first time I laid eyes on you, all I've been thinking about is what you would taste like . . ."

He leans in.

I move back. "Here." His right hand reaches up, and then the rough pad of his thumb touches my lower lip. "But now that I've tasted you . . . I want to know what you taste like here." As he whispers his fingers lower to cup my face all while continuing to swirl soft patterns on my skin.

I shake my head. The thought of him devouring me is too much right now. I feel like a raging inferno.

"Is that what you want, Sun?"

"Stop calling me that. Unless you tell me why."

"You don't want me to taste you here?" He kisses my jaw ignoring my plea. "What about here?" He kisses the hollow of my neck. "What about here?" He lifts his face away from me, and his eyes darken. There is no iris at all now, just the pupil. "Do you want that?" He lowers his head. "Do you?"

"We can't," I whisper. "You kidnapped me. I don't want you," I say, but there is no conviction in my words. His jaw tightens, and then I feel his hands trying to pull my legs apart.

"Are you sure about that?"

I nod.

"How about I check to see if you're lying?" His eyes light up with mischief because both of us know what he'll find. My face warms as I feel his fingers press gently against my core.

"Admit you want me. Admit you want this."

Then his hand is cupping me.

I watch as his lip tips up. "Tell me."

"I want you . . ." My voice is low, and he lifts his eyebrow.

"Louder." He begins to rub on the bundle of nerves hidden beneath my leggings.

When I don't answer, his pace increases, the pressure getting harder and harder, and I can feel myself losing the battle of wills.

"Say it again."

"I want you!" I shout this time because there is no denying it. I want him. I'm desperate for him.

I need him.

"Then you'll have me."

I expect him to undress. To pull my legs apart and fuck me on the desk. Instead, he gets down on his knees.

"W-What are you doing?" I stutter.

"Tasting you." The cold air hits my legs, and that's when I notice he's pulling off my pants. "Tasting your lies."

Once I'm bare before him, he spreads my legs wide.

It's agonizing torture as I wait.

Then I feel it. The first swipe of his tongue against my skin.

A sigh escapes my mouth, or maybe a groan. I can't hear over the sound of my pounding heart.

He tastes me. Devours me. Feeds off my essence. A man in a drought. Parched and desperate.

He drinks me up as if I'm what he needs to live.

He consumes me with each swipe of the tongue until a wave builds inside me and I'm crashing against the earth.

I open my eyes to find him staring down at me. He lifts his hand and wipes away the remnants from his lips. Then he lowers his head, pressing his lips to mine and letting me taste my lie. I'm not sure what I expect next, but it's not for him to take a step back.

"What are you doing?" I ask, and he smiles. "I thought . . ." I trail off.

"You thought I would fuck you?" I don't answer his question, my face warming at the conversation. "I will fuck you. But not here and not like this."

"Then like what?"

"When you are begging me."

He touches his finger to my head. "You are still fighting this right here, and until you let go, until you are ready to ask for it, beg for it, I won't fuck you. Taste you . . ." He kisses me again. "But not fuck you. When you are ready, you will come to me."

And then like that, I'm left alone again, on his desk, needy and desperate for Cyrus Reed.

CHAPTER THIRTY-THREE

Cyrus

FUCK ME . . . I CAN STILL TASTE HER ON MY LIPS.

Still feel her coming apart on my tongue. It took everything in my power to walk away, but I had to.

This needs to be her decision and not when she's floating off the high of coming on my face.

I'm an asshole, but I'm not that big of an asshole. I take, but never like that. So, as much as my dick hates me right now, my brain knows I did the right thing.

A criminal with a conscience. Oh, the fucking irony.

I'm in my room, staring out the window like a love-sick fool.

I should call Z and have him bring the boat around. The weather isn't bad right now, and who knows how long it will last.

They're calling for another storm this weekend. As much as I'm needed back at the main estate, I can't fathom leaving Ivy all by herself.

She asked me again why I call her Sun.

The words were on the tip of my tongue to tell her, but when I tasted her, I realized how far from the truth it was.

So instead, I diverted the question yet again by licking her with abandon.

She came apart in front of me, the way a flower finally opens her petals when it blooms.

Erotic, sensual, a sight I will always remember even long after.

Her cheeks are a warm shade of pink as she comes down from her high, fueling the need inside me.

My cock grows hard in my pants, and I know without a measure of a doubt that I'll have to finish myself off in the bathroom.

With an exhale, I walk toward the shower and turn on the water.

The scalding hot water will only fuel the heat inside me, but I have no other choice. If I go to her now . . .

I won't see her until I'm sated.

Standing under the hot water, I desperately need to find my release. Watching her come has me ready to ignite.

The pent-up need is unrivaled.

Closing my eyes, I fist myself in my hands and imagine what it will feel like when she finally gives in and admits she wants me the way I want her.

I imagine what it would feel like to thrust in and out of her. Dragging myself through her heat.

With my dick in my hand, I grip myself tightly in my palm.

Pulling from root to tip, slowly, I fuck my hand.

I tighten my grip. My hips rock up. My back goes rigid as I chase my high.

It's building. I can feel the end is near.

The sound of the shower door opening pulls me out of my haze.

"What are you doing in here?" I growl.

Her lip tucks in between her teeth.

Gone is the self-assured Ivy. She's nervous, and she should be. Once she says the words, I will ruin her.

I will take her. She'll be mine. I'll consume her.

"I want you," she whispers.

"Are you sure?"

She nods. Still timid. Still scared.

I don't know what demons she battled on her way in here, but I'm not sure it's enough.

"No," I respond, and I hate myself for being the man that I am right now. I should fucking say yes, grab her, and pound her into the shower tile. Instead, I turn off the shower and grab the towel and head out the door.

"Where are you going?" she asks quickly as she follows me into my bedroom, and I turn to face her.

"I will not fuck you like this."

"Like what?"

"Unsure." I move toward the cabinet to grab clothes. With my back toward her, I rifle through the shirts. I can hear her steps behind me. Then I feel her hand on my back. My spine straightens, willing myself not to let loose a beast and grab her.

Let her come to you, the voice in my head says.

The voice that stops me when I know I will go too far.

You need her to come to you.

"Cyrus," she says, and I don't respond. Instead, my lungs expand with an inhale. "Turn around," I hear from behind me. Her voice is not weak this time. It sounds like the Ivy who's been fighting this attraction between us has finally gotten the memo: this will happen. I turn around as she's asked and look at her. "I want you."

Narrowing my eyes, I study her. Her chest heaves as her breath comes out heavy, and her pupils are dilated as she licks her lips. There is no questioning it this time. It's written all over her features. She wants this. But I'm a dick and saying it isn't enough.

"Prove it." I smirk.

Then she drops to her knees.

Thank fuck.

CHAPTER THIRTY-FOUR

Ivy

I DON'T KNOW WHAT HAS COME OVER ME, BUT THE FACT THAT he rejected me and walked away was too much to handle. I sat in the room for what seemed like forever, but really was only a few minutes before my brain finally caught up to what was happening.

I needed him.

Yet when I found him in the shower, pleasuring himself, that's when I knew what I needed to do.

As much as I wanted him, though, I'm not the best with men, and apparently, it showed through with my indecision or shyness. It's funny how bold I can be in certain aspects, but with men, not so much.

Now, I kneel in front of him, and as he looks down at me, the only thing I can imagine is what he will taste like.

What he will sound like when I drive him as crazy as he drove me.

It makes me feel bold with need, so I grab the towel around his waist, pull it down, and meet his eyes.

The look he's giving me is enough for me to combust. It makes me feel like a flower as the first ray of sunlight in the morning hits it. I want to reach for him and show him what he does to me, so I do.

I make sure not to be tentative. There is no way I'm letting him reject me again.

When I take him in my hand, I don't give him a second to

think or say anything. Instead, I pump my hand up and down, and then lean forward and place the tip in my mouth. A groan of satisfaction is enough to urge me on.

My feelings of desire and the need to bring him to his knees consume me. With every moan that he expels, I feel bolder. Placing him fully in my mouth, I devour him. His hands find purchase in my hair, tugging lightly as he finds his release.

I love the way it feels.

I love the power I possess *over him.*

It's nothing I have ever felt before.

Before I know it, he's pulling me off him.

"I need to be inside you," he grunts before picking me up under my arms and throwing me down on his bed. I watch through hooded lids as he prowls over to the bedside table and grabs a condom.

He rolls it on slowly and then stalks to me, grabbing my legs and pulling off my leggings in one move.

"Shirt. Off."

I scramble to remove it, and then I'm lying on my back fully naked before him.

"I'd taste you again, but I can't wait. Open your legs for me, Sun."

I shake my head and do as he commands.

He crawls up my body, aligning us, and then I feel him at my entrance. With one quick thrust, he's inside. I let out a gasp at the sudden movement.

Nothing happens for a moment. We breathe together as he allows me to adjust.

Looking up at him, I nod, and then he moves inside me. He lowers his mouth to mine as he starts to fuck me, brushing our lips together. I open, and he swipes his tongue. Before long, he's kissing me at a frantic clip, plunging his tongue into my mouth. He tells me with his body and mouth how much he wants me.

He gives me exactly what I want and need. Moving at a delicious pace, he slowly drags himself in and out.

When he goes to leave my body yet again, I wrap my legs around him, pulling him back in.

He lets out a hearty laugh. A laugh I have never heard leave his lips before.

I love the sound.

With that, he pumps faster.

I claw at his back, pulling him closer.

He thrusts harder.

Faster.

In. Out. In. Out.

Slowly dragging me over a cliff. No, more like throwing me. My breathing becomes frantic, and I'm so close, but just not close enough.

"More," I pant. "Need. More."

He answers my pleas by placing a finger where I need him most. I'm so close. He presses harder and firmer against me, swiveling his hips and picking up his pace.

The building feeling spreads through my body.

My heart beats faster as I climb toward my release.

He must be close too, because his movements become more erratic.

Together, we fall over the edge.

"Fuck," he grunts as he twitches inside me.

We stay entwined in each other's arms for a few more minutes, allowing our breathing to regulate.

When we both calm, he pushes off me, and I miss his weight immediately. But at least the view is good as he leaves. His ass looks amazing as he walks into the bathroom, and I stare in awe. A second later, I hear the same chuckle.

"Did I ruin you?" he asks playfully.

"Was that what you were trying to do?" I ask.

"Yes."

"Ruin me from what?"

"Everyone. I want to ruin you for everyone but me." He crawls back onto the bed, and this time, he has a towel in his hand.

When he cleans me, I all but die at the surrounding intimacy.

Yes, I healed him, and I saw him at his weakest, but this feels like so much more. Cocking his head, he stares at me before he gets back off the bed to dispose of the towel. I stand and move to leave the room.

I know we just had amazing sex, but I'm not sure what that means.

"Where are you going?" he asks from behind me.

I stop my movements and look back at him. Still naked. My heart flutters behind my breastbone.

"In the bed now. Keep the clothes off. I'm not nearly done with you."

Wide-eyed, I obey, dropping my clothes and getting back into the bed.

There I let him keep me up all night long. He shows me over and over again just how much he wants me, and I let him.

I don't know how long we lie in bed. Cyrus draws soft circles on my back. It's the next day. I don't think either of us slept. Well, I know I didn't. My mind was racing too much.

Too many questions run through my brain. It's like a never-ending stream of consciousness. A loop on repeat. It's like a damn kid's train on a track that keeps going and going.

I need it to stop, but the only way to do that is to grow a pair of balls, which, for obvious reasons, I don't have.

I want to ask him.

But something stops me. Something makes the words die on my tongue.

"You're thinking too hard." He stops his movements and places his hand on my shoulders to turn me around.

Now facing him, he looks down at me. He's up on his elbows with his brow furrowed.

"What's going on in that beautiful head of yours?"

When I say nothing, his jaw tightens. "I'm not ready to tell you," he says, knowing what I want to ask.

"I thought I wasn't ready to hear."

He leans forward and places a kiss on my lips.

"I'm not sure you are, but right now, I'm not either." His admission makes my heart flutter like the wings of a hummingbird. It's flying fast, but I need to hold it back. I need to put it back in the cage.

"Why?"

"Because if I tell you, you'll be upset and then you won't let me touch you, and I really want to fucking touch you right now."

"You are touching me." I raise a brow.

His hand reaches under the blanket. "Not there, Sun."

"Cyrus," I say, but it comes out as a pant as he runs his fingers over my sensitive nipples.

"Sun?"

"Stop trying to distract me."

"Cyrus." I move my hands to stop him. His hand is now on my lower abdomen. "Please."

"I will." *Lower.* "Just let me have you a bit longer before you ruin it." His hand travels lower.

"How long?" I pant.

"As long as it takes me to get my fill."

"That's not an answer," I say. My breath hitches as he parts my legs and teases me.

"It's the only answer you are going to get. Now shut up and let me in."

I part my legs farther and do. His mouth finds mine, and he silences me.

When we come up for air sometime later, the questions still weigh heavy in my mind, but I know he's right.

Talking about the kidnapping is an inevitable thing, but once we breach that topic, everything will change.

No matter what he says, he's a criminal.

I have allowed the haze of my desire to cloud my judgment. Once I hear it, once we talk about it, I will have to stop pretending I'm living in a bubble where Cyrus and I can make love and nothing else matters.

Since I'm not ready for it to end yet, I table the conversation.

Denial is a wicked thing, but since he's the devil himself, I might as well indulge for a little longer.

I must have fallen asleep because when I open my eyes Cyrus is not in bed, so I stand, grab his discarded shirt, and head out to look for him.

I wonder how much longer he'll stay.

Does he have to head out?

My footsteps echo through the quiet of the house, and I find him in the kitchen.

He's cooking.

It's crazy to see him.

Most of the times he came to see me, prior to when he was hurt, he was always in a three-piece suit, but now he's in sweats. They may be fancy sweats, but they're sweats all the same.

He's wearing no shirt, and his rock-hard and cut abdomen is on full display.

He must hear me because he lifts his gaze.

Even though he's cooking, he still appears deep in thought.

I wonder if he ever really lets go.

Sometimes he does.

For me, he laughs, smiles, jokes.

I wonder if he does those things for anyone else?

When he does these things, it's like seeing a whole different side of him. That's what warmed my heart toward him. The secret side, the real side, he doesn't share. Each laugh thawed the once icy feelings I had toward him.

"What are you doing?" I ask as I step into the kitchen.

He lifts a brow. "I mean other than cooking yourself breakfast." I laugh because my question really was stupid.

"I'm making *you* breakfast," he answers with a shrug.

My mouth drops open at what he just said. Did he really wake up early to make me food? It seems so out of place. Or does it? Maybe in the beginning, but recently, he's been caring and thoughtful. Still, it feels strangely domestic and out of character . . .

"You are?" I question.

"Yes. I am. Now sit down."

I stroll over to the table and take a seat. *In my spot.* Another thing that's odd. How can I refer to this seat as mine? It's crazy how I now consider this my spot. These thoughts shouldn't be in my mind, but regardless, they are. I feel comfortable here— on this island, in this house—with him.

Cyrus is quietly cooking. Cerberus is eating from his automatic feeder on the floor. It's oddly quiet right now. A part of me expected small talk to be made, but apparently not.

It seems that even after sex, he's back to being his grumpy self, but I think that's just who he is. Grumpy. Gruff. Isolated.

I know he doesn't leave his main estate unless he has to. I wonder why?

I wonder what happened to make him this way.

A few minutes later, he places the plate in front of me, and I look down to see eggs and toast.

Simple. Like him. Lifting the fork, I take a bite. It's surprisingly good.

"Are you going to eat?" I ask.

He shakes his head.

"Do you not eat?" I know he does since he ate when he was hurt, and when we had dinner together before I tried to escape but maybe that was just to appease me.

There is so much I don't know about this man.

Other than the obvious.

"What's going on, Sun?" He inhales deeply, placing a mug of coffee down in front of him.

His features have darkened. It's as if a cloud has formed around him. Hovering close.

A storm is brewing. Not just in the room, but outside. The sound of thunder makes me shake.

"It's going to rain," I say, looking out the window.

"It will be over soon."

I turn back to Cyrus, but he's not looking outside. He's watching me.

It's strange to have someone watch me so intently. I'm not used to it. As much as I like the attention from Cyrus, I also feel like a zoo animal on display. Maybe if there were no secrets between us, I wouldn't feel this way. Or maybe I would feel worse. Once I know the truth, it will hang over us, casting a shadow of darkness and doubt. I shudder inwardly at that thought. I don't want this to end or change.

"I want to know things, but I'm not ready yet."

He nods.

"But that doesn't mean I don't want to get to know you. I might not ask the whys yet, but before I do, before everything changes, I just want to know you."

He stands, charging me, lifting me up from my breakfast.

His mouth attacking mine.

"All you need to know is this." He devours my mouth. "This." *Kiss.* "Is all I'm willing to tell you now." He kisses me again. His tongue attacks mine. Then I hear the dishes hitting the floor, and I'm lifted onto the table.

And before I can object, my legs are parted open, and he descends.

CHAPTER THIRTY-FIVE

Cyrus

JUST AS PREDICTED, ANOTHER STORM ROLLS BY. THIS TIME, bringing fierce rain. It's officially spring, and we have crappy rainy weather to prove it.

I have business to attend to and going back to the mainland isn't something I want to do now. The weather is a perfect excuse to stay. I haven't had my fill of Ivy, and until I do, I hope the weather doesn't turn.

Picking up my phone, I make my way into the office and call Z.

"Boss," he answers.

"I will not be needing the boat today."

"You won't . . .?" He trails off. The way he draws out the word makes an implication of why.

"No." I know he wants to ask, but he won't. Although he is the closest thing I have to a friend, we don't talk about women.

Actually, that's not true. We just haven't talked about one for a long time.

"Anything I should know, boss?"

"No," I say sterner than I mean. We are not females, and we will not be gossiping.

"What about the meeting with Mathis?"

Mathis is one of my clients. He runs all sorts of illegal businesses here and in Europe. According to the United States government, he owns nightclubs, hence the large sums of cash that I clean for him and hold in my bank. The truth is, he is a club owner, but his money comes from all sorts of shit he has his hands on. Including distributing a hefty portion of Tobias's cocaine.

"He wants to meet next week."

"Do I have any other meetings this week?" I ask.

"Not that I'm aware of. Oh, wait, Alaric. Maybe Tobias as well. I'll have to check and get back with you," he says.

"Very well. What about the game, who's playing?"

"So far, it's the usual suspects . . . a few trustees."

I start to pace the length of my office. "Trent?" He better not be, not after everything I've done.

I hardly think he would appreciate knowing I've fucked his sister while I'm supposed to be protecting her.

"Nope. He hasn't been back since you spoke with him."

"Good."

I'm happy he hasn't pressed the issue. I'm still not happy I have to deal with it, but as long as he's not making it worse, Ivy will be okay. *Safe and sound in my bed.*

Once I have my fill, I'll decide what to do with her. Trent is gathering the money to pay Boris. Once that's done, she can go back to her life.

A pit forms in my stomach at the thought of letting her go. She was never supposed to stay. She is a means to an end. Walking over to the chair in my office, I plop myself down and lift my hand to rub my temples. A headache is forming just thinking about this shit. "And Boris? Any word on that front yet?"

The line is silent, and I look down to make sure the call hasn't dropped due to the impending weather.

"Still putting feelers out."

I don't like this. No one should be this hard to find. It never bodes well. Usually, it means war is coming.

"The Russians have been too quiet. Do they know I have her?"

"Doubtful," he answers, but I wonder if that's true. The lack of control I have over this matter is infuriating. Taking back the reins is the only way this is going to work, but how?

If they find out I have her, I'll be fighting two fronts. I need to find leverage on them and ultimately bait them, but until I have what I need, I need to lie low and come up with a foolproof plan.

Z has one, but I'm not willing to go that route. At least not yet.

"It wasn't supposed to happen this way," I say on a sigh. Because it wasn't. None of it.

"I know."

I look toward the door. Ivy is now standing there, her blond hair flowing down her shoulders.

"I have to go."

"When should I come back for you?" Z asks.

"After the storm," I say. After the storm, another will brew, but this one will be different. This one, I'll use to my advantage.

I hang up the phone, and Ivy's nose is scrunched. I'm not sure how much she heard.

"Everything okay?" she asks as she takes a step into the room.

I nod.

"If you want to talk about it . . ." she starts, but the idea of unburdening on the woman I've kidnapped sounds ridiculous.

I shake my head.

"Are you leaving again?"

I stand from my chair and walk toward her. Leaning down, I place a kiss on her lips. "No. Not yet."

Pulling away, I take her hand in mine. It looks so small. "There's a storm rolling in. You're stuck with me for a few more days."

She nods silently. I wonder if she's happy or sad about that fact.

I don't ask because I don't want to know. Soon, this will be over, and she'll be gone. Once again, the light will go out. But until then, I plan to bask in her warmth.

I start to lead her out of the room.

"Where are we going?" she asks.

Instead of answering, I pull her beside me and tuck her under my arm. Then together we walk to the great room.

With large windows that face the outside, the clouds looming in the distance are present.

"Sit," I say before heading across the room.

"What are you doing?" she asks.

"I'm going to start a fire for us," I say over my shoulder as I head where the logs are in the corner of the room.

"And then what?"

I stop and look over my shoulder toward her.

"Are we going to talk?" I hear the apprehension in her voice.

Turning back around, I grab a log and then prepare a fire. I was never a Boy Scout, but I still taught myself how to build a fire. A trait I learned as a child to warm my house whenever my father forgot to pay the heat.

The question still lingers in the air when I'm sitting beside her a few minutes later.

Her chin is tucked down as she stares at the fire that has started to take life.

"Soon, okay?"

She looks up, her eyes large. "Really?"

"Yes. With the storm coming, I don't want the truth hanging over us too. Once it passes."

She nods her head in understanding.

We both go quiet then, both staring into the flames, lost in our own thoughts. I try to find a solution to the problem dangling above my head. What to do with Ivy once the truth is out and what to do with the Russians.

I'm not sure where she is mentally, but I can see little lines have formed between her brows.

Finally, after what seems like forever has passed, she turns to me, cocking her head.

"Tell me about yourself?"

Her question takes me off guard, but I'm not sure why. It's not like we've never spoken, but a part of me expected her to ask me about the reason I took her again.

"What do you want to know?"

"Everything."

"That's a vague question, Sun."

She leans forward, resting her elbows on her knees. There is a mischievous twinkle in her eye. This should be interesting.

"Spit it out. Whatever you're going to ask." My lips tip up into a smirk. "But no promises I'll answer."

"Why are there chains in the basement?"

"It's cute that you think I'm going to answer that." I laugh. She'd hate me if she knew.

"Come on, just tell me."

I grow quiet, trying to think of an evasive answer to this question. No wonder Ivy is wearing a shit-eating grin. All the times when we played questions and answers over food, I was able to sidestep all her questions, but this one won't be as easy. There is no plausible answer other than the truth that would do.

But I can't tell her the truth. That I have chains in the basement because in order to become the banker to the underworld, I had to become the monster my competition was and take anyone down who got in my way. I can't tell her that in order to get the contacts I needed to have men like Alaric on my Rolodex, I needed to lie, steal, and apparently torture. Nope. That won't be my answer. Leaning closer to her, I place my hands on her face, tilt her head back to expose her neck, and then kiss the pulse that thumps heavily beneath my touch.

"They came with the house."

"Seriously, you won't answer." She lets out a puff of air. "Fine. But I'm not done asking questions."

CHAPTER THIRTY-SIX

Ivy

I EXPECT HIM TO SAY NO AFTER MY LAST QUESTION. TO BE honest, I expect him to actually stand from the couch and leave. I'm just barely scratching the surface of who he is, so to put him on the spot like that . . .

The thing is, ever since we both finally gave in to our desires, I want to know more about him.

But I don't just want to know what his part in my life is. I want to know everything.

Most people would think I'm crazy. Hell, half the time, I think I'm crazy. The man kidnapped me, for fuck's sake. But for some reason—and the reasons elude me completely—when he said he was protecting me, I believed him.

I still do.

Cyrus Reed might be a cold man. He might also be the villain in most people's stories. Heck, he could even end up being the villain in my story, but I'm not afraid of him.

I shouldn't think he wants to help me after everything, but I do.

Some people might look at me and think I'm a foregone conclusion, a weak woman with a weak mind who fell for her captor, but I think it's the opposite. I know what I feel, and Cyrus isn't the bad guy.

Yes, he might act that way sometimes, but I also know what I see when I look into his eyes, and that is a protector.

He wouldn't hurt me.

I know the truth still hovers over us, and once I find out, it will surely change things, so that's why I don't press. Because like him, right now, I'd prefer to live in this fantasy bubble just a little while longer.

That doesn't mean I don't want to know more, and being stranded on an island alone with this man is the perfect excuse.

"Or we don't have to talk at all," he offers up gruffly.

I tilt my head in his direction, allowing my left brow to lift. "We aren't having sex again."

If Cyrus Reed could pout, he would, but since that's not on his list of facial expressions, I have to assume by the way he furrows his brow that he doesn't agree.

"Talk first, sex later?" I suggest with a raise of my shoulders.

He studies me for a minute in full thought before he nods his head. A man of many words.

"By agreeing to my terms, you will answer anything?" I joke.

"No. I will answer what I want."

"You aren't very fun."

"You're wasting your chance. Goad me, and I'll have you on your knees. That will shut you up."

I lift my hand up in the air. "Fine. Fine. Jeez. You're no fun."

Cocking my head, I look at him and try to decide how to use this opportunity. I need to ask him questions, but at the same time, I don't want to ruin the remainder of the time we have together.

"Do you watch TV?" I ask. His brown eyes widen, and it makes me laugh. Yep. That was not what he was expecting. "See? No questions about chains." I wink.

"No."

Now that answer I was expecting.

"Why do you ask?"

"You're so serious. I can't imagine you lying in front of a TV and being able to rest."

"I rest."

"No . . . you don't."

He doesn't say anything for a minute, and then he inclines his head. "You're right. I don't." His hand lifts, and he runs it through his hair. "The first time I have rested in years is here with you."

"That hardly counts," I respond, rolling my eyes.

"Of course, it counts."

"You were dying." I throw my hand up in the air dramatically. He scoffs at my display.

"First of all, I was not dying. Second, if I'm not working, I'm resting."

"And what is it you actually do, Cyrus?" I cock my head to the side and raise a brow with a full smirk lining my face. I'm teasing him, goading him.

"You know this. I run a bank." He looks bored by my line of questions.

"There has to be more than that," I say.

Because no way does it make sense. Why would a billionaire banker want me? That's not to say I'm not good enough for him, but I have always known there is more.

People talk about Cyrus Reed in passing. At least Trent does. It's as if he's a legend.

"I hold a very exclusive and private poker game." He shrugs.

"More."

"The rest I can't tell you."

"Or what? You will have to kill me," I joke, but the moment the words leave my lips, I realize just how not funny they are.

He surprises me when he takes my hands in his and lifts them to his mouth. A kiss is placed on each knuckle. The move is slow, soft, and completely out of character. "I would never hurt you, Sun."

"Why Sun? You told me it's not because of my sunny personality, so then why?"

"As I'm sure you know, I speak many languages. When I first saw you, spoke to you, you were like a poison the seeped into my veins. I knew you would be bad for me. So, I called you Sun."

"I don't get it."

"Sun means poison in Somali. But that isn't why I call you Sun now."

"You called me Sun 'cause I'm poison."

"Yes, Ivy. When I first met you, you were like poison ivy that creeps into your skin, burning you. But over time, and as you took care of me, it changed."

"And now why do you call me Sun?"

"Because you brighten my dark world. You make me feel like maybe . . ."

"Like maybe?" I beg him to continue, but instead, he stops, then stands and pulls on my arms.

"What are you doing?" I ask, confused by his change of topic.

"Taking you outside." He starts to walk, still holding on to me.

"It's raining," I whine.

"And you say I'm no fun," he jokes, and his playful voice warms my heart.

"You want to go outside and what, dance in the rain?" I stop walking and so does he, looking back. His face serious.

"No, I want to go outside and fuck you in the rain."

Holy.

Yes. Please.

But then I let my lip tip up. "Dance first, play later." And then I take off, knowing full well he will follow.

I run as fast as I can into the greenhouse, grabbing the supplies I need. I know Cyrus doesn't like me being in here, but I want to do this, so I will.

Grabbing a tarp, I head back to where I left him and then walk toward the outdoors.

"What are you doing?" he asks, his footsteps sounding from behind me.

I'm at the front door now.

"Why are you holding a tarp?"

"Wait and see."

"Ivy."

"Not Sun? Am I not brightening your day?" I waggle my brows at him. He just shakes his head like he doesn't know what to do with me. "I have cabin fever. You mentioned going outside, so I'm taking you up on your offer."

"And doing what with the tarp? Going fishing?"

I roll my eyes at him and continue my trek. "Hardly. What fun would that be?" I ask before stopping again to make sure he's following. When he doesn't move closer, I furrow my brow. "Were you ever fun?"

He stares at me blankly.

"Okay, better question. Were you ever a kid?" It's a dumb question. Of course, he was a kid, but I wonder if he ever was different. Or has he always been this way? I've seen him let loose and relax, but more often than not, he's uptight and angry.

Again, his expression doesn't change. However, his jaw

tightens, and I file that away. Cyrus doesn't want to think about his childhood.

I push the thought away before I take a step outside, tarp in hand.

"Come on, when I was searching for an escape off the island, I found a smaller hill to the beach."

"And . . .?"

"I thought we could make a slip and slide."

When he says nothing, I go on. "Like when you were a kid. Okay, fine, maybe not when *you* were a kid, but when I was. When we were younger, we used to live by Central Park. When the weather was like this, Trent and I would grab one of Mom's tarps, and we would go to Central Park and slide down it."

He doesn't look at all amused. "We didn't have a lot of toys. Dad thought they were beneath us. There was a time when he was present. When he would laugh and play with us . . . but that stopped when I was around ten. But Mom . . . she used to come with us, help us."

I let out a small sigh.

"Do you miss her?" His voice is softer than normal. Filled with compassion, I don't often hear that in his tone.

"Yes." I nod. "Trent too."

"And your father?" This time, there is no mistaking the bite to his words; he doesn't like my dad. I'm still not sure why, though. It doesn't make sense, but maybe as a man, he thinks my dad should have protected me from him. He's right. He should have.

"No," I answer truthfully.

He nods as if he understands.

"Soon," he says, and I'm not exactly sure what that means. Will I be going home soon? Is it safe for me? He still hasn't even explained what wasn't safe, so I don't understand. I give him a small smile. I don't want to go there now. No. Now I want to have fun because I know everything will change soon.

"My mom used to hold down the top end." I continue to walk toward the hill through the path of trees until we're almost at the beach.

Most of the hills are too steep, but this one will be perfect. Here, the land isn't too high, but it's high enough to gather water.

"Come on. I won't bite," I joke, and his dark eyes get even darker if that is even possible.

I think that's exactly what he wants me to do, but we have been playing by his rules today. In the rain, we will play by mine.

The wind is starting to pick up. Small raindrops fall from the sky, and my hair clings to my forehead.

Soon the storm will come, but for now, it coats the tarp as we wait.

It doesn't take long. With each passing moment, more rain falls from the sky until the tarp has a constant stream. I'm happy it's warmer today because if it wasn't, the rain would feel like little needles against my skin. Luck was in my favor because I couldn't stay inside another second.

I love the fresh air.

Even with rain, I can smell it. Spring.

Tilting my head back, I allow the water to drip down my face and off my nose, and then I look down. Cyrus is leaning over, holding my tarp, and I smile at him before I step up to where he is and slide down.

I close my eyes.

And right now, I'm not on an island.

No. Right now, I'm a little girl whose mother pushes her to be different, to be herself, and to be whoever she wants to be.

I haven't done this since my mom became the shell, but doing it now, even with Cyrus, makes me feel closer to her.

When I'm at the bottom of the hill, I look up to see Cyrus standing there. He's still dressed casually, but that's not what does me in. It's how he looks so large on the hill, more than life. Like a god.

He looked that way the first time I saw him too, but now I know the man.

He once reminded me of Hades, the god of the underworld.

He still does, but now I think Hades was misunderstood.

When I walk back up to where he was standing, I lift my hand. "You're next."

"No."

"Come on, live a little."

He stands firm, looking at the slide like it's beneath him. I take his hand in mine. "With me. Together."

I know he wants to say no, but I don't let him. I grab him and pull him to the ground. I know his clothes will be muddy, but so will mine.

"Please." I look at him through the pellets of water cascading down my cheek.

He nods, pulling me into his arms and placing me on his lap. Then he pushes off. Mud is everywhere.

Rain starts to pound down on us, and we go.

As I try to close my eyes, Cyrus tightens his arms around me, keeping me steady.

Laughter breaks against the wind, spilling out of my mouth, but as we make our descent, I realize I'm not the only one laughing, and it warms every part of me.

Before long, we are on the edge of the tarp. I'm still in his arms when he turns me to look at him.

Gone is the smile.

Gone is the laugh.

All that I see are lust, desire, and most of all need.

CHAPTER THIRTY-SEVEN

Ivy

THE DAYS HAVE PASSED. THE STORM A DISTANT MEMORY. I know it's time for Cyrus to leave once again.

I should be happy, but I'm not. The time we have spent together has actually been some of the best of my life. I don't even know how that has happened.

How that can be true.

I should hate him. But as much as I know I should, I can't help the way I feel, and I can't help the simple truth: I believe him when he said he was protecting me.

But from what?

Am I ready to ask, and the better question, is he ready to tell?

No. I'm not ready yet.

Instead, I enjoy the time we have left. Like now, in his arms.

I think this is my new favorite place to be.

It's crazy how only a few weeks ago I would never have said that. Hell, a month ago, I would have kicked him and ran . . . okay, swam for my life.

Life changes so fast, but the more I get to know Cyrus, the more I truly see his real self.

To some, he might be the bad guy, but he's no monster to me.

Rather, he's the guy I have come to trust.

Right now, his arm is wrapped around me as we sit together in the den, staring at a fire Cyrus started. It's something we have been doing every day together, that and chess. It's nice to have, even though it's not that cold, but the fire gives an intimate feel I love.

The nice thing about being with him is we don't have to talk. Neither one of us needs that to fill the silence.

Instead, he strokes my arm with his hand, and I close my eyes. His movements are slow and leisurely, as though he has all the time in the world.

"That feels good."

"Mmm," he responds.

I open my eyes and tilt my head up from where I am in his arms. I can't see his features, but I can tell he is looking toward the fireplace in the center of the room.

For a moment, I watch also, mesmerized by the red sparks bursting up from the wood. Time stands still at that moment as the fire flickers.

A sound has me looking in the other direction. When I see who is watching me, an involuntary shiver runs up my spine.

Z.

His right-hand man.

But it's not his presence that has me feeling like this; it's the look in his eyes. The darkness that lives behind them.

"Are you cold?" Cyrus says from beside me, wrapping his arms tighter around me. A part of me wants to close my eyes and not let this man come into the bubble Cyrus and I have created, but I can't. Something tells me Z wouldn't let me.

I shake my head before saying, "No."

At my one-word answer, Cyrus removes his arm and looks over his shoulder.

"Z. Why are you here?" The bellow of his voice reverberates through my body.

"I came to check on you," Z responds as I pull away from Cyrus's grip and move to stand.

"And where do you think you're going?" Cyrus places a kiss on my shoulder, halting my retreat.

"I'll give you guys a minute." I force myself to smile over my shoulder at Cyrus, who seems appeased by this.

"Very well," he answers.

I stand, straightening my shirt, and start to walk out of the room.

As I pass Z, I note the look of disdain in his eyes. Why the animosity? I'm not sure, but I don't care to find out.

Whatever issue he has with me, he can take up with his boss.

Instead, I head in the direction of the greenhouse.

With Cyrus preoccupied, it's the perfect time to water the plants.

Doing that always calms me and makes me feel better, and after the way Z looked at me, it's exactly what I need.

CHAPTER THIRTY-EIGHT

Cyrus

I PUSH UP TO STAND AND WALK OVER TO Z. MY FACE IS unreadable as per usual. Stone cold. Calculated. Angry. With Ivy, my walls come down, but now that I am standing in front of one of my men, I need to right that shit.

The surest way to lose everything is for someone to underestimate me and try to take what's mine.

Z wouldn't do that. He's been with me way too long. He knows the consequences for crossing me, but one can never be complacent. Not even with your most loyal and trusted.

"What are you doing here?" My voice leaves no question of how I feel about the interruption. I'm not happy, and he needs to give me a damn good reason.

"I came to make sure you were okay," he responds.

Not a good answer. I narrow my eyes at him before responding, "Now that you have, you can leave."

He's been dismissed, but surprisingly, he doesn't go.

Instead, Z looks toward the fireplace. I follow his line of vision. I watch as the wood cracks and explodes under the mantel, burning fast. It reminds me a little about Ivy and me. It's not just the fire, though; Z coming here also reminds me how this is temporary.

Soon, she'll ask me the question that will change everything.

Then like a log that burns into the night, we too shall burn away and be left with only ash.

I wish it didn't have to be this way.

Truly, I don't.

But it will.

I took her. No matter what happens, nothing will change that.

Not how I feel. Not how I act.

Time is limited. We are mere grains of sand running through an hourglass, and soon, it will run out.

At least until she speaks, until she asks the questions I don't want her to, we can pretend, but Z being here will impede on that.

"You missed a meeting." He finally speaks up, and that has me lifting my gaze to meet his.

"With?"

"Alaric. I handled it. But I shouldn't have to. While you're here playing house, you have forgotten what's important."

Anger rises inside me like a dormant volcano ready to erupt. "And what is that, Z?"

"Your clients. Your business. Taking down the organization. Bringing people to their knees."

"Not that I need to answer to you, but that is exactly what I'm doing."

"It looks like you're pussy whipped," he mumbles under his breath, low enough that he doesn't think I can hear. But he's underestimated me. I hear everything. Know everything. I might as well be a fucking god.

Before he can even fathom what I'm doing, I have him in a headlock.

"I understand what this means to you, so that is why, this one time, I will give you a pass. But know, I'm not weak for making this choice. Question my authority again, and I will kill you. No matter our past, I will snap your neck."

I remove my hands from his body and step back. Z lowers his head.

"I'm sorry I overstepped." He looks defeated as the words leave his mouth.

I nod. "Was there anything else you needed before you leave the island?"

"Boss," he says.

"*Boss.* So you remember your place after all." I narrow my eyes at him, and at least he has the decency to appear remorseful for speaking out of turn. "Speak. Tell me what you wanted to say."

"Can we discuss Matteo?"

"What about him?" Striding over to the side table, I grab a glass and the decanter of scotch, lifting it up to Z. To most people, it would seem I'm indecisive, but Z knows me. I said my piece and now we move on. Business as usual. I don't hold grudges; they are beneath me.

When he nods, I pour us two glasses and then take a seat in a chair in the corner of the room. Z grabs the one I prepared for him and then accompanies me.

"What's going on?" I ask as I lift the glass to my mouth and take a drink.

"War. Apparently."

This is news to me. Not that I should be surprised, though. There is always a war brewing within the mafia.

I set the glass down and lean forward. "How so?"

"From what I hear, he and his cousins are at war over who will take over the new territory they took from the Irish."

"War is good."

"It is."

"Have you crunched the number?"

"Maxwell says if they go to war, with the guns Matteo will need from Alaric, we are looking at bringing in a fuck ton of money."

"How much are we talking?"

"Fifty million, give or take."

"War is inevitable, and it always pays to be on the right side. Matteo runs the East Coast. If he expands into the Midwest, is there any chance his cousin will win?"

"No."

"Good." I lean back in my chair and bring the glass up to my mouth. "Any other business you want to discuss, or can we now enjoy this hundred-year-old scotch?"

His eyes dart to the bottle of Glenlivet on the console across the room. I'm usually a cognac drinker, but Z prefers scotch, and seeing as I only minutes ago had him in a headlock, this is my peace offering.

"Nope."

"Perfect."

With war on the horizon for one of my clients, I can't stay on the island that much longer. The time is coming to finally come clean and tell her the truth.

The only problem will be convincing her it's in her best interest to stay, even if I'm not here.

But something tells me when I do finally give her the choice, she will make the wrong decision.

CHAPTER THIRTY-NINE

Ivy

It's been a day since Z came, and I can no longer pretend. His visit brought reality home. His hatred for me seemed deep rooted, and I have to believe it's connected to why I'm here. I tried my hardest to stay in my little bubble with Cyrus a little longer, but things are different now.

I need to know what is going on and he needs to tell me.

It's time.

My head has been buried in the sand long enough, but I need to break free and find out the truth, even if that truth hurts me.

With my mind made up, I stand from where I'm kneeling over the freshly potted plants and go in search of him.

I find him where I always find him.

He's in his office. Or what I assume is an office. I'm not sure how much work he gets done when he's here. Maybe he did in the beginning when he locked me in my room.

My stomach tightens at the memory, but then the muscles loosen as I remember that even then, even when he was the devil, he still never harmed me.

Never once did he touch me in a way I didn't want. Even before I would admit it out loud, he didn't.

It seems like so long ago

How long have I been gone?

"What month is it?" I ask as I enter the wood-paneled room and step to where he is sitting behind the large oak desk.

"April."

"And the day?"

"Why are you asking me this?"

Still standing, I walk to where he is. He swivels his chair so I can step between his legs.

He places his large hands around my thighs, holding me to him.

"Why, Sun?"

"I'm ready," I say. There is no need to clarify what I'm asking for.

His hands drop from my thighs as though they are burned by a flame.

He's quiet. The silence screams between us, ripping at my ears and begging for words. Any words.

A part of me knew that we were a foregone conclusion, I'd eventually have to deal with reality and find out why he's holding me here, but another part hoped we could live in the bubble forever.

But the truth is, no matter what he answers, I need to know the truth, no matter what that truth does to me.

I step back and then look down at him.

He gives me a nod before he moves to stand, steps around me, and starts to walk out the door.

"Where are you going?"

"Outside."

I follow him out of the office, down the hall, and into the grand foyer.

Once we are outside, he takes my hand, and I'm surprised by this gesture. He seems so far away and closed off. But still, I welcome the warmth it brings and follow him blindly.

It's odd that I do.

Most wouldn't follow their kidnapper.

Even though we have spent the past week entwined in each other's arms, it doesn't mean he won't kill me now.

But I know he won't.

But deep down in my heart, I know he would never hurt me, so I follow him through the trees and up the gravel terrain until the trees clear. We have walked some ways, and when I step out into the clearing, I'm not surprised we have come to the highest point of the island. I remember seeing the steep slope from the beach up when I tried to find a way off, but I never ventured this way.

From where we are standing, I can see the whole island, and I was right; there is no place to go.

The trees are too dense to land a plane, and if you were to jump . . .

I shake my head, not thinking of that.

I'm not sure why he's brought me here, but I know it's not for that.

"See over there?" He points into the distance. I look and see what appears to be a large mansion in the distance. That must have been where the lights were coming from.

"Where is that?"

"That's my estate." At his words, I turn toward him. That's where he is when he is not with me. Why does he keep this place?

I have so many questions, but the truth is, those questions are about him, and this is about me. I don't ask. Instead, I cock my head. "Why are you showing me your estate?" I ask.

"That's where it all began. That's why you're here." He gestures his hand to the ground beneath us. "Sit."

I do as he asks, and when he sits beside me, I know whatever he is going to say will be bad.

"Every Friday night, I have a poker game," he starts.

"I know." I didn't know it was every Friday, but I knew Trent went, and I knew it was often.

"The poker game is only one piece of who I am. Of what I do. See, I'm also a banker as you know."

I nod, still not understanding what this has to do with me. "My clients . . . let's just say not all are law-abiding citizens. Without going against their trust, some use the poker game for their needs. Cash is exchanged, dirty cash . . . for clean."

Now I understand. A feeling of foreboding coursed down my spine as I think of my brother being involved with this, but I push it away.

Trent, who never does anything wrong.

"A few months ago, your brother came to my game, but this time, he wasn't alone."

My heart rate picks up.

The blood in my veins thumping just a little bit stronger.

"Who?" I ask.

"Your father." He inhales deeply, and I can tell whatever he needs to say is weighing deeply on him. "This wasn't their typical game. The guest of this game . . ." He trails off, and I want to cover my head with my hands. Close my ears.

"He placed a bet, and he lost."

"What was the bet?"

"It's not a what, but a who."

I feel like the world is closing in as my mouth opens. "Who?"

"The bet was for you."

A heavy pain sits on my chest, and I feel like I'm suffocating. Like I'm drowning in a pool of water, I can see the surface, but as much as I kick, I can't break free. I can't breathe.

My father bet me.

The man who was supposed to love me unconditionally, placed a bet and I was the stakes. My heart thumps madly as tears well in my eyes.

Don't cry. Don't cry. Don't cry.

I pull my legs in tight, my arms wrapping around my knees as I begin to rock.

My father doesn't deserve my tears.

I take a deep breath and try to relax; there is more I need to know, and I can't lose it now.

I swallow and find my voice. "You won me?" I choke out. "I'm a game." The tears I thought I had stopped threaten to fall from my eyes.

He shakes his head.

"No. Ivy, I didn't win you in a bet."

I don't understand what he's saying. My mouth feels like it's wired shut, and my throat feels like it's closing, but no matter how much it hurts to open it and speak the words, I do.

"Then who?" Barely audible words, but they come out regardless and he hears them, because he closes his eyes before speaking.

"The Butcher."

The blood in my veins turns to ice, and my whole body starts to shake uncontrollably.

The Butcher.

I belong to The Butcher.

You would have to be living under a rock not to know who The Butcher was.

Even though I don't go out much, I've watched the news enough to know of him.

"Isn't he like Russian mafia or something?"

When I don't speak, he leans forward and buries his head in his hands.

"He is."

"Why would he want me?"

"He takes women."

Thump.

"Sells the lucky ones."

"And the unlucky ones?"

Thump.

"He keeps them for his own sick amusement. They don't call him The Butcher for no reason."

"H-He . . ." I stutter.

"He carves them up, rapes them, and then throws them away when he's done."

Fear slithers in my veins, poisoning and killing off the remainder of peace within my body.

"What does this have to do with you?" I ask. Was he a part of this? Was he holding me for him? I push to stand, my back straight and my body tense. "Are you going to give me to him? Did you have your fun, and now it's time for me to go?"

He stands and comes toward me, but I lift my hands in the air to stop him.

"How can you say that?"

"How can I say that!" I scream. "You kidnapped me. Now you tell me I belong to The Butcher, and you have the nerve to ask me how I could say that. It all makes sense." I take a step back. "You wouldn't touch me, probably because you were scared of The Butcher finding out."

He stalks me like a predator stalking his prey. Grabbing me, he yanks me toward him.

His lips inch toward my ear, his breaths tickling my skin. It sends a shiver down my spine as he speaks. "I'm not scared of him or anyone who tries to take you. And do you want to know why?"

His arms wrap around my front, and he slips his hand into my leggings. When his fingers find my core, he speaks. "Because you're mine. Understand me, Sun. You are mine. Not his. And I will fucking kill him or anyone who tries to take you from me."

I bite my lower lip at his words, stifling the moan threatening to expel.

He parts me with his finger. "Do you understand me?"

My head falls back, and my eyes close. "Tell me you understand, Sun."

I let out a whimper. His fingers stop their ministrations. Instead, they hover over where I need him, teasing, toying, but not breaching. "Tell me."

"I understand," I pant.

"And who do you belong to?"

"No one," I say, and he thrusts his fingers back inside me.

"Wrong answer, Sun." Behind me, I can hear him rummaging to free himself. "Hold on to the tree."

I open my eyes, placing my hand on the tree inches away from us.

He grips me by the waist and pushes me forward to angle my ass up. I'm shaking with need as I wait for him to touch me again.

A primal moan escapes me as he thrusts inside me.

His thrusts are hard and fast.

Violent. He is telling me he owns me.

I'm his.

I arch my back, letting him take me deeper.

One hand lifts from where it is resting on my hip, and he grabs my hair, pulling my head back until his lips find mine.

Our tongues dance together.

The insanity is unlike anything I've ever felt before. Nothing has ever felt like this.

No kiss. No touch.

This is different. *This is primal.*

Desperate.

I need this right now. My world is spinning out of control and I need the power Cyrus yields.

I need the pain. The control. I need him.

My eyes roll back from the frantic need building inside me as he slams into me over and over again.

A wave begins to grow inside me. "*Betatee,*" he growls again, and I'm not sure if it's the way he moves inside me or how he says the words I don't even know, but I fall and crash, spiraling over the edge to oblivion.

He must find his release too because as I return to Earth from my haze, I notice the warmth inside me, and he's stopped moving.

Together, we catch our breaths.

Slowly, he pulls out of me. "I won't let him take you from me."

I straighten my pants.

"I'll protect you." Relying on him isn't easy for me. I've learned over the years that I can't rely on anyone. "Trust me. I will protect you."

I'm not sure he will. I'm not sure anyone can.

CHAPTER FORTY

Cyrus

I TOOK HER LIKE AN ANIMAL AGAINST A TREE.

I don't know what the fuck got into me. Normally, I'm more reserved and don't show my emotions like that. But her doubt made me see red, and all I wanted to do is mark her as my own.

I couldn't control myself. This girl has gotten to me in a way I never predicted or anticipated. I'm not sure how I feel about it. Maybe it's time to go back to my estate and distance myself from her.

Right now, we lie in bed together. We haven't spoken since what happened outside. I'm sure she has a lot to process after what I told her.

The silence stretches around us. It's not unwelcome. I have a lot to think about too.

Last I heard, Boris has gone underground. If I can't find him, I'm not sure how I can accomplish my goal. There has to be a way to draw him out.

"Why?" she asks.

I turn toward her. She's watching me with wide eyes that are red from unshed tears. I can't imagine it's easy to hear that your father has sold you.

No. I know it's not.

"It's time to tell me why you took me."

"Isn't it obvious?" I respond, arching a brow.

"Not to me. You run a poker game, an illegal one. It doesn't seem like you care who plays, so why this? Why me?"

"I saw you . . ." My eyes close on their own accord as I try to remember exactly what went through my head when I did. Why did I take her? It was more than her looks; it was the energy that wafted off her. "Trent asked me to help you."

She sits up from where we are lying and tilts her head in question.

"There has to be more."

She's right; there was. But the idea of saying it tastes bitter on my tongue. It's so far from what I'm feeling now. The fact I even thought it at any point doesn't sit well with me. Ivy Aldridge will never be a means to an end.

Still searching her eyes, I remember the feeling that spread through my chest. That's the real reason, but at the time, I wouldn't admit it. But here and now, with the future so uncertain, I decide to be honest about at least one thing.

"When I finally looked at you, so serene and beautiful, I couldn't fathom a world where you didn't exist. So, I took you."

"But—"

I lift my hand, stopping her. I never thought I would do this, but with her, I find I want to. Looking into her blue eyes, I find myself speaking.

"Let me tell you a story."

"Okay."

"There once was a man and a woman. They were very happy and fell madly in love. This man and woman loved each other so much that they decided to have a baby. They loved the baby and for years tried to have another. Years passed, but it didn't seem like that was in the cards. The man had given up. He was happy, but the woman was desperate. She wanted a son. A son to look like the man she loved. And one day she grew pregnant . . ." My throat feels like it is closing as I push down the emotions swirling inside me. I haven't spoken of this ever, and I find that it's harder to get the words out than I thought.

With a cough, I continue. "When the baby was to come, there was a complication. The mother finally had her son, but as she held him, she took her last breath. The man always resented the boy. He was angry and sad, and started to drink and gamble. After he lost his job, he became even angrier and turned to crime.

"Luckily for the boy, the sister was there to raise him. The father became a criminal, dealing drugs, but often, he did more than he sold. He took loans and owed a Russian billionaire hundreds of thousands of dollars.

"By this point, the little boy was now a young man, and one day, he came home from school, and his sister was gone. He searched everywhere. Then he found his father."

I pause. Ivy must realize this part is harder for me to say because she reaches her hand out and takes mine in hers. With a small squeeze, I continue.

"He was drunk, and when the boy asked him, he said to the boy, 'You took my wife from me, so I took her from you.' It turns out, the girl was sold to a vile man who made her his wife. There was nothing the little boy could do. No one could save her."

"What happened?"

My eyes close. The memories assaulting me as I speak. "She was found dead. Shot in the head." I look at her. "The woman was my sister." She blinks, and that's when one tear escapes her blue eyes. "But more importantly, she was a mother to me. She was my home. She showed me love. She was everything good in the world. Growing up, I knew there was more to life because of her. But her light faded and so did mine. I never saw sunlight until I saw you that day. I saved you because I couldn't save her."

When I stop talking, I wait for her to say something.

But she doesn't.

Instead, I hear a small sniffle.

Pulling back, I see that she's crying. My hand swipes against her face, catching her tears.

"Don't cry for me," I say, my voice gruff and tight from retaining my emotions.

"How could I not?" She lifts her hand and touches my jaw. "You were just a boy."

"It made me a man."

"What happened to your father?" she asks, but I know she probably already knows.

"He's dead."

The unspoken question is there. What kind of man grows up to kill his father?

I'm not sure if she's ready to hear my words, but I tell them anyway. She should know the man she got in bed with. I am no hero. I'm a villain.

"I killed him, and then I took his business contacts and started my bank."

"That's what I don't understand."

"I vowed never to be him. Never to need money so badly that I would resort to that. So, I became the bank, and I don't trade flesh."

"Then why was The Butcher at your game?"

It's a good question, but I'm not ready to tell her that part of the story. So instead, I lean forward and silence her with my mouth.

CHAPTER FORTY-ONE

Ivy

H E REFUSES TO TALK. INSTEAD, HE SHUTS ME UP WITH HIS mouth, but I push back, removing my mouth from his.

"Let me see all of you, Cyrus." I lift my hand to touch his face, to run my fingers along his jaw down to the pulse on his neck. "Please."

I can feel his heartbeat accelerate as it jumps under my skin. There is so much more to Cyrus Reed, and I want to see him, all of him. I know there are levels of depth he doesn't show, but I want to see them. Need to see them.

"You have." He tries to remove my hand, but I shake my head.

"No. I want to see the parts you don't show anyone. The parts that you fear will scare me. I want to know all of you."

"You won't like what you see. The darkness you see."

His deep brown, earnest eyes seek mine. They are dangerously ominous. Somber and full of emotions I can't comprehend, but I want to. I move closer until our lips touch. "Let me be the judge of that." *Kiss.* "What are you hiding from me?"

"I'm a bad man, Sun. I don't deserve to bask in your light. My hands are dirty. They're not clean enough to touch you."

"Not true. You're too blind to see what I see." A sudden chill descends on my words and what he will say next.

"I killed to become the man I am." There is a vulnerability to him when he admits this, and it makes me fall for him even more.

"I know," I whisper back.

"I murdered men."

My head tilts down in contemplation. "Did you murder children?"

"No."

"Women?"

"Fuck no, but that doesn't absolve me of my sin. In order to be powerful, I took the power."

I take his hand in mine. "Why did you need the power?"

"For vengeance," he responds, his face clouded with unease. "But I am no saint. I didn't do it just for that. I now control the underworld. I'm the one who holds the coin for the most powerful men in the world, and in turn, I rule everyone."

I shake my head and then kiss his fingers. "Say what you will, but you won't convince me otherwise."

"It started off as a way to have the power to save my sister," he admits on a sigh, defeated.

"It was your father's job. You were just a boy. But you see, this is why there might be blood tainting you, but it will never consume you. You are a good man, Cyrus." His hand drops from mine, but this time, I reach my hand out and trail my finger over a scar that tarnishes his chest. There is one round one that looks like it was caused by a bullet. I had noticed it before, but never felt comfortable asking about it. "This scar—"

"Is my monster."

"No. That is your hope. It is your strength. It is your love. Each scar on your body *inside* and out was placed there because you loved your sister enough to try not to let this ever happen again."

My fingers trail over his stomach, up his torso.

I touch his jagged scar first, then I drop a kiss on it followed by the rest of his chest. To all his exposed skin, blemished and unblemished. Because I know that even behind the muscle are scars I can't even comprehend. There are stories that Cyrus believes makes him a monster, but I know the truth. They might tell a story, but they tell the story of a boy who lost everything. A boy who deserves love.

The scars didn't take away from his beauty. Even with them littering the surface of his skin, he's still beautiful. If anything, now that he told me a little bit about each one, he is more beautiful.

When I finally reach his mouth with mine, he kisses me. He kisses me like I'm the last bit of oxygen before he dies.

"Your father never deserved a daughter like you. You're beautiful, Sun."

He kisses my lip. "*Gamilla,*" he whispers as he flips me over so he's on top of me.

"What?" I question.

"It means beautiful." Then his lips find my jaw. "*Amar.* Gorgeous." His lips trail over my throat. He kisses the hollow of my neck. "*Noor Eineya.* The light of my eyes." And then he places his lips on my heart. "*Tu es à moi.*" His words cause my heart to swell, making me want to give that boy my love.

But can I?

He says he's a monster, and I know he's not.

But is he mine to love?

Will he ever be?

He took me for the right reasons to protect me, but what happens next?

Will he love me?

Can he?

Or like the list of women in his closet, will my name just be added?

When I wake up the next morning, I find Cyrus's part of the bed empty. Without him here, it feels like a blinding fog has lifted from my eyes.

Last night still lingers in the air. All the truths we spoke, and what it means for the future.

I'm falling for Cyrus Reed. A part of me already has, but there is one part that can't reconcile the man who took me, who kept me here all these months.

What do I really know about him?

A lot, actually.

Probably more than most.

He told me about his job, about his sister.

But still, something feels unsaid.

I stand from the bed and grab his button-down shirt that lays on the chair. Once it's buttoned, I head into his closet.

Last night, I was consumed with him and his demons, but now in the light of the day, the things I tried to push away come rushing back in.

The list.

I never asked him what it meant.

How can I move forward without knowing what this means?

Sitting on the floor, I pull the box out from where it is hidden and start to rummage through it again.

Cyrus caught me the last time, but this time, I will ask him point-blank what the list is. Who are the women?

I need to know.

So many feelings are circulating through my body. Feelings burst out of me, but I can't let them take root and grow, not until I have all the truths.

Not until I know what this is.

He says beautiful words I don't really understand.

He makes love to my body and touches my soul. It would be so easy to fall in love with him, to admit that this is what I am feeling, but until I know that I am not another notch on his belt or, better yet, another name on a list, I need to tamp down the feelings that threaten to spill forth from my heart.

I need to erect those walls.

Because once they come down, once I give every last part of myself to Cyrus, I'm not sure I will ever be able to rebuild them again.

I'm there for a while, on the floor of the closet, staring. When I hear the sound of a gasp behind me.

The woman.

The one I haven't seen in weeks, ever since Cyrus started feeding me himself, is here.

I look up at her like a deer in headlights, but she's not looking at me. She's looking at the picture in my hand. I follow her line of vision, from her to the photograph, that's when I finally see it.

Why the woman looked familiar.

Much younger, but still recognizable.

It's her.

Pulling out his list of names, I see Mariana. Wasn't that what Cyrus referred to her as?

My heart starts to hammer in my chest.

Does he employ his ex? Or is it worse than that? I can feel the muscles in my stomach contract as bile threatens to rise. A new thought pops into my head; a dark and disturbing thought that chills me to the bone.

Is she his captive too?

Was everything a lie?

No.

It couldn't have been.

The blood thumping through my veins makes me feel dizzy and weak. I fear I might pass out.

Last night, we broke down walls, and he told me his truth. There has to be more.

"It's not what you think," she says, and I look up at her, my mouth hanging open when she does.

"You-you speak English," I stutter. "But . . . why?" Then it hits me in the chest. "Cyrus." It all makes sense, yet makes no sense at all. Why wouldn't he want me to speak with her? Was he trying to isolate me? Did he not want me to know I am one of many?

She steps forward and shakes her head. "It's not what you think."

"Oh, no. Because to me, it sure does look like it." I gesture to the pictures. "To me, it looks like Cyrus is full of shit, and he took me because he likes to take women. Not protect them." The pain that radiates through my body is not like anything I have ever felt before. "Was it all lie?" I feel like I'm drowning. As if cold water is slowly filling my lungs. "Did my father—"

"Stop," her voice cuts in. "Mr. Reed is a good man. He saved you. Just like he saved me." She rolls up the sleeves over her arms. "He saved you from my fate."

The scars on her arms scream at me that there is a truth so much bigger than even I can fathom.

"Those women, he saved all of them in some way or an-other. Some from poverty. Some from being so hungry that they were going to sell themselves on the street. Others from drugs. And for me, he saved me from a fate worse than death."

"Boris?" I whisper.

"No. This was my husband's doing. He was an abusive man who worked for Cyrus. Cyrus didn't know at first that he beat me, cut me, burned me. But once he did . . . Cyrus lost someone close to him, and he vowed to help women who couldn't help themselves."

My eyes widen as her words hit me in the gut.

Each woman on this list represented something that reminded him of his sister. He saved them because he couldn't save her.

Like me.

He never was lying.

He really was protecting me.

"Cyrus Reed is a good man," she says again as she moves to leave the closet.

He helps women.

Now that I'm alone again, my mind is going a million miles a minute.

Standing, I place all the pictures and the list back in the box and leave the room.

I need to go for a walk and think about all I learned today. Stopping in my room, or at least what used to be my room, I grab a pair of leggings and slip them on, then socks and shoes.

Now that it's April, the weather should be nice enough to not need to have a coat, especially with Cyrus's long sleeve button-down on.

Fresh air will do me good.

On my way out of the house, I pass by Cyrus's office, but it's empty. Mariana must have heard me come down because she walks up behind me.

"He's not here." Her voice startles me. There is a long, brittle silence that stretches between us as I think of a response. She lied, which means Cyrus probably lied. What else could he be lying about?

My mouth opens and shuts, like a guppy trying to eat food. All I muster out is an, "Oh?"

"Yeah, when you were sleeping, he headed back to the house. That's when I was dropped off."

A part of me wants to leave the room without asking the question that burns on my tongue because ignorance is bliss after all. But that's not the girl I am, so I incline my head, narrowing my eyes at her.

"Why didn't you tell me you spoke English?" I ask.

"Cyrus was worried I would tell you the truth about your father."

"Wasn't that my right?"

"It is, but—" She stops herself, swallowing and then meeting my gaze. "He thought he was doing right by you."

I nod, and then walk past her. "I'm going for a walk."

Cerberus chooses that moment to walk up to me. Well trained. "Kom," I say to him, and he follows me outside.

I don't mind him coming, though. He makes me feel safe and cared for.

I had started to feel that way about Cyrus, but all the lies, or omissions of truth, still sit heavy in my heart.

By the time Cerberus and I make it up the hill through the trees to the clearing, my mind has started to clear.

Once I'm sitting, I stare out at the ocean. It's vast, but in the distance, a small glimpse of land appears. Where it all started. How I got here?

He did everything to protect you.

As if the air has cleared me, I feel emotions I have not felt in a long time. For so long, I have been the only one looking out for myself, but now, Cyrus has shown me he too has.

I feel special. Cherished. Loved.

Love?

I never thought I would feel this way, but Cyrus has shown me so much. My chest flutters as an overwhelming feeling pours through every molecule of my being.

Until I can't not say the words out loud.

"I love Cyrus Reed."

Even if he's a monster, he's my monster, and I love him.

CHAPTER FORTY-TWO

Cyrus

As per usual, I'm working. Which, unfortunately, means leaving Ivy alone in my bed. I had to head back to the estate to get some files, but now I'm back, knee deep in shit.

Holding the money for the mafia would be a full-time job as it is, but couple it with the fact that I also do business with the cartel and arms dealers, and it could take two lifetimes to do what I do.

It's why I'm so damn successful. Because I have no life.

Well, that's not true. Recently, I have finally let myself indulge a bit, but today, even though I'm still on the island with Ivy, there is plenty to be done for my clients.

Turning dirty money clean isn't as easy as everyone thinks. But luckily, I am damn fucking good at what I do.

Today, I'm helping broker a deal between Alaric and Matteo.

Alaric has guns, and Matteo needs guns. Although this isn't my typical day's work, it benefits me regardless.

Not only do I make money off Alaric's deposit with the interest I charge for him to keep his money in my bank, but I also get a cut of the sale.

Think of it like a finder's fee or kickback. Whatever the fuck it is, just money in my pocket.

"Are you busy?" I hear from the doorway.

Yes. I want to say, but I can't. Not when my eyes meet hers.

She's so fucking stunning, and it knocks the words right out of my mouth. Her hair is pulled back in a disheveled bun on the top of her head.

There is something dark on her nose, though.

I stand and make my way to her.

"What's this?" I swipe the dirt off.

"I was gardening."

"Oh, were you now?" But then it dawns on me where she was, and my jaw tightens.

She drops her head, her blond hair falling over her face as she looks at me through the wisps. The way she stares is unnerving. She is really looking at me, like she can see past every lie I have ever spewed.

I'm not sure how I feel about it. In the past, I would have hated it. Fuck, if anyone else looked at me like this, I would, but when Ivy does, it's different.

"Why do you hate it?" she asks, her voice low and uncertain that she can talk about this.

Feelings. God, I fucking hate them, but just thinking about going in there brings them up.

I shake my head and walk past her, toward the door. This is not something I want to get into right now.

"Cyrus." I stop and turn to look at her over my shoulder. "What is it?" she asks.

"It was hers," I grit.

She looks at me with confusion, but then it must hit her because her eyes go wide.

"Your sister's."

"I lied when I said I bought this home because of the proximity to my estate. This was my family's summer home." I bury my hands in my pockets.

"Can I tell you something?" she asks, and I don't answer, so she continues. "When I was a little girl, my mother taught me how to garden, but as I got older, I didn't like to go out there with her anymore. I wanted to live my life. It wasn't until she had her mental breakdown and I came back home to live with her, to take care of her, that I stepped foot in a garden again. I was eighteen. The first time I stepped foot in it, I sobbed. I lost it right there because everything reminded me of the mom I lost. Then I pushed past the pain, and I started to dig. It was hard at first, but as I planted my first seed, I remembered her smile. I remembered the jokes she used to tell when she was happy. From that moment on, it no longer made me sad."

She pauses, and I see a tear in her eyes. I lift my hand and catch it.

"When the flowers bloomed that summer, my mom spoke to me. A woman who hadn't spoken to me in months spoke. From then on out, I knew the pain was worth it. Let me show you."

I think about her words for a while and then with reluctance reach out to her. Hand in hand, she leads me to the greenhouse. As soon as I step in, the smell hits me. The smell that reminds me of Sybil.

She's everywhere in this room. So much so, I feel like I'm suffocating.

"I have to leave," I say, emotions clogging my lungs.

"Let me help you," she says, and she hands me the shovel and leads me to a fresh pot filled with dirt.

"This dirt is the beginning of something new. Think of your sister, of all she thought of you, and of how she protected you, and grow something in her honor."

I close my eyes, afraid to show emotions, but with my eyes closed, I see everything Ivy said I would see.

I see my sister laughing, smiling, living.

Opening my eyes, I dig. I break through the earth, through the pain. I can feel my eyes becoming moist, but I don't cry. Instead, I live.

After divulging so much to Ivy, I sequester myself back in my office. It's not that I said much, but she saw a part of me I have never shown anyone before. It felt like I took a knife, cut my heart open, and bled all over the dirt I planted in.

Feeling vulnerable is not a feeling I like to have, nor is it one I want a repeat performance of. Which leads me to the here and now, sitting behind my desk under the guise of working.

You're avoiding her.

I'm building my walls back up because I will be useless to her in this state. It's bad enough that I have yet to come up with a viable plan on how to bring the asshole down.

My fingers drum on the wood surface of my desk. The one thing I know is I have to be smart about it. He won't come out for just anything. He's heavily guarded at all times.

It's not something I can't do, but it's not ideal.

My thoughts are cut off by the sound of footsteps, I look up to see Ivy leaning in the doorframe.

"Penny for your thoughts." She smiles.

"There isn't enough money in the world to tell you some of the terrors, I think."

Her smile fades, turning into a thin and tight line. "What can I do to help you?"

"Take my mind off things." Before she can object, I motion to the chessboard. "Play me?"

"Okay." Her voice is low.

The board is set up, and I let her go first. She's gotten better. Her moves are calculated, and analytical. She's no longer thinking in the present, she's steps ahead. She maneuvers her pieces around the board as if she were playing for years, the way I would have if I were her.

When it's my turn, my brain is not here, I'm far off, thinking of what the future will be. But that's my demise, because my mistake will be her win.

Again, it's her turn, and I follow, but it's too late for me.

"Check," she says, surprising me yet again.

The thing to remember is even acting on the best plan can bring a negative outcome. I thought I knew the right move, but in the end, Ivy backed me into a corner.

It reminds of taking Ivy. At the time, I thought I saw five steps ahead, but I could never anticipate how I would feel for her down the line, how much I would want to protect her. She might have been the pawn, but the more I know her, the more I see her as much more.

She's the queen.

———— • ————

An hour later, she's gone to garden and I'm picking up my phone, Z answers. "You ready for the boat?" I can hear the bite in his voice. He's not happy.

He doesn't understand why I'm dragging my feet. Why I haven't solved shit yet.

Good thing I'm the boss, so he really doesn't have to understand.

"Not yet."

"It's time, boss."

"Oh, so you do remember who's boss?"

He's silent, and I think he might cut his losses and not push his agenda. I know he has one. It's not much different from mine. We all have our own, but ours just run in the same direction. It's actually how Z came to be my employee.

"We going to use the girl?" he asks.

The idea of using Ivy doesn't sit well with me. Not after everything. She makes me feel too much, and while a part of me hates that she has opened up this part of me that I've wanted closed, I'm not willing to risk her.

"No," I answer.

"It's a solid plan to lure him in. He's keeping her for himself . . ."

"We don't know that," I respond back.

"She's his type. We have to use this to our advantage. Give her to him."

My fists ball on my desk. There is no way I will let that happen. "No."

"Why not?"

The sound of my hands banging on the desk echoes through the room. Loud. Violent. But the idea makes me want to kill someone. Anger spreads through every molecule of my body, reminding me of a fire. Scorching, blistering, and burning.

"He can't have her," I grit.

Z needs to shut the fuck up. He's lucky he's nowhere near me right now, or I would bash his head in.

"It will never be done until we stop him. You will never have peace . . ."

"That might be the case, but I won't."

"He would come. Then we—"

"Enough!" I shout, before taking a deep breath to calm the raging inferno building inside me. "Using her is a last resort."

I understand the merit of his suggestion, and once upon a time, I suggested it too, but it makes me fucking livid now. It makes me want to rip someone apart, or better yet, it makes me want to grab a gun and shoot someone in the head.

"Just think about it," he presses.

"She would make good bait." I'm about to tell him why it doesn't matter, though, when I hear an audible gasp.

Before I can object, I look up to see Ivy running toward the door. I bolt after her, grabbing her by her arm to stop her.

"It's not what you think," I say, and she shakes her head, pushing my hands out to escape my grasp.

"I don't care." She looks down at the ground, but I don't miss the way her jaw trembles from unspoken emotions. I place my fingers under her chin to lift her gaze to meet mine.

"It's not like that. You aren't bait."

"But I was." She lifts her eyebrow, challenging me to object.

Unfortunately, I can't. She's right.

Originally, the thought had crossed my mind. Had I not become so enamored by her, she probably would be.

I don't speak because what is there to say. She might not be here to be bait, but I would be lying if I tell her otherwise, and I never lie. I'm a lot of things . . .

A crook.

A criminal.

A murderer.

A villain.

A liar isn't one of them.

She shakes her head side to side; the movement making my hands drop.

"It's fine. You said you weren't a nice man when you took me. You held me here. You never lied. I'm the idiot who thought there was more."

"Sun."

"No, don't 'Sun' me." She air quotes. "You were always the villain, but I just forgot. It's fine."

I step toward her, and she steps away.

"It was a fun distraction." She shrugs, then turns away from me. "Don't you have work to do? Go back to your castle and leave me alone."

She doesn't wait for me to say anything else before she turns and sets off up toward the high point. The same point where I told her the truth.

I grab my cell from my pocket. "Send the boat."

"For both of you?"

"Mariana too."

He's quiet, and I wonder if he will tell me to bring her and set a plan in motion. He thinks she is bait.

She's not.

She's so much more than that.

CHAPTER FORTY-THREE

Ivy

MY HEARTBEAT IS ERRATIC. I FEEL LOST, AS IF I'M A floating balloon lifting off the ground, and I'm not sure how I'll ever be grounded again.

It's hard to walk away.

Each step feels more painful than the last.

That's the problem with falling in love with a criminal. He might not have meant to hurt me, but he did anyway.

Bait.

I was meant to be bait. Even though a part of me knows the truth—that he would never use me as bait—it still hurts to hear it.

Regardless of how I feel about him, I have to leave. I can't stay. My walls need to be up. It will hurt. Because we have an expiration date.

So I do. My eyes fill with tears. I already miss the feeling he brings out in me.

It's over.

It's time to walk away and let him go. It's time for me to figure out a plan, but that's a little harder. As much as I hate it, I need his help. I'll discuss it with him once we've both cooled down. The thing is, I wasn't off.

He was using me. But in the end, I know deep down something changed. He didn't deserve my words. When he comes back, I'll say I'm sorry. I will walk away, though. It will hurt, and I'll miss him. I'll miss what he makes me feel. But it's time to go home and live my life. Not that I have much to go back to.

A father who sold me.

Shit.

I haven't had time to even process that.

My feet take me up to the spot on the top of the island. I stand in the same place where he opened up to me only days ago. I shake my head. He wouldn't have opened up to me if things hadn't changed between us.

Obviously, it had to mean something.

But my defense mechanism kicked in, and I didn't let him explain. I look down at the ocean. A boat in the distance.

He must not have left yet.

If I go now, I can apologize.

I know he's not a good guy, but I don't think he'd hurt me.

No.

I know he won't. I was a fool for saying what I said.

Maybe.

Maybe I can catch him.

I start to head back down the hill. Through the trees and shrubs. My pace picks up.

Almost there. I dash forward.

Thump. Thump.

The boat is approaching. My gaze skates the distance. He should be somewhere near, but I can't find him. Maybe I beat him here. Just as I'm making it through the clearing, I see someone emerging from the boat. I take a step back on instinct. Slowly, to not be seen.

The sound of my shoe hitting a fallen branch screams into the silence.

Fuck.

My gaze is still forward, praying this stranger didn't hear, but his head rises.

Dark, menacing eyes meet mine, and the left side of his mouth tips up, showing teeth in a snarl.

"Hello, Ivy. It's about time we become acquainted."

Without another thought, I turn around, dashing toward the house. Cerberus is inside, if I can get to him, he will protect me. Now I'm alone with this man, and I don't need an introduction to know exactly who that man was. Boris.

A man known to cut up his victims. As I head back to the estate, branches and twigs scrape against my limbs, cutting into my skin.

Burning.

But I don't let that stop me.

I need to find Cyrus. I need to get away.

But then my stomach drops. If that boat wasn't for Cyrus, that must mean Cyrus isn't on the island.

I run faster. My legs burning with pain.

I can't hear his footsteps behind me over the pounding of my heart.

It rattles violently in my chest, telling me to go faster.

Run harder.

I don't need to hear him, though, to know he's gaining on me. I can feel it in my bones. In the ice that travels through my veins.

I don't stop, though. I push past the pain. Through the aches and scrapes. I'm so close.

I can see the large oak door. If I can just get to the door.

What?

What will I do? I'm stuck here.

No weapons.

No escape.

I push down the thoughts and keep going.

I'm not weak. I will never be weak. I will fight with everything I have before I let him take me.

I'm there. So close. My hand reaches out, and my fingertips touch the cold knob. But then I'm slammed forward. My head ricocheting off the wood that should have been my salvation. I can't see the blood, but I can feel the bite of my flesh ripping. His hands bracket around me, pulling my limp body to his. Bile travels up my throat. A ringing sound echoes in my ear.

"You will be fun to break," he whispers in my ear.

Making my stomach roil. A metallic taste infiltrates my mouth.

No.

I can't let him take me.

"Get your hands off me."

I kick.

I shout.

I throw my head back. But it doesn't stop him from grabbing me and pulling me toward the boat.

My arms burn in the sockets, and I'm sure if I fight harder, I'll dislocate my shoulders.

I try to struggle, but it's no use. It's hopeless as he throws me on board. My body grabbed by another man as The Butcher pulls my arms behind my back and secures them with zip ties.

He looks down at me.

There is nothing but malice in his eyes.

I had thought Cyrus was a monster, but this man is truly one.

Cyrus.
My gaze turns the island as the boat pulls away.
Will he look for me?
Will he find me?
Will he even care?

CHAPTER FORTY-FOUR

Cyrus

I SHOULD HAVE ANSWERED HER. I SHOULD HAVE TOLD HER the truth. But the words died on my tongue. What could I have said anyway?

Truth.

A part of me did want to use her.

Fact.

But that changed, and I should have told her. Another truth, I didn't want to. A dark feeling spread through my chest at the accusation.

How could she doubt me? I had borne my inner turmoil to her. She saw my demons and embraced them only turn me away. Did I deserve it? Fuck yes.

But it didn't make the pill any less bitter to swallow. So here I am, with my head up my own ass, avoiding her.

A grown-ass man.

A man who fucking holds the money and fortunes of the world's worst men in my hands, and I'm hiding from a little girl.

A girl who makes you feel.

Sun.

She started off as a poison in my life, a means to an end, a sick obsession I needed to exploit for my own gains, then she became someone to protect, someone to care about, someone to cherish.

How the fuck did I let it get this bad?

Never did I think this type of distraction was in the cards for me.

Z is actually right. I have an objective, and playing around with a girl, no matter how beautiful and alive she makes me feel, is a bad idea.

I open my computer, checking the figures in a few off-shore accounts. Then I fire off an email to Trent, letting him know his sister is okay and checking in on the millions of dollars I have him investing for me and my clients. Holding their money isn't enough. Increasing and cleaning is why they come.

An hour passes before I can no longer pretend my mind isn't elsewhere. I wonder what she's doing.

Is she still pissed at me? Or has she calmed enough for me to explain? If she knew the truth, how would she feel?

Why am I acting like a little bitch? Because she means something to me, and I don't want to hurt her.

The truth is, she means so much more than I will ever admit, and the thought scares the fuck out of me.

A gun to my head doesn't scare me this bad.

I stand from my desk because there's no reason to pretend I'll get shit done. Stalking out of the office, I go in search for Z. When I find him, he's pacing the drawing room, looking out to the ocean.

"Tell Maxwell to bring the boat around." Z's body stiffens at my voice before turning around and facing me.

"You're going back?"

I cock my head at him, daring him to say something else. His jaw is tight. He doesn't agree with my decision to keep her. By the tic under his eye, I know he wants to tell me that.

He's not happy.

We have always seen eye to eye on what to do about business and other shit, really. He thinks she's a distraction.

Well, he's right. She is.

But I don't fucking care.

He nods his head and then shakes it in disbelief before he stalks off to get the boat. Now alone, I look toward the island. I'm going to have to let her go, but I need to see if Trent has settled shit with Boris yet for his father.

Pulling out my cell, I make the call.

"Cyrus," he answers.

"Do you have the money?" I ask. There's no reason to pretend we like each other. No reason to keep up the false pretenses.

"I do."

I don't want to know how he came up with that money right now, but I'm sure it's not something too far off from what I deal with.

Trent's resourceful.

He probably has a Ponzi scheme going. As long as it's not with the money he's taking care of for me, I don't give a fuck.

I will gut him if it is, but he knows better than that.

"Have your father call Boris and set up the drop. Once it's done, I'll release your sister. But if I ever see him in my house. If I ever hear—"

"I know."

"I won't hesitate to kill him, and then after, I will kill you for allowing it to happen."

"I know."

With that out of the way, I hang up. There is no question in my mind that if this man puts Ivy in danger—I don't care if she loves him—I will torture him slowly. Very fucking slowly.

I might not be The Butcher, but I'm just as fucking lethal. Killing and torturing when I need to.

The sound of shoes in the hall has me pulling my gaze away from the window and back to Z.

"Ready?"

"Yep," he responds, his voice tight with anger.

Z has a massive fucking stick up his ass, but I don't give two shits. If he has a problem with me, he can keep that shit to himself. I don't pay him for his opinions.

I pay him to have my back.

Having my back means shutting the fuck up, getting my goddamn boat, and taking me to my girl.

My girl.

Shit.

When the fuck did I start referring to Ivy Aldridge as that?

The faster that fuck Trent pays off Boris, the faster I can send her back and stop this insanity.

Once on the boat, it doesn't take long with the wind.

I'm not sure how long I'll stay this time, but since the meet is happening soon, I make a new plan.

"Stay by the dock." Maxwell nods, and Z turns to face me. "Trent is making the exchange, so I see no reason why she can't come back to the house with me tonight."

There is that tic again.

"Do you have something you want to say?" I level him with my stare.

"No, boss."

Once we pull up to the dock, I head up to the house.

I'm about to open the door when I notice a faint red mark.

Is that blood?

My stomach drops, and I wonder if after I left, she hurt

herself on her walk. Throwing open the door, I don't expect her to come running into my arms, but I do expect to find her on the main floor.

Ever since we reached an accord when I got hurt, she no longer secludes herself in the bedroom. I walk through all the rooms on the main floor, yet no one is there.

I go into my room next.

Nothing.

Maybe she's so pissed she's in her old room. When I swing the door open, I find nothing at all. The feeling that hit me when I saw the blood starts to intensify.

If she's hurt, where could she be?

I go to walk back outside when Cerberus runs out of the house. Maybe he knows where Ivy is, but instead of stopping, he runs off barking. He heads in the direction of the beach.

I follow him.

Running behind as he barks.

The first thought is that, once again, she tried to escape. She tried to leave me.

But when I get to where the beach starts, every muscle in my back tightens.

Footprints.

They are not hers. They are much larger. Another set trail as if she was being dragged.

Emotions I thought I had buried deep within me rise to the surface.

I can't push it down.

Before her, I didn't feel, but now that I have met her, found her, and lost her, I can't control myself.

The raw emptiness inside me was finally starting to fill with her in my presence, and now it feels like a knife has stabbed me, emptying once again but unlike before when I closed off the pain, this time, the pain is real and tangible.

I head back to the boat.

Both my men look at me. They instantly draw their guns and are on high alert.

"She's gone."

"What? How. . .?" Maxwell asks.

"I don't fucking know!" I scream. "I want all the surveillance tapes. Get me the fuck home and find out how that fucker found her."

The ride back is tense.

No one speaks.

When I'm finally back in the house, my worst nightmare comes true. There is nothing on the cameras. A glitch, whatever the fuck that means.

"Fuck!" I bellow as my fist flies through the air, punching the wall. The plaster concaves in, leaving behind a bloody hole.

Not knowing what else to do, I call Trent.

"Hello," he answers.

"Did you give him the money?"

"What? No. Not yet. I can't get through to him."

"He has her. That's why he doesn't need your fucking money. He fucking has her."

"Who?"

"Boris."

The line goes quiet. My heart tightens in my chest. "What the fuck am I going to do?" My hard voice cuts through the silence. I'm not usually at a loss, but this time, I am. I don't know.

"How did he find her?"

"I don't know, but I'm sure as shit going to find out."

A part of me always knew this was a possibility, and even Z had mentioned it. Using her was a good way to lure him in. Finish him and everything he stood for.

But I never anticipated what she would mean to me.

She's my sun.

I realize now I was just fooling myself.

With a deep inhale, I calm all my nerves. This is not who I am. I tamp down any emotion I have for her because I won't let them blind me to what I need to do.

This is a war now.

He came onto my property and took something that was mine. Because yes, Sun, Ivy, is mine. And I'm going to get her back. I will use every last resource I have. It's time to do that.

I grab my phone and dial the one man you need standing beside you during a battle.

Matteo Amante.

"Cyrus Reed, to what do I owe the honor? It's not often you call unless . . . is everything okay with the money?"

"Yes, Matteo. This is actually a different matter. A personal matter."

The line goes silent. It's as if he is weighing his options of whether to humor me on this. We have worked together for a few years, but I have never called in a favor. This is practically unheard of. Cyrus Reed doesn't ask for help, nor does he help others. At least not for free.

My reputation is what precedes me and why men fear me.

"Now you have me intrigued."

Of course, he's intrigued, and at this point, I'm desperate. Not a good combination.

"I need your help," I say on a sigh. Bitter words. An even more bitter pill to swallow.

"More intrigued." This time, he chuckles. Not good. He will bleed me dry for his help.

"Something of mine was taken. And I need your help to get it back."

"Old friend, I would love to help you . . ." He trails off.

"But it will cost me."

"I can't be doing business for free."

The fact that he's right sucks, but it's the nature of the beast. I wish there was another way, but I'm all out of options.

"I respect that. Consider yourself interest-free for your next deposit."

"Life."

"One year."

"Five."

"Deal."

Five years interest-free comes out to a shit ton of money, but her life is priceless to me.

The next phone call I have to make is going to be harder, but some things don't add up. I hit the contact on my phone and wait.

"Cyrus," Alaric answers.

"Did you do it?" I ask.

"Do what?"

"Did you sell me out?"

"What? Fuck, no. What the hell are you talking about, man?"

I lean forward in my chair. "The island."

"One, I have no fucking clue what you're talking about. Two, think really carefully about your next words will be. They very well may be your last."

I consider myself a good judge of character, and nothing in

his pitch indicates he's lying. I let out a deep breath. "If that's the case, I need your help."

"Cyrus, we have worked together a long time, and out of respect for those years, I won't kill you for questioning me . . ."

He's right, and I know he's right.

In this business, you're only as good as your honor, and by questioning his, I should be a dead man. I won't apologize because that's not me, but I fucked up by accusing him before I had proof. Ivy's disappearance is making me act recklessly.

"Thank you."

"Tell me what the fuck is going on, and how I can help." The fact that Alaric is willing to help after what I accused him of speaks of his integrity. I'm not sure I would be that forgiving. I'll owe him, but somehow that fact doesn't bother me.

"I need guns and I'm prepared to offer you the same deal I gave Matteo."

"Which is?"

"No interest for five years."

"Done. What else?"

"Care to go to war?" I ask, and he chuckles through the phone at my request.

"Where and when. I'll be there."

War it is.

CHAPTER FORTY-FIVE

Ivy

I BLINK A FEW TIMES TO HELP MY EYES ADJUST TO THE DARK. As the room starts to focus and the foggy haze that I've been in dissipates, confusion sets in. I'm staring at a wall. On a bed?

My head is pounding. My muscles ache. Where the hell am I?

Something bites at my skin when I try to move. That's when I realize I can't move.

A scream escapes my mouth.

"Help." I kick myself up and try to leave the bed, but I don't make it far, only a mere foot before a wave of nausea hits, making me retch.

I move in the opposite direction, trying to find something to illuminate the room.

The shackles bite my skin, rattling every time I try to move.

Where am I? I try to move again, but my distance is limited. I need to try to get them off. Sitting back down, I try to pull at them, but it's impossible. They are on too tight, and even if I could manage to get out, I'm too dizzy to escape.

I must have lost more blood than I thought.

Lifting my chained arm, I touch my head. I rub at my temples and then bring it back down. Dried, caked-on blood is present on my fingertips.

The throbbing intensifies; the pain is too intense.

Tears run unbidden down my cheeks. I swipe them away.

I move to stand off the bed, but even that is too much. I'm feeling light-headed and all I have managed to do is sit up. I wrack my brain for memories of what happened to me.

Tears roll down my cheeks as it comes crashing back.

My fight with Cyrus. The boat.

Boris.

He found me.

And now I'm chained to a bed, waiting for him to come back. To hurt me. I bring my knees to my chest and rock back and forth. What am I going to do? My head shakes violently.

Fight.

You will fight. You will fight even if it's with your last breath.

My body slumps to the cold bed. I don't have enough energy to stand, plus I'm not sure how much distance I can even go, but I need to try.

How to get out of here.

I don't even want to know why there is a bed in this place. What is this place?

My breathing picks up, and I will myself to calm.

That is, until I hear something. My grip tightens on my chains.

The door squeaks, and a glimmer of light appears in the dark room. Fear bursts through my veins like ice-cold water from a faucet.

Thump. Thump. Thump.

My heart beats so hard it might explode. I might pass out.

No. I can't. If I pass out . . .

The door opens. More light streams in and a large figure strides closer to me. I recognize him, and it makes bile form in my mouth when I see what he's holding. In Boris's hand is a knife. But it's not just any knife. No, it's a butcher knife. I move away from him, launching my body as far away as I can.

I refuse to scream again, though. There is no way I will give the maniac that. My screams are his aphrodisiac, and I won't give in.

There must be a way out. I might lose a part of myself in the process, but I will get away.

Or I will die trying.

"Here," the bastard says as he throws me a bottle of water. I don't want to drink it. Fuck, I don't want anything from this monster, but my mouth is parched, and I have to keep my strength up if I have any shot of ever getting out . . .

Grabbing the bottle, I drink it way too fast, choking on the water and coughing it back up.

It settles in my stomach, making it turn.

Once I swallow, I look back up at him.

He steps closer, and I can see the look in his eyes as he looks me up and down.

His gaze makes me feel ill as it settles on my breasts.

"Too bad," he says as he steps closer. "I would have liked to fuck you, but *he* wants you for himself. He wants to see what's so special about the girl who brought Cyrus Reed to his knees."

My shoulders drop for a second at his words, but when he lifts up the knife, they tense again.

Adrenaline floods my blood as I wait. Beating fast and heavy. Making me feel dizzy. Saliva thickens in my throat as each second passes.

"But just because I won't be able to, doesn't mean I won't ruin you. I'm still allowed to play and since you aren't being picked up for a few days, we can have some uninterrupted fun."

I won't scream.

I won't scream.

I won't scream.

Fear chokes me like a tight necklace around my neck. Cutting off my supply of oxygen, he approaches me like a cheetah, faster than I can ever imagine. My chains are tightening in his arms as he reaches into his back pocket and pulls out another set. This time, I'm stuck in place, and I won't be able to move.

I kick and try to break the chains, but as I'm secured tighter to the bed, I know it's futile. I won't break out.

The first slice comes. Breaking through my efforts. My shoulder burns from where he left the gash. His blade hovers against my skin. Across my shoulders, down my bicep.

Slash.

Slash.

Slash.

My breath comes out choppy. Liquid dripping from where I was cut.

I pray it will end soon.

CHAPTER FORTY-SIX

Cyrus

TWO DAYS.

Two long days.

I haven't eaten. I haven't showered. I haven't fucking slept. Time drags on in a never-ending loop. It melds together like a form of torture.

I wish I didn't care.

I wish I didn't feel.

But this girl changed everything. All I can think about is her. What he's doing to her. If he's broke her. I know I'm too late. He will have taken all the parts I love . . .

My movements stop.

Fuck.

My hand lifts to my head.

Love.

I fucking love this girl.

Slowly, she pulled me from my darkness. She has shown me what it is to bask in the light again. I stand from my chair. The legs scrape against the floor as I head to where my men are.

I find them where they have been for days, except this time, Jaxson Price is here too. He's supposed to be one of the best hackers out there. He better be, because I need him to find Ivy.

He's using the intel Matteo has gotten to pinpoint the GPS location of Boris's phone. Apparently, the thing is not turned on, and when it is, it's untraceable. But I know if anyone can find her, it's him.

Alaric is also working with them to try to lure Boris in with a new shipment of guns, and Tobias is here as well. Pays to have the mafia and the most ruthless men on speed dial.

"I got something," Jaxson announces, pivoting in his chair to look at me.

I step closer to where he's sitting in the room. "What?" I'm in his face now. I know I shouldn't be, but I am. As if I think threatening Jaxson Price will get her back any faster.

I'm a fucking mess.

"Here." He points at one of the computer monitors in the surveillance room. "When Boris called to schedule the pickup of the guns, he pinged this location."

"Yeah. We know this, but there are too many buildings."

"I hacked into a satellite."

"Your point?" I have no idea what he's going on about, but if he could just get to it. So much time has been wasted already. We need to find her. I'm about to bark at him that he needs to clarify when he lifts a hand and points at the screen.

"See the red?" In front of me on one of the monitors is what appears to be a building. The image is a live feed taken from above. There are small red dots moving around. "That's a heat index," he clarifies. "There are bodies moving in that building."

"How do we know it's them?"

"We don't."

"I'm going." Trent stands.

And I follow him out the door, grabbing his shoulder. "No, you go in there, you die. I won't have that shit on my shoulders because when I get Ivy back, she will have my balls if I let her brother die for this shit."

He lets out a long-drawn-out sigh. "Then what?"

"I'll go in. With my men. You'll stay here."

"I—"

I lift my hand. "She will need to know you are safe. You are staying here."

He nods in defeat, but he won't argue with me. He's only ventured a moment in this underworld. I live my life here.

I turn to Matteo. "How many men can you spare?"

His lip tips up, and I know it will cost me.

"I don't fucking care." I might sound weak, but she's it for me. She's mine, and if it costs me every penny I have ever made, I will gladly pay the price.

He cocks his head. "Done. And it won't cost you anything else."

I turn to my men. Fifteen of my most trusted men are here. Awaiting orders.

"Alright, everyone, fall out."

With Matteo's men and Alaric's guns, we are heavily loaded, expecting war, but I don't think it will come to that. That's not how the operation works.

The ride from my compound in Connecticut to the warehouse in Jersey is a lot longer than I want, but the use of helicopters is out of the question for now. The sound it would make would give us away for sure. So instead, we have them on standby just in case we need them. We're not sure what condition we'll find her in. I shake my head. Nope. I'm not going to think about that now. I need my head in the game if I'm going to get her out of there alive.

The minutes pass slowly, and it's agony. Even though I tell myself not to think about what I'll find in that warehouse, I can't help it. My stomach is in knots. I have never felt this lost before. My brain is on an endless loop of what-ifs. It's like I'm lost in a maze of my own thoughts, one of the mazes with tall shrubs and no exit.

All the possibilities hitting like a ton of bricks.

"Almost there," one of Matteo's men says, and I finally focus back on the road ahead of us. "We are a few miles outside the radius."

There is no longer a highway. Now, we are on the side roads. Roads that seem deserted. The car slows to a stop, and then it shuts off.

"We get out here and go the rest of the way on foot."

We all get out, and then we move in. It takes us fifteen minutes on foot to make our way through the trees that surround the warehouse.

This place is isolated. We made the right move by driving in.

Silently, we access the location. Luckily for us, Jaxson Price, who is still at our headquarters at my estate, is guiding us using the satellite he has accessed.

We could have gone in guns blazing, but then we risk casualties. Instead, we scope out the location, and once it's clear, I nod. It's time.

"How we getting in?"

Alaric holds up a grenade.

Leave it to him.

The plan is sound. Blow the door, storm the building.

"On three."

And then it begins.

Mayhem. Complete pandemonium. My ears ring as debris starts to fly. The door completely gone now. Smoke billows out through what must be the hallway. Even with smoke, I can make out the way. I run, not wanting to spare another minute, and then I turn the corner and run some more. It doesn't take me long to reach the only door in the hallway, and I kick it down. It bursts open, and lifting my gun, I storm in.

What I see has my movements halting, my muscles tightening, and an unnatural anger forms inside me. Tied to a bed is Ivy. She's still dressed, thankfully, but I see splotches of dried blood on her skin.

Her hair is disheveled, and her eyes are wide. I turn to the other presence in the room. Then I see him. Boris.

He has his butcher knife in his hand.

"Z," I say, motioning for him to secure Boris before I head to my girl.

Slowly, I pull her to me. "I have you now," I coo.

She winces at the contact.

"You're safe." She turns her head.

I expect her to cower, but instead, she pulls back, looking at Boris.

"Give me the knife."

My eyes go wide, but I don't move.

"Give me the fucking knife, Cyrus."

"Don't," I say, looking down. "You don't want his blood on your hands. Let me take this burden for you."

"But then it's on your hands."

"My hands are already stained with blood."

She gives me a nod, and I turn to face Boris. He looks from me to Z, who is holding the knife in one hand and a gun in the other.

"You can't kill me. Without me, you won't . . ."

A gunshot goes off, smoke rising from the gun in Z's hand. "I didn't want to hear him speak."

"We needed him." I shout.

"We don't need him; we still have her," he narrows his eyes in Ivy's direction.

I'm about to step forward to silence him when I feel a hand on my arm and the clank of the chains. I stop what I'm about to say and grab the keys in Boris's pocket.

She feels weak in my arms. Barely able to lift her head up at all. I want to cradle her to me, kiss her head, and tell her I will never let her go.

Gone is the man I've always been.

Strong and unfeeling.

He's been replaced by a man whose heart has been opened.

I don't even care who can see me. All my men and Matteo's. All I care about is Ivy.

Pulling her closer to my body, I undo every chain on her frail body. Then I stand, Ivy in my arms, and walk out the door.

I'll leave Z to clean up the mess. All my thoughts are on my Sun. Getting her home. Protecting her.

Over my shoulder, I look at Maxwell. "Call the doctor. Have him meet us at my house. Also tell the helicopter they can land."

Since the threat is taken care of, we can return home faster this way.

Even though it's only been two days, Ivy feels lighter in my arms. I wonder if he fed her.

If I could kill the bastard again, I would.

I cross the distance and get us into the helicopter. Keeping her in my arms, we take off and head toward my compound.

She doesn't speak during the ride. Instead, she snuggles in closer to me. Broken.

I was too late.

The marks on her body prove it.

My fists clench, and I want to kill her father next. This is his fault. Ivy deserves justice. But I know that has to be her choice. She has to decide her father's fate. If he lives or dies.

Personally, I wouldn't allow the fucker to live. If it was up to me, I would drop off Ivy and go straight to his desolate brownstone and put a bullet in his head. But even that would be too nice. Ivy has multiple cut marks on her upper body, and he deserves the same.

Before long, the helicopter lands, and I'm carrying Ivy into the house. I don't stop until I'm on the second floor in my bedroom.

I walk over to the bed and place her down before moving to get a towel.

Her hand shoots up when I try to leave. "No," she croaks, her voice strained. "Don't leave yet."

I look down at her, and her gaze is on me. Her eyes haunted by whatever horror she endured.

"The doctor is coming," I tell her.

She nods but grimaces at the movement. "He didn't—"

She starts, and I shake my head. "You don't need to tell me."

"He didn't rape me," she says, and I let out a sigh of relief. "He hurt me, but not that."

I lean down and kiss the top of her head. "Let's not talk now. Let me clean you up and tend to your wounds."

"Okay." Her voice is soft like a whisper, and her eyelids flutter shut.

I use the opportunity to head to the bathroom and grab a towel.

When I return, she's sleeping peacefully. Her mind finally shutting down.

Slowly, I remove her shirt. I pull the blanket over her chest, only exposing her upper arms to me. I wipe the dried blood off her limbs. The cuts aren't that deep. He made them deep enough to bleed, but they won't need stitches. The Butcher was known for toying with his prey. First with superficial cuts and then escalating.

It seems I got to her in time. Of course, there is damage, but it could have been so much worse.

While I clean her, I hear a knock on the door.

"Come in," I say, followed by the sounds of footsteps. The doctor is the type of doctor who doesn't ask questions. He's on my payroll as well as Tobias and company.

He keeps his head down and stays out of everyone's business.

"I'll leave you."

A small hand touches mine, and I look down to see crystal blue eyes staring up at me.

"You can stay," she whispers.

"Are you sure?"

She gives me a small nod.

The doctor is quiet as he assesses her injuries, but before long, he leaves. She's bandaged up, but just as I figured, any scars will fade over time. The scars inside her might not. But Ivy is strong. Bright like the sun, she will be okay. I know it.

"Are you okay?" I ask, sitting down on the bed and pulling her close to me.

"No, but I will be."

She is very quiet for a moment. "It will never end, right?"

"What do you mean?" I ask. "You're safe with me."

"He didn't rape me because I wasn't meant for him." My blood runs cold. Words dry on my tongue as I try to think of something to say.

"I will keep you safe," I repeat.

"I don't want to lie in wait." She pushes away and looks down at me.

From this angle, she looks fierce.

"Okay."

"Use me."

"No. Absolutely not."

"This isn't your choice, Cyrus Reed." She moves to stand and leave the bed. "If you won't, I'll use myself."

"Sun . . ." I pull her back, burying my face in her neck. "I can't lose you too."

"You won't. But I can't wait for the other shoe to drop. I won't be anyone's scared victim. Use me as bait and then finish it."

I know she's right. I know it's the only option. But I still hate it.

"Say yes." She turns her face to kiss me on the lips.

"Yes."

One word. One word that changes everything. Because that one word means there is nothing I wouldn't do for Ivy Aldridge.

She will be my doom.

CHAPTER FORTY-SEVEN

Ivy

I CAN'T BELIEVE I AGREED TO THIS. ACTUALLY, WORSE . . . I can't believe this was my idea. Tomorrow morning, I'll be putting myself on the chopping block. I'll pretend to be docile and scared, but in truth, the anger inside me is so deep, I'm not sure how I'll do it.

Acting is not my strong suit.

Never has been. If I don't like you, you know it. If I do, I'll do anything for you.

It's a trait I like about myself, normally. But now, when it could cost me my life, not so much.

"What's going on in that head of yours?" Cyrus asks, pulling me closer to him in the bed.

"Nothing." I have so many things I want to say to him, but I just don't know how to. It's not the time.

It should be easy, but the emotions I feel for this man are suffocating me.

He saved me.

For that, I owe him my life. But it's so much more than that . . .

Emotions are running high tonight, so as much as I want to say things to him right now, I can't. Both of us need to be in a good headspace.

"It's not nothing, Sun." He cuts into my inner ramblings.

"You're right. It's not."

He leans forward and kisses my head, a gesture I have grown to love.

Love.

The words hover inside me to say out loud, but how can I know if this is love? It might be. The circumstances leading to our relationship are strange, to say the least, but that doesn't mean they aren't real.

They are.

But still, the words stick to the roof of my mouth, refusing to leave.

I swallow with difficulty, trying desperately to find my voice and say the thoughts plaguing my brain.

"What if something goes wrong?" My voice drifts from my mouth in a soft whisper.

"It won't." There's conviction in his tone, but I'm not sure I believe him. Not after everything I've been through. Nervously, I bite my lip.

"You can't know that for sure."

"I can. And I do. I will not let him have you. Ever. Do you hear me?"

I nod silently, and he lifts his hand and strokes my cheek.

"Words. Say you understand."

"I understand."

"You're mine, and no one takes from me." His words are final and resolute. But I wonder how long he'll want to keep me.

I expect him to try to chase the demons away by kissing me, but it never comes. Instead, he holds me tight and rocks me in my arms. It's not what I expect from him, but it's so much more. It's exactly what I needed, even though I didn't know it.

He makes me feel cherished, safe, and most of all, even if it's temporary, he makes me feel like I'm his.

The next morning comes before I'm ready for it. Sunlight streams in from the closed blinds being pulled back. When I open my eyes, I'm temporarily blinded.

"Good morning," Cyrus says as he crosses the distance. He makes it to me in two steps, his heavy footsteps making me smile. Before I can think about it, he's placing a gentle kiss on my mouth.

"What time is it?"

"Four p.m."

"What? That's not morning. Shit. I have to get up." I jump up too quickly, forgetting that I had hit my head only days earlier.

Although I'm feeling dizzy, I refuse to show it. I know if I do, Cyrus won't let me help him.

Failure isn't an option on this.

This sicko was going to take me, and my worst nightmares can't tell me what he would do if he got me.

I'm not dumb enough to think another woman won't take my place if we don't get him.

Slowly, I walk to Cyrus's bathroom.

When I step inside, my steps falter at the reflection of myself in the mirror. Boris might not have touched my face, but the remnants of my capture are clear all over me. From my hollowed eyes and the dark circles, my skin looks drab. But it's the sight of the bandages on my arms that makes my blood turn cold.

There are at least five on each arm. I remember each cut, and a shiver works its way down my spine.

"What are you looking at?"

When I don't answer, he steps up behind me. "I asked you a question. What are you looking at?"

"How I look," I whisper.

"And how is it you think you look?" I turn my head to look at him, but he follows my movement. "No. Don't look at me. Look at yourself."

He steps up closer, so close I can feel each inhale and exhale of his body.

In the reflection of the mirror, his eyes beg me if this is okay. I nod, and he puts his hands on my hips.

"Look at yourself."

I do.

"You know what I see?"

I shake my head.

"I see a survivor. I see a strong woman who didn't break. Yes, you are bruised, but you didn't break. I see a woman who, even though she should be scared, offers herself so that no other woman would have to endure what she has. Now look at yourself. Do you still see anything else? On top of being the strongest woman I know, you're also the most beautiful."

"Hardly."

One hand lands on my back, tilting me forward. The other shimmies up my T-shirt, exposing my panties to him.

I catch his stare in the mirror as he slowly lowers them down my ass until they pool on the floor.

"Is this okay?" he asks, and a part of me melts right there. Even through his haze, he won't take.

I nod.

"Words."

"Yes, Cyrus."

"You are the sun. You shine brighter than anything in this universe. You burn so hot that when I touch you, I'm sure I'll melt." His hand parts my legs, and then his finger teases my seam. When he dips inside, I swear I will combust from the heat growing inside me. "See that flush? See the way you look? The haze in your eyes." He pumps his finger in and out. "You are gorgeous. This is the most beautiful you have ever looked."

I hear him moving behind me, and then he leans closer to me, flicking his tongue on the skin by my ear.

He removes his fingers, and just as I'm about to beg him not to, he thrusts to the hilt inside me. I lean forward over the counter, my face close to my own reflection. My pupils are wide.

He thrusts in and out of me like a possessed man.

"Like this . . ." He fucks me harder. "Like this, with me inside you . . ." *Thrust.* "You are perfect." *Thrust.* "You are everything." *Thrust.* "You are my light." *Thrust.* "*Entee albi.*"

His moves become more animalistic at that, and I know we are both close.

Together, we fall over the edge.

CHAPTER FORTY-EIGHT

Ivy

THE PLAN IS IN MOTION. WE ARE HEADING TO THE location we found on Boris's phone. Apparently, and I don't know all the details, Cyrus hired some ridiculous hacker to break into Boris's phone. From there, they impersonated Boris, saying the girl was ready . . . the girl being me.

I'm not sure exactly what was said about me, but after Cyrus received the text, he threw stuff. Broke a table and didn't seem too happy. Yet the plan is still on, so it must have worked.

When I asked, he didn't say one word about it. He just told me not to worry and that he would take care of me.

Whoever we are meeting will be ambushed, but that's not how the plan will go down.

I'm still bait.

So that means, right now, I'm chained up again.

The only difference is these chains are for show.

They aren't secure, and I have a gun on my back. Not that I think I will use it, but the security of knowing it's there is worth it.

I'm still not sure how much I like this plan, or if I think it will work, but either way, I support Cyrus.

It feels like an eternity as I wait, arms fatigued from being behind my back.

"Incoming," I hear, and I know that Cyrus isn't in the room right now.

Instead, one of Matteo's men is here with me. Matteo thought that they would send a man in first to make sure I was here. This is the part of the plan that should scare me.

But instead of letting it, I breathe in slowly, not allowing it to.

My heart beats rapidly in my chest as I hear the sound of footsteps, and then I hear more. Craning my neck, I see five men walking toward me, and in the center is a handsome man in a suit.

This must be the leader. He's getting closer and closer, and all the nerves in my body feel like they are on edge.

"Magnificent." He's close enough that I can smell his cologne.

"Where is Boris?" He turns to Matteo's man. "He did well."

"Boris is on his way," Matteo's man answers. Lies, more like it. Boris will be going nowhere anytime soon, but he plays his part perfectly in the deception.

The man looks back at me and then turns to the other man. "How long have you been working for Boris?" he asks.

Whatever the man does or says has things going tense.

I can't understand what he says, but something is not right. Before I can reach for the gun tucked in the back of my pants, I'm grabbed from the front.

"Out." I hear, and I'm being forced forward.

That's when all hell breaks loose.

Cyrus and Tobias's men come out. It's pandemonium. Shots are fired. Bullets fly through the air.

It's an all-out war. Bodies start to drop. I try to run away, but the man holding me, the man in the suit, grabs me and pulls me in front of him.

Cyrus steps out from where he was fighting.

It almost reminds me of an old-fashioned showdown, except I'm being held hostage.

If only I could grab my gun.

But I know it's impossible. Even from this angle where this

man holds me in front of him, there is no way I'd be able to get to it. Especially since I have a knife cutting my neck to stop me from moving

"Cyrus Reed," the man states. He knows him.

"Alexander."

But the voice holds no warmth, just malice.

"She's quite lovely. I have to assume Boris is dead."

"You assume right."

"Well, then I thank you for delivering my new pet."

Cyrus's jaw clenches.

"Hopefully, she outlasts the last few. Few last long. None as long as—"

"Shut the fuck up." Cyrus lifts his gun.

"You always did have a soft spot for my pets," the man I now know as Alexander says. "I wonder if when I fuck her in the as—"

"I said shut the fuck up."

"Oh, this one is important. Dare I say more than Sybil?"

Sybil?

My brain tries to catch up to what I'm hearing. Who is Sybil? It sounds so familiar.

Sybil.

Cyrus steps forward. He doesn't have a clean shot. The only way to shoot him is through me.

But by the look in Cyrus's eyes, it's a possibility.

"Dear Cyrus. Why all the theatrics? Is that any way to greet your brother-in-law?"

And then all the pieces click together.

His first pet.

His favorite pet.

His broken pet is Cyrus's sister.

The knowledge swirls inside me like a venomous snake with a need to strike, and before I can think of why I shouldn't, I do. I strike. Not caring what happens to me, I move my body. Throwing my head back, I bash his nose, then drop to the floor.

"Don't ever speak of my sister." The gun raises, and the shot is fired.

The sound of his body hitting the floor ricochets like the bullet flying.

Cyrus dashes toward me, his arms coming around me.

"Why did you do that?" he asks.

"You were talking too much." I laugh.

"You could have died." He lifts his finger and swipes the blood from where the knife grazed my skin.

"But I didn't."

"Thank you," he says. Lowering his mouth to mine, he says, "Thank you for bringing me peace."

I know what his sister's death brought him, and this was my way of thanking him.

CHAPTER FORTY-NINE

Cyrus

I CRADLE HER IN MY ARMS. TIGHTLY. THAT WAS CLOSE. TOO close.

But in the end, Ivy, being Ivy, did what she had to do. This woman will be the death of me. She is strong, smart, and she is my equal match. Now if only I could keep her.

I can't, though, and I know this. If I do, she will always wonder if what we had was real. I will always wonder it too. We came together because I took her. She never came to me of her own free will.

I know what I have to do.

I have to let her go. There is just one thing I need to do first.

Pulling out my cell phone, I hit the contact. "Bring him in."

Ivy is still in my arms, but at the sound of more feet, she takes a step away from me.

"Dad?" Her voice rises a pitch.

"What we do with him is up to you," I tell her. She looks at me, her eyes wide. No daughter should ever have to make this choice, but I won't take it away from her. She deserves it. Everything that has ever happened to her is because of this man.

"Help me, Ivy."

At that, she laughs. She pulls completely away from me and stalks toward him. When she is standing in front of him, I notice the gun in her hand.

I step toward her, putting my hand on the barrel and turning it toward the ground.

"What are you doing?" she asks me.

"I can't let you do that."

Her mouth opens and closes before I take the gun out of her hand.

"You will get justice."

"Will you kill him?" she asks me. "I don't want another death on your hands."

"Why?" I say, cocking my head at her.

She leans up and places her lips on mine. "You are a good man."

"I won't kill him."

"What will you do with him?"

"Death is too easy for him. I will make him pay for the rest of his life."

I lift the gun and aim it at Aldridge's head. "I thought you said you wouldn't kill him."

"I did, but I will kill someone."

My hand moves and takes aim exactly where it needs to be, to the blood I will spill today. Right now.

"Boss."

"Did you really think I wouldn't know?" I say, aiming right between Z's eyes.

The traitor.

"She was a distraction. She was clouding your judgment. Sybil deserved better. She raised me too, she was like a sister to me. I couldn't let your whore—" he starts to say, but I shut him the fuck up.

Bang.

His body drops to the ground. Aldridge starts to shake uncontrollably. I turn to Maxwell. "Set it up." I don't need to say more because he knows the plan. What the plan has always been since Ivy went missing from my island.

Z's death.

Aldridge framed for it.

"I'm taking her home," I say to Alaric. Wrapping my arm around Ivy, I lead her out of the warehouse.

"Cut out his tongue," I hear Tobias say as we walk out. Ivy shivers in my arms, but she doesn't object. She knows this is what needs to happen to protect us. To protect her.

Tobias doesn't like people to talk, and I can't say that I blame him. All the deaths will fall on Aldridge, a sale gone wrong.

She will finally be safe. Now to tell her.

CHAPTER FIFTY

Ivy

SOMETHING IS WRONG. SOMETHING IS VERY WRONG. CYRUS won't look at me. He won't speak to me. He won't even touch me.

He held me as he walked me to the car, but now we are driving, and instead of talking to me, he stares out the window.

"Cyrus . . ." I start to say, but I don't know what to say after that.

A weird foreboding feeling claws in my skin.

"Are you okay?" I ask.

How could he be? I'm not. After everything that has happened, I'm not okay. He killed the man responsible for the death of his sister, the man who took me, the man who wanted me. The past few days have been a shitshow, so I understand why he's like this, but still, I expected more.

I expected him to hold me.

Comfort me.

I wrap my arms around myself.

I turn to look out my own window, and that's when I see it. We aren't heading to his compound; we are entering the city. In the direction of downtown.

Where I live.

"Why are we going this way?" I ask, looking back at him. He, however, is staring out his window. His jaw is tight, shoulders tense, but it's his clenched fists that worry me.

"It's time for you to go home." His voice is robotic, lacking all the warmth I have come to know.

My hands reach out to touch him, but I stop myself before it connects with his skin.

"Why are you acting like this?" I ask, but he doesn't even glance toward me at the sound of my voice. "Look at me, goddammit."

That makes him turn.

Still, he doesn't speak, and I'm transported to a time before. When his walls were down.

They are once again in place, and I hate it.

"Please don't do this. Talk to me." I reach out my hand and go to touch him, but instead, he takes my hand in his and places it back on my lap. The movement infuriates me.

"Don't make this harder." He turns his head to gaze out the window. He won't look at me.

"Make what harder? What is this?" I say, demanding he speak to me.

"I was wrong about you being the sun, you are a blazing comet in the sky. You burn bright, but you aren't meant to stay with me. I'm letting you go."

Those words feel like daggers in my heart. "What if I don't want to be let go?" I whisper.

"It's not your choice."

"Like hell, it isn't. Look at me. Tell that to my face."

I hope when he does, I will see the lie. But when he looks at me, I feel like ice has spread through my veins.

"Sun."

"No. You don't get to tell me it's over and then call me your sun."

"What do you want from me?"

"I want you to admit you love me. Because I—"

"You want me to admit I love you. Of course, I fucking love you. I will and have killed for you. You are my everything. You are the only light I see in my dark world. But it isn't fucking enough."

"It is to me because I love you too."

"But do you? You don't know if you do. And if you stay, you will never know. Right now, you might think that, but next week, next month? Next year."

"So, this is a test?"

"It's not a fucking test. I love you, and I'm letting you go. No test. No tricks. I'm doing the right thing for once."

"How could you?"

He's quiet. "It's for the best."

"For who? For you. You're taking the easy way out."

"You need to go home. You need to think about what has happened. You need to be with your family . . ."

The car pulls up to my house, and the door opens from the outside. He doesn't move. Not one inch.

"This is it?" I choke back the sob that has lodged itself in the back of my throat. It hurts. It hurts so bad I want to scream. I want to shout at the injustice, but more than anything, I want to fall down onto the street and cry. Not only because of Cyrus, but because of everything. The past few months crash into my chest. Beating down on my heart.

"It's the way it has to be. I took you . . ."

He's right. No matter how angry I am, I know he's right. He took me, and this is the only way it can be.

I turn back to him.

To the man who proved himself to me. Who protected me. The man who loved me enough to let me go.

A tear falls from my eyes, then another one as I step out of the car. The door still open as I walk the few steps to the front door. By the time it opens and I'm in Trent's arms, my face glistens with a never-ending current of tears.

I cry for yesterday; I cry for today, and I cry for a future without Cyrus.

It isn't until the next day that I finally feel the full weight of everything that has happened to me. It's not until I'm alone in my bedroom that I stare at the cuts and bruises from everything I went through.

As much as I don't want to be away from him, I realize now how fucked I am from my ordeal.

I spend the first day crying in bed.

I don't eat.

I don't sleep.

I don't even want to speak.

By day two, things get a little better. I'm now able to look at myself in the mirror without crying. Food has taste again.

I beg for Trent to bring back my mom, but he says I need more time. That I need to be stronger.

It isn't until day five after my return that my mom walks in.

It's been months since I've seen her. She looks good. For the first time in forever, her hair is brushed, and her eyes are clear.

When she sees me, she smiles, and of course, that makes me cry again. She doesn't talk, but that's okay. A smile is enough to bring the light back inside me.

It takes another week before she starts to talk, and when she opens her mouth and says my name, tears fall from my eyes.

We're outside and the sun is shining bright. She blooms in front of my eyes.

"Your father is gone, you know?" she says and my heart lurches in my chest.

I lift my hand from where it is in my lap and take hers in mine. We're sitting on the back patio, staring at the flower buds that are growing in our garden.

"I finally feel like I can breathe," she whispers.

She might be able to, but now I can't.

Time passes slowly when you miss someone. I thought that when I left Cyrus behind that day, the empty feeling in my heart would fill over time. But instead, the longer it is, the more my heart feels like it's breaking in two.

It's been one month.

I've spent my time bringing my mother's garden and my mother back to life.

With my father gone, my mother has finally gotten to a better place.

It didn't happen overnight, and maybe the flowers helped, but now, we stand together outside watering the plants.

They are in full bloom now. Spring is thick in the air. The smell of flowers permeates through my nostrils, making me feel alive. But as much as I do feel alive, there is still something missing. My mother is my priority, though. She needs me now. With my father in jail, she can't be alone.

"It's beautiful," she says.

I turn to the flower she's looking at. "See this flower here." She points at a closed bud. She must have planted it without me as I haven't seen it before.

"It's evening primrose. During the day, it closes. Sometimes it even withers, but that doesn't mean she won't flourish." She holds the closed bud to me. "It's in the dark when it comes alive. Some of the most beautiful things grow in the darkness."

I look up to find her gazing at me.

"Go to him," she says, and I don't even know how she knows.

"I might not have been here." She points at her head. "But I heard. Go to him."

"But who will take care of you?"

"Ivy, when I named you, I would never know how true your name would mean. Do you know what Ivy means?"

I shake my head.

"It means faithfulness. You are everything an Ivy should be. But you put yourself last. It's time you stop thinking about me. Be true to you."

"Go."

I look back at the flower, the evening primrose, and then I go.

CHAPTER FIFTY-ONE

Cyrus

ANOTHER FRIDAY NIGHT. ANOTHER POKER GAME. I'M SICK of the pretense. I never loved being here, but now what little I liked is gone.

It's like all the light in my world has been robbed from me. It's like the sun that my life orbits is gone, and in truth, it has. Letting her go was and is the hardest thing I have ever done.

There isn't a second that I don't think I should change my mind, break into her house, and take her back.

But I don't.

Instead, I wait for her to decide. I need her to come back to me. To tell me again that she loves me. To love me now that it is her choice.

I'm standing in the same place I have stood for weeks, watching as bets are made and money is lost and won.

Alaric is at the table and beside him is Matteo and Tobias. I have grown used to them here now. Ever since they helped me, I owe them, so they always have a spot at my table.

I keep to myself as always, drinking my cognac. Cards are being drawn when I see him from the corner of the bar.

What the fuck is that fucker doing here?

He is no longer welcome at my game.

I know it's not his fault, but rules are rules. Maxwell sees him at the same time I do, and both of us start walking to the entrance of the room.

That's when the crowd parts, and I see he's not alone.

My fists unclench.

Trent looks up at my men surrounding him. "Call off the dogs."

With one signal of my hand, they stand down as I approach Trent and Ivy.

She's even more beautiful today than she ever was in the past. Her skin has a healthy glow as if she's been out in the garden too long and her cuts have faded.

"What are you doing here?" I ask probably gruffer than I should, but I can't help it. If this is a mirage, I don't want it to fade. But I also don't want to get my hopes up.

I have lived in the dark too long to see a glimmer of light and then be thrust back in.

She steps closer, and the smell of a freshly bloomed flower hits my nose. I want to inhale her and never let her go.

She opens her mouth to speak, but I lift my hand.

"No. Not here," I say. "Follow me."

There are too many people here. I don't want this—whatever this is—to be done here in front of people I don't trust. These men will use my weakness against me if I'm not careful.

"She's not going anywhere with you."

I level Trent with my eyes, about to tell Maxwell to take him out back when I feel a soft hand touch me.

"Trent." Her hand is still on my arm. "I'm going with Cyrus. Thank you for bringing me here, but I need to speak to him alone."

He looks at her for a second before reluctantly nodding.

Once he steps away, I grab her hand and pull her out of the ballroom and up the stairs to my office. I don't know what this is, so that seems like the best place to go.

When we are inside, I turn to her. "I'm listening." She

doesn't deserve my attitude, but I'm too wound up to tone it down.

"I love you," she blurts out, and that's enough for me because as soon as the words leave her lips, I pounce. Pulling her toward me, I wrap my arms around her and seal my mouth to hers.

"Took you long enough," I grit out, and her blue eyes widen as she pushes back to look at me.

"I had to know," she whispers.

"And do you?"

"I do."

The space that separates us shrinks as I move toward her again, until our bodies touch and I can feel her inhale of breath.

"You know I will never be anyone other than the man that I am. I don't leave my compound."

"You've left for me." Her mouth twitches with amusement.

"Yes. Only for you or if I need to." I lean down and kiss her small nose. "Life won't be easy with me."

"I don't care."

"It might be darker than you're used to."

She wraps her arms around my neck, lifts up to her tiptoes, and brushes her lips against mine. "Then I will be the evening primrose." I cock my head, not understanding her words. "I'll live in the dark. I'll bloom in dark. All I need is you, Cyrus."

I kiss her again. "All I need is you. I love you, Sun. I stopped believing. Long before you, I stopped believing, I thought I would always live in the blackness, but you brought me light."

And she has.

She's all the light I will ever need.

EPILOGUE

Cyrus
Four years later.

FROM ACROSS THE DISTANCE, I CAN SEE HER. SHE'S STILL just as beautiful as she was that first time. Actually, even more so. She was pure light. As bright as the sun.

I took her then.

Made her mine.

I've never regretted that decision because she illuminated every dark crevice of my mind, of my heart, and most importantly, of my soul.

Am I still the villain?

Fuck yeah, I am.

But with her, never.

She has shown me that no matter how dark and twisted I am, she will love me anyway, and even the monster can get a happy ending.

I stroll toward them without a care in the world. One thing I decided when I made Ivy my wife, three weeks after she came back to me, was to never let her go.

She fought me at first, claiming she needed to see her mom. That her mom would fade away again if she wasn't there.

I compromised.

So, every summer, we move to the island estate with her mother in tow. They spend the days gardening and playing out on the beach. Ivy did eventually open up that flower shop she always dreamed of. It's back on the mainland and the flowers she grows in our greenhouse she sells there. Her mother runs it for her when Ivy can't be there. It's given her something to live for and it makes my wife happy to see her mom flourishing.

It's perfect.

This island that once caused me pain is now my safe haven.

Here in this bubble, I'm at peace.

That doesn't mean I don't have to work, and I still hold my Friday night game.

But I don't let that touch my life.

That's business, and this . . . this is family. I wouldn't trade it for a second.

Endless hours away from them is worth it to see them in the middle of the open grass. Knees on the dirt. Planting.

I walk up behind them before she sees me.

Primrose. Rose for short.

Named after a flower that grows in the dark, or so Ivy said.

"Daddy!" She jumps up, pulling away from her mom and grandmother, and flying into my arms.

"Momma teaching me how to plant."

After she lets me go, she steps back to point at the ground. To the pile of dirt that Rose has dug up.

Her whole body is covered in mud, including her face.

"Momma is letting me put the seeds."

"I see that, baby."

My mother-in-law stands up from the ground and takes Rose's hand. "Let's get you cleaned up," she says, and then they walk away toward the main house.

Ivy is still on her knees, patting the ground, when I reach my hand out to help her stand.

She's not as dirty as Rose, but there is a smudge of mud on her face too.

Lifting my hand, I rub off the smudge and lean down and place my lips on hers.

Her mouth opens against mine.

It's like coming home.

"Everything I am, everything I ever could be, is because of you and your love. You have given me a family." I look at where her mother, who has become a mother to me as well, plays with our baby, and then I place a hand on her rounded belly. "You have given me peace." I lean down and kiss her. "Thank you." She smiles against my mouth again before pulling away.

We carry our past with us. It's in every inch of our skin. Our scars. Some you just can't see, but they are there. I used to wear my scars as if they were the only part of me that mattered. But because of Ivy, I wear them like a faded memory. Sure, they are there, but they no longer define me.

Ivy taught me to no longer live in the past, but instead, to live for today. Live for right now. Just plain live.

ACKNOWLEDGMENTS

I want to thank my entire family. I love you all so much.

Thank you to my husband and my kids for always loving me. You guys are my heart!

Thank you to my Mom, Dad, Liz and Ralph for always believing in me, encouraging me and loving me!

Thank you to my in-laws for everything they do for me!

Thank you to all of my brothers and sisters!

Thank you to everyone that helped with Corrupt Kingdom.

Jenny Sims

Angela Smith

Gemma Woolley

My Brother's Editor

Marla Esposito

Champagne Formats

Lori Jackson

Hang Le

Thank you to Chris Davis and Mike Jukes for such a great picture.

Thank you to Sebastian York, Ava Erickson, Kim Gilmour and Lyric for bringing Corrupt Kingdom to life on audio.

Thank you to my AMAZING ARC TEAM! You guys rock!

Thank you to my beta/test team.

Gemma! Thank you for your help!

Livia: Thank you for everything!

Parker: Thank you for everything you do for me.

Leigh: Thank you for always being there.

Sarah: Your input and feedback is always amazing! Thank you!

Kelly: Thank you for all your input.

Jessica and Lulu. Thank you for your wonderful and extremely helpful feedback.

Jill: Thank you for all your help.

Melissa: Thank you for everything.

Harloe: Thanks for always being there.

Mia: Thanks for always plotting.

Thank you to Jing Kemp, Hanan Abskharon, Clarissa Wild and Maïwenn for helping me translation a few sentences for Cyrus.

I want to thank ALL my friends for putting up with me while I wrote this book. Thank you!

To all of my author friends who listen to me complain and let me ask for advice, thank you!

To the ladies in the Ava Harrison Support Group, I couldn't have done this without your support!

Please consider joining my Facebook reader group Ava Harrison Support Group

Thanks to all the bloggers! Thanks for your excitement and love of books!

Last but certainly not least...

Thank you to the readers!

Thank you so much for taking this journey with me.